JULIE[illegible]

was born in Cornw[illegible]. Her
ancestors were a mix of professional musicians,
miners and matelots, of Welsh–Cornish
pedigree.

After a brief but varied Civil Service career in Whitehall and The City, marriage, two children, and a degree as a mature student, she became a teacher. Her poems have been published in magazines and anthologies, and she has broadcast her own scripts on local radio. *Invaders of Privacy* is, however, her first venture into novel writing.

Julie Burville

INVADERS OF PRIVACY

The Thriller Club
T.004

Aspire Publishing

An Aspire Publication

First published in Great Britain 1998

ISBN 1 902035 12 7

Printed and bound in Great Britain by Caledonian International Book Manufacturing Ltd.

Typeset in Palatino by Kestrel Data, Exeter, Devon.

Aspire Publishing – a division of XcentreX Ltd.

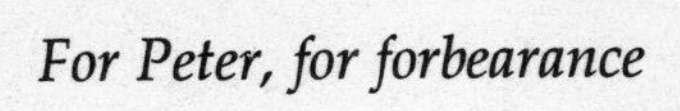

For Peter, for forbearance

Chapter 1

'Which one, darling?'

The question came from a scruffy-looking man in a grubby white raincoat, its cut proclaiming it had seen smarter days. A cigarette, dangling from his lower lip, challenged the clearly displayed NO SMOKING signs, and his sharp features distorted in the effort to divert the smoke from his eyes. The lift's control panel indicated fifteen floors; Kate Rider asked for the third. Her fellow passenger turned to study her.

'And what would a nice girl like you want with the third floor?' The accent was hard, Irish, north of the border.

The lift was swift and the doors had already opened to let her out. She emerged into a long corridor and was surprised when Scruffy-Raincoat joined her there. In case he was a colleague, she decided to be friendly.

'I'm reporting for work, it's my first day.'

'Welcome aboard.' He thrust out a sticky paw. 'Jack Brymer, crime desk hack.'

She wondered if he were pulling her leg. Jack Brymer's scoops were legendary. He was the slickest crime reporter in the business, and it was rumoured that senior policemen read his columns to get their leads. He was still holding her hand, hindering her progress.

'And you are?'

Smoke from his cigarette drifted into her eyes, making them water.

'Kate Rider. I'm joining Mr Colson's team, on the home-news front.'

'As what?'

'As a journalist.'

This prim response made him guffaw.

'Straight from university, are you?' He gave her no time to reply but went on, 'And what gives you the idea you've got what it takes to be a reporter?'

Jack Brymer or not, his condescending attitude riled her. 'I graduated more than five years ago and I've been a practising journalist for all of that time.'

'Now there's a funny thing, how come we haven't met?'

She wished she had not boasted about her professional experience, the details were unlikely to impress. 'I worked in the provinces, on the *Tamar Advertiser*. You won't have heard of it.'

'West Country rag?'

'Yes, out of Plymouth.'

'And today you're joining Kev Colson's team on *The Flag*, full of ambition and hoping to make a name for yourself on the nationals. You should have stayed in Devon, darling. This scandal sheet is the ruin of aspiring, bright young things.'

It was not an auspicious welcome. At last, he released her from his sticky clasp, bequeathing a damp residue. She walked on along the corridor, resisting the temptation to wipe her hand on her jacket.

'This is my bolt hole, he said, in step with her. 'Yours is the main office, second on the right.'

She knew, but thanked him just the same and continued on her way.

He called after her, 'You're a pretty girl; watch out

for Colson. He thinks editorial powers extend to inserting his bits wherever he wants, if you get my drift.'

She had hoped to make an impressive entry into her new office, but, thanks to Jack Brymer, she arrived blushing and flustered.

Though the circulation of the *Tamar Advertiser* was nothing to boast about, it was a respected paper in her home city, and its readers were well acquainted with Kate Rider's name. For the past two years, her lively style had been aired in her own gossip column. The mug-shot that headed her weekly contribution showed a pretty face, dark lashes, tomboy haircut and the winning whiteness of even teeth. What that grainy portrait did not show was her five-foot-six-inches of indisputable femininity.

There was no immodesty in her claim to journalist status. She was no raw cub-reporter, but a talented writer who had served her apprenticeship. She knew how to fake veracity and combined a deft questioning technique with a manner that instilled trust. Nine times out of ten she established a friendly rapport with the people she interviewed. West Country big-wigs, entertainers, sportsmen, politicians, businessmen and even the local aristocracy had opened their hearts to her and revealed their secrets. Though she exploited the confidences so-gained by making them public, she did so skilfully, careful to ensure all revelations were illuminated in a flattering light. It was not unusual for her to be rewarded with the thanks and compliments of the celebrities she featured.

The *Tamar* column had led to many glamorous assignments. At first, it had been exciting to rub shoulders with celebrities, but interviewing the small-pond fat and famous had its limitations. Soon, she became heartily sick of covering charity galas, balls, dinners, theatrical events and conferences, and yearned to work on some real news. To this end, she had hawked her curriculum vitae around every London-based national daily. The broadsheets had ignored her and so had the tabloids, with one exception. When she hauled her banner up the mast, it was *The Flag* that had responded.

The Flag was a product created for the new millennium. To enliven its pages, its multi-millionaire owner had head-hunted the smartest editors, the slickest journalists and the most-talented photographers. The tabloid's politics were exactly what its label suggested: it was a flag-waver for the British national interest and a fingers-up at European federalism and monetary union. Its only concession to unity was its support of closer trading links with continental partners. This more serious political purpose was garnished with the sensational and the salacious. The combination was proving a successful formula, for, in the sixteen months of its existence, the new daily's circulation had grown to challenge that of the two best-selling newspapers in the land.

At her *Flag* interview, Colson had told her that he liked ballsy women who could sell themselves. Kate could scarcely believe her good fortune when he offered her a job. It was a success that induced some envy among her *Tamar* colleagues, but not even their sniping could sour her elation. Before her departure, Phil Kitto, the bumbling and good natured editor, ran a half-page feature about her, headed, TAMAR REPORTER, RIDER, FLIES THE FLAG. The local girl made good had become a minor celebrity.

* * *

When Kate next crossed paths with Jack Brymer, three weeks had elapsed and the lift was travelling in the opposite direction. His predictions were not unfounded; already she was disappointed in her expectations.

'So, how are you feeling, Miss Fleet Street Experience?' he asked.

She wasn't sure if he was being facetious or had merely forgotten her name.

'Fleet Street experience? Chance would be a fine thing. All I've been allowed to do for the past weeks is play at assistant sub-editor, correcting and tidying other people's trivia.'

Jack laughed, good humouredly. 'It's called serving an apprenticeship, acquiring the house style.'

'Straight-jacketing, more like.'

'Sounds as if you need a drink. Come on, I'll buy you one.'

She was flattered. It would do no harm for the new girl to be seen with the respected Jack Brymer.

He bustled her into a nearby watering hole and, without asking what she wanted, bought her a pint of bitter to match his own.

'Told you you'd regret leaving Devon. At least they serve cream teas down there.'

'Cream teas can be too rich a diet. Perhaps I hanker after more basic things.'

'Well, you've come to the right place for that, darling. Unfurl *The Flag* and all human life is there; its more sordid bits anyway.'

He tilted his glass and half the contents disappeared down his scrawny neck. She sipped circumspectly. She would have preferred pilsner to bitter and usually drank halves.

Though he seemed interested only in drinking, she attempted to draw him into conversation.

'What got you started on your career, Jack?'

'Don't remember, all too long ago, but I'll tell you something for nothing: in our game you won't achieve much unless you're prepared to go out and make the news yourself.'

Again he tipped his drink and opened his throat. Seconds later, when he righted the glass, it was empty.

'Make it up, do you mean?' She was aware that she sounded censorious.

'No, make it happen.'

'How do I do that?'

'If you can't answer that question yourself, you've chosen the wrong career.' He looked mournfully at his empty glass. 'Another?' he suggested.

Brymer's damning assessment of her aptitude only served to kindle her determination.

Returning to the noise and bustle of the office, she cornered her editor, Kevin Colson, to list her complaints.

'You employed me as an investigative journalist,' she pointed out, 'instead of which I've been tied to the office computer, performing sub-editorial duties. I'm growing stale with all this inactivity, I should be out there bringing in my own stuff. I have the appropriate qualities, I'd like to show you what I can do.'

'Then you've come to the right man.' Colson smirked. 'I like to put spirited young fillies through their paces.'

Her eyes flashed with annoyance at his innuendo. 'I'm serious - give me the opportunity to bring in a story and you won't regret it.'

The best she could extract from him was the promise that when something suitable came up, he would push it her way. At the end of a month, she was still correcting the syntax and punctuation of reports faxed in by freelances from the provinces. It was a bitter irony.

She tackled Colson again. 'I'm still waiting for the assignment you promised.'

'My, what an impatient Miss you are,' he teased.

'All I'm asking is that you let me out in the field, so that I can do some investigating of my own.'

'Fair enough, if that's what you want. Come back later, when the paper's put to bed, and we'll discuss your career development.'

Jack was not the only one to have warned her about Colson's reputation. It was common gossip that the editor was inclined to amuse himself with the young women on his staff, in the belief that their position was, quite literally, beneath him. But, imbued with all the arrogance of successful youth, Kate had no qualms about negotiating with her rakish editor.

She found him tieless, his shirt sleeves rolled. He waved her to a chair and poured two generous quantities of scotch into glasses. She accepted hers, but left it untouched waiting to hear what he was offering, hoping that it was something other than his body. Pouring himself a top-up, he came and sat on the arm of her chair. He was so close she could smell his masculine body odour. It was not unpleasantly stale, merely evidence of a hard day's work.

'Have you an assignment for me?' she enquired.

'Oh yes, something very suitable.'

His hand dropped to her knee, after examining the bone structure there, he began to smooth her stocking, with each stroke his fingers pushed her skirt a little higher. Her restraining efforts failed, and when his exploring fingers reached her thigh, she sprang from the chair. Whisky spilt down her skirt.

'I thought we were talking about an assignment for the paper.'

'We are, Katie, we are. Let's just say you scratch my back and I'll scratch yours.'

Clichés were part and parcel of *The Flag's* house style too.

By discarding his whisky glass, Kevin had freed his other hand and was deftly unbuttoning her blouse. She opposed him single-handed, her right hand still clasping the overfilled tumbler of scotch. He was breathing the same fiery spirit into her face.

'I find it much easier to be generous to girls who don't play hard to get.'

'Do you mean that I have to submit to this before you allow me to write my own copy?'

His hands were under her breasts as if weighing them.

'Of course not, that would amount to sexual harassment. Be a good girl, unwrap the goods, I like to preview what I'm bidding for.'

Ambition overruled personal scruples, and her hesitation was brief. Yet, so foreign was this method of career advancement, she detached herself from the action, by pretending that the young woman unhooking her brassiere was someone other than herself.

Chapter 2

Colson was a busy man, and she was obliged to pounce on him as he passed her desk between conferences.

'You won't forget you promised me an outside assignment,' she reminded him.

There was no acknowledgement and smarting with wounded pride, she wondered if she had been fool enough to have given him what he wanted for no reward. Later in the day, however, he put his head into the general office and she received a personal summons.

'Rider, there's a job for you.' The use of her surname was a ridiculous formality after their intimacy. 'Get down to Wimbledon as quickly as you can. Another toddler has gone walkabout from his nursery, but this time he's wandered onto a busy road with fatal consequences. I don't care what angle you choose, just make sure you find someone to blame.'

He handed over a piece of paper. It bore the name and address of the nursery school. Grabbing her jacket she made for the lift. Jack Brymer was entering it and he held the door for her.

'You look purposeful,' he observed.

'Kevin's given me my street permit. I'm off on an outside assignment.'

Jack narrowed his eyes, examining her in an

exaggerated way that seemed to be assessing how she might have persuaded her editor to agree to this concession.

'What's he given you?'

Blushing, she wondered if Kevin had blabbed or if Jack was merely familiar with her editor's modus operandi. She decided to ignore the ambiguity of the question.

'Nothing earth shattering, just an unsupervised infant who toddled out of its nursery and under a car.'

'A local tragedy that you're expected to turn into a national drama.'

'That's the intention, though I doubt if there'll be scope for that much hype.'

Brymer pushed through the swing doors ahead of her, but waited on the pavement.

'A word of advice. If you want to turn in a good story, you have to dig deeper than the rest of the rat-pack. Find your perpetrator and delve into their past. Everyone has a skeleton.'

'Thanks, Jack, I'll do that.'

She did want to turn in a good story. The previous evening she had palmed Colson off with a half striptease and hand job. Though he was a handsome man, not unlike the Hollywood heart-throb whose name he almost shared, she had provided neither service with even a faked enthusiasm. She deserved to be employed for her writing talent alone, and it was distasteful and belittling to have to prostitute herself for her career. In the back of her mind lurked the fear that next time she might not escape so lightly. It gave her the creeps just thinking about it. Under the hard-nosed newswoman lurked an orthodox romantic for whom sex had never been a recreational activity but an expression of love.

Despite having advanced in age to the ripeness of twenty-six years, her sexual experience was somewhat limited. In the biblical sense, she had known only two men: her first consummated affair was at university, when she had dated the same fellow undergraduate for five terms; the second came as an engagement package that had lasted two years. That commitment had ended when her fiancé, impatient over the indefinite nature of their engagement and peeved by her refusal to name the day, had issued an ultimatum: marriage in three months or separation. Following her gut instincts, she had opted for a career and freedom. With such a restricted sexual history, the idea of becoming a convenient outlet for Colson's excess testosterone was repugnant. If she could prove her worth in her professional capacity he would have to respect her. She was determined to make her Wimbledon debut a centre-court performance.

Taxi, train and taxi later, she was dropped at the address written on her piece of paper. It was a large, detached, four-storey property. A board affixed to the gate proclaimed, *The Cedars' Nursery School, Proprietor Mrs Caroline Kershaw.*

As she paid the fare, the inquisitive taxi driver took in the scene and asked, 'What's been happening here then, love?'

'Just another road accident statistic.'

It was an unfeeling response, but inwardly she was cursing Kevin. So much for her hope of an exclusive. The lead he had given her was stale: a small circle of reporters were gathered about the front door, pestering the uniformed policeman guarding it. Two cellophane-wrapped floral tributes were already propped at the kerbside, and a group of gawking onlookers milled on the pavement.

As her taxi sped away, a television, outside-broadcast crew drew up. Kate wondered why they were wasting their time, for the scene hardly provided a photo-opportunity. Apart from a saloon car with a shattered headlight parked at an odd angle to the kerb, and a series of chalk lines drawn on the tarmac by policemen with tape-measures, there was nothing to record.

Instead of joining the competition Kate mingled with the crowd but could not unearth a single witness. It was an affluent residential area. Most of the spectators looked well-heeled, and from their conversation it became obvious that a number of them were local residents, but no one had heard anything of the collision until the arrival of the ambulance and the blaring of police sirens. A senior police officer appeared at the door of the house to be greeted by a battery of Japanese technology. Kate hurried to add her own mike to the others that were thrust into the spokesman's face.

His statement informed the waiting press that the victim of the accident was a three year old boy, Toby Edmunds. Yes, he had attended The Cedars' Nursery School and yes, his family had been informed. Death had been instantaneous, and no, there was no evidence that the offending car had been speeding. The driver could not be named until the precise circumstances of the accident had been investigated. And until the police enquiries were complete, Mrs Kershaw, the school's proprietor, could not be interviewed. No further statement was likely that day.

The policeman withdrew and the rat-pack broke up. Intent on pursuing the dead child's grieving family, they headed en masse for the nearest call box to check the numbers of subscribers called Edmunds.

Kate, still interested in obtaining a vivid eye-witness account, did not follow them; instead she scanned the two large properties opposite. At a first-floor window, a face withdrew. Instinct urged her to check it out. This might be the witness she sought.

The house was an almost identical building to the one that housed the nursery school, and its single bell-push declared sole occupancy. The six foot Afro-Caribbean with neat dreadlocks who opened the door was a surprise, chiefly because he was wearing a frilly apron.

'What's de problem, gal, ma pinny or ma skin colour?' There was no aggression, he was grinning at her.

'Neither, you look fetching.'

'I just love pretty compliments, lady, so I'll ask what I can do for you.' The heavily accented West Indian was gone from his voice now.

'Did you see anything of this morning's accident?' She turned, indicating the road.

'You a reporter?'

She admitted the fault. As the door began to close on her, she stuck out a foot.

'I wouldn't do that if I were you, doll, this is a heavy-weight door.'

'Please, I noticed someone at a first-floor widow, she might . . .'

He cut her off, 'You people are nothing but ghouls. A kid died out there this morning and you want to make money from it.'

'I want to write an accurate report of what happened, that's all.' The lie came easily, smoothly.

'We have nothing to tell you, so if you wouldn't mind moving your dainty foot . . .'

As if in confirmation of his use of 'we', a woman's voice called down the stairs.

'Who is it, Winston?'

It was Kate who responded. 'Good morning, my name is Kate Rider,' she called up the stairs. ' I've just been asking Winston if I can talk to you.'

There was a momentary hesitation, then the same voice commanded, 'Show her up, Win.'

'She's a reporter, Ma.'

Ma? Kate wondered if she had misheard, the voice hadn't sounded at all West Indian.

'So? She won't bite will she? I'm bored with my own company. I'd like to see her.'

Kate beamed her triumph and Winston shrugged. 'You'd better follow me.'

Both the entrance hall and first-floor sitting-room to which she was escorted were elegantly furnished with antiques, but Kate had eyes only for her elderly hostess. She looked every inch the stereotypical English aristocratic, her demeanour and dyed-foxy hair reminiscent of Queen Elizabeth I. The wheel-chair in which she was seated was no surprise, for the chair-lift installed on the stairs had prepared Kate for some form of disability.

She treated the invalid to the sunniest of her open smiles. 'It's very good of you to agree to see me.'

'You don't look like a reporter.'

'Don't I? Perhaps that's just as well. There are people who don't have a very high opinion of the press.' She looked pointedly at Winston as she spoke. Instead of withdrawing he seated himself in a chair. She noticed that he had removed the apron.

The woman chuckled. 'Have you been rude to this young woman, son?'

Kate found it impossible to believe that this ancient, most English-looking woman with her upper-class accent was truly Winston's mother.

'I told her the truth, Ma – that they were a bunch of ghouls, squeezing a story from a child's death.'

'She's far too pretty to be a ghoul. You had better apologise by pouring us all a sherry.' Turning to her visitor, she commanded, 'Sit down, my dear.'

Kate waited for Winston to serve the sherries before beginning her questioning.

'I noticed you sitting at the window, Mrs . . . ?'

'Blakeney, Irene Blakeney. Yes, since the accident, I've been spending far too much time looking out of windows. I am referring, of course, to my own accident; that was a car too, but I wasn't run over, I was inside it.'

'I'm sorry . . .'

'There's no need to be. I'm a fortunate woman, and life is bearable, even for a cripple. And of course I have Winston to console me.'

She looked towards Winston affectionately as she said this, and Kate wondered anew about this odd relationship. Mrs Blakeney could not possibly be his mother. It was not just a matter of race; the woman was in her seventies, while Winston was young, around Kate's own age.

'You saw what happened outside, this morning?' Kate asked.

'Unfortunately, I did. It's years since I saw anyone killed. There were so many deaths in the war, but I've never witnessed the death of a child before.' She continued, without prompting, 'I could see it unfolding before me, but could do nothing to prevent it. A man in overalls came out of the house, one of the interior decorators who have been at work over there for the past week. The little fellow came hurrying out after him. At first I thought the child was trying to catch up with the workman, but then I saw that he was actually escaping.'

'Escaping, why do you say that?'

'He was looking back, as if fearful of pursuit. The decorator's vehicle was parked on the road.' Kate followed Mrs Blakeney's glance out of the window. 'It's since been removed. The workman went to the van and opened the rear doors, quite unaware of the child following him, I'm sure of that. While he was busy at the back of the vehicle, the child ran out from around its bonnet. I could see a car, coming sedately down from the direction of the common and realised it was on a collision course with the child. It's odd, you know, it was as if time lengthened, everything went into slow motion: the little boy advanced straight into its path, I counted his every step. I doubt if the driver had time to react, he wouldn't have seen the child until the last moment. It was like watching fate unfurl, as if the convergence was destined to be. An elderly clergyman and a small child.' She sighed. 'Do you believe in fate, Miss Rider?'

Kate didn't respond to the question but asked one of her own, 'You said a clergyman?'

'Yes, he was wearing a dog-collar. In fact, I think I recognised him. I believe he was the retired minister from St. Anselm's down the road, but I couldn't be sure. He was no sooner out of his car when he collapsed in the road. He was carried off in the same ambulance that took the little boy.'

Two casualties and one of them a clergyman. It was an additional angle, and Kate's journalistic instincts sharpened.

'How ghastly for you, to be witness to all that,' she commiserated.

'But how lucky for the lady reporter,' came, sotto voce, from Winston. Mrs Blakeney appeared not to hear.

'Is there anything you can tell me about the proprietor of the nursery school? Is she the owner of the house?'

'Good lord, no. Mrs Kershaw simply has a tenancy agreement to use the basement as a nursery. It started up only a year or so ago. At the time, there was considerable opposition to it from certain of the residents.'

'The Nimby syndrome,' Winston interjected.

'That's right, it doesn't matter whose backyard as long as it's not mine. You know the type; they believe that any commercial enterprise would lower the tone of the neighbourhood. All nonsense, of course. We are directly opposite but never hear the children. There has been an increase in traffic at delivery and collection times, but it's hardly a problem.'

'I don't suppose you know where Mrs Kershaw lives?'

'She's fairly local, I believe. The Armstruthers, her landlords, mentioned that she comes from the Putney direction. I suppose she will be hounded, poor woman, though apportioning blame hardly helps.'

Kate felt obliged to defend her own position. 'The little boy was her responsibility, she had an obligation to ensure his safety. Giving publicity to the failure of security here could save other young lives.'

Mrs Blakeney was keen to explore this justification, but Kate was equally keen to get on the trail of Mrs Kershaw and the collapsed clergyman.

'Would you allow me to use your name in my report?'

'I'd rather you didn't, dear. The police might want me to attend the inquest if they found out there was another witness. The workman was on the spot, he can tell them everything they need to know. He must know that the car wasn't speeding.' As an afterthought she inquired, 'Which newspaper do you work for?'

'*The Flag.*'

Kate heard Winston scoff.

'That's the new one isn't it?' Mrs Blakeney said. 'I always read *The Telegraph* myself. Well, it was nice to have met you, my dear. Good luck.'

Winston showed Kate out, following her onto the front doorstep. 'You'll respect Ma's wishes – you won't name her as your source?'

'Of course not, I've given my word. Goodbye and thanks.'

'Hang on a minute,' he called. He popped back into the hall, returning to hand her a card. It bore the legend "The Spice Mill" and an address in Richmond.

'What's this?'

'A club – young, professional clientele, live music, classy stuff. If you find yourself at a loose end any Tuesday, Thursday or Friday night, come along. Tell the doorman you're Win Blakeney's guest.'

Win Blakeney. He used Irene's name, perhaps he was her adopted son. 'I might take you up on that.'

And so she might. The Blakeneys intrigued her. Maybe the real Wimbledon story lay with them.

Chapter 3

The crowd on the opposite pavement had dispersed. Only the television crew and a handful of spectators remained. A very plain, female reporter was talking into a microphone, and the camera was rolling. As Kate watched, the camera-man swung his lens through ninety degrees to focus on a piece of staged action: a young girl, obviously under direction, approached the place where the little boy had met his death. Solemnly, she placed a floral tribute at the kerbside. Kate recognised the bouquet as one of the two wreaths that had already adorned the spot when she first arrived. The cheapskate television crew had borrowed one of the tributes as a prop and then recruited a bystander to act out a homage that had already been paid. If Winston were watching, his jaundiced views on the media would be confirmed.

Consulting her London street-atlas, Kate located the two nearest hospitals. For once her random choice paid off: the first Accident and Emergency Department that she tried proved to be the correct one. Staff on the reception-desk confirmed that a clergyman had been admitted, but refused to divulge information about his condition. Kate fumed with disappointment; she should have claimed a blood relationship.

Leaving the building by its revolving doors, she caught up with a distressed- looking, middle-aged priest. As always, intuition served her well and encouraged her to try a long shot.

'Excuse me, but don't I know you from St. Anselm's?' she inquired.

The priest came out of his reverie. 'I'm sorry my dear, I didn't recognise you. Are you one of my parishioners?'

'I can't really claim to be that.' The lie came easily. 'I haven't attended much since the last vicar retired.'

'Oh dear, so you knew Stephen Langton?'

'Knew?' Kate's interest quickened. 'Surely he isn't dead, he passed me in his car only the other day.'

She was soon in possession of everything she needed to know. The Reverend Stephen Langton had been admitted that morning, having suffered a massive stroke. Earlier, he had been involved in a fatal road accident that had induced his seizure. His death had occurred within an hour of arrival at the hospital.

The clergyman, who was the Reverend Langton's successor at St. Anselm's, comforted Kate. He even invited her to read something at the memorial service.

Though Kate's grief was contrived she was genuinely sorry – a second death heightened the tragedy but it didn't add much in terms of human interest. An interview with a priest-become-child-killer, however unintentional that killing had been, would have made a far better story.

She made her way back to the nursery school. The road outside was clogged with parked cars. The young pupils were just dispersing. It was a fortuitous timing that Kate, ever the opportunist, intended to exploit.

She adopted the posture of another waiting parent and listened. The fatal accident was the single topic of conversation, and some of the mothers were obviously hearing about it for the first time. Many of the women appeared distressed and agitated, though sorrow was not the only emotion being expressed.

An indignant mother declared, 'I'm withdrawing Melissa. It's simply not good enough, considering the fees we pay.'

This sentiment was echoed by others. Apparently such mishaps were only supposed to occur at state-run nurseries that offered free places.

Two nursery assistants handed the infants directly into the custody of the waiting mothers They were challenged by the mother of Melissa.

'How could you have let it happen?'

The two helpers looked miserable but said nothing.

As they dispatched the last child, Kate accosted the pair. 'Good afternoon, may I speak to Mrs Kershaw please? I've just moved into the neighbourhood and I'm looking for a nursery place for my three year old.'

Mrs Kershaw's employees shifted uncomfortably, but the older of the two was polite.

'Would you mind waiting outside for a moment. There's been a problem today, and she's very busy, but I'll find out if she can see you.'

They left Kate standing at the open door, but as soon as they disappeared down the basement stairway, she followed.

In the basement a deeply distressed, motherly-looking woman was being comforted by an elegant but anxious-looking blonde.

'Rose, believe me, no one blames you. If that man had closed the main door after himself, it would never have happened.'

Rose clung to her comforter, her ample frame wracked with sobs.

'But it was me who took them to the toilet, I knew

Toby was hyper-active and inclined to run away, I should have kept a special watch on him. How *could* I have failed to notice that he didn't come back with the others? Oh, Mrs Kershaw, I feel terrible.'

The blonde, thus identified as Caroline Kershaw, detected the intruder and challenged her, 'Who are you? What are you doing here?'

Kate appealed wordlessly to the two helpers to sanction her presence. One obliged. 'She's a parent, come to inquire about a place.' She frowned at Kate. 'I asked you to wait outside.'

'I'm sorry,' Kate apologised to her accuser. 'I didn't think you would mind if I came in to look at your facilities.' Her interest in the playroom wasn't pretended. Little details, like *the rainbow-coloured playhouse that Toby had been playing in, prior to his death,* would add the authenticity of inside information to her reportage.

Mrs Kershaw, a woman in her thirties, brushed aside the wisps of stray blonde hair that had escaped from her bun and invited the prospective client into her office.

'You must be wondering what you've walked into. This is usually a welcoming place with a happy staff. Unfortunately, you've come at a very bad time.'

Kate was all wide-eyed innocence. 'You've obviously had a spot of bother.'

'We've had rather more than that.' Tears welled into the grey eyes. 'One of our pupils was killed this morning.'

Kate feigned ignorance. 'Do you mean a child has been murdered?'

Caroline Kershaw's already ashen face turned a shade whiter. She appeared to be trembling.

'No, of course not, it was an accident. A car.'

Kate was relentless. 'How awful for you all. And the poor mother; how distraught she must be.'

The sympathy loosened Mrs Kershaw's tongue. 'She is. What makes it even worse is that she's suffered a double tragedy. Only two weeks ago, she miscarried a baby. Now to lose Toby is just too cruel.'

There was no doubt that her informant's grief was genuine. For Kate, however, the additional misfortune was excellent news. The human interest aspect was growing. The emotive sentences that would embellish her story were already forming in her head.

'How unfair for tragedy to strike the same family twice,' she murmured. The glib words were a cover for her enthusiasm.

Mrs Kershaw became more business-like. 'I'm sorry, I shouldn't be burdening you with all this. But, as you can imagine, we are very upset.' She offered a brochure, taken from her desk-top. 'Perhaps you'd like to take a copy of our prospectus? There's an application form at the back.'

The glossy prospectus would provide useful background detail. Kate took it a shade too eagerly.

Mrs Kershaw's eyes narrowed.

'Do you have a son or daughter?'

'A little girl.'

Though Kate's hesitation was slight, it lasted a shade too long for the perceptive Mrs Kershaw. 'Would you mind giving me your name and address,' she said stiffly. It was a demand rather than a request and her voice was positively hostile.

'It's the wrong time to be pestering you.' Kate beat a retreat, calling over her shoulder, 'I'll return when it's more convenient.'

Caroline Kershaw came after her. 'You're not a prospective parent, are you? You're a bloody reporter. Why can't you people stop hounding me? Surely there are enough villains in the world. Why do I warrant so much attention?'

Kate accepted her ejection from the nursery school without protest. In walking away, she averted her eyes from the house across the street. She felt mildly ashamed.

Kate pondered the Kershaw woman's agitation. What had she meant about warranting so much attention? During the course of the day, the police had protected the nursery school from the gathered reporters. So why was she claiming press persecution? A possible answer was that she had been previously subjected to media harassment. What, Kate wondered, could there be in Caroline Kershaw's past to arouse such interest?

Jack Brymer had advised her to dig for skeletons and it certainly looked as if she had unlocked the cupboard that hid one. It was a start, but not enough. She needed to uncover the whole rattle-bag if she were to read the bones and turn-in an exclusive.

A framework for her story was completed in her head as she loitered on the leafy roads between The Cedars Nursery and Wimbledon Station. It was probable that at least one of the nursery assistants would take that route home. Her anticipation and patience were rewarded. It was the small break she needed, the key to turning a twelve-liner into a news sensation.

Mrs Kershaw's young assistant was preoccupied and completely unaware of the stalker at her heels. She started perceptibly when Kate spoke.

'I thought I recognised you. I do hope I didn't get you into trouble by barging into the nursery school like that.'

The girl was indignant. 'You lied, you said you were a parent.'

'I know I did, but I really want to help and I couldn't think of any other way of speaking to your boss.'

The girl was red-eyed from weeping. 'You say you want to help. How can you do that? Nothing will bring Toby back.'

'But the school shouldn't suffer, should it? It was the workman who left the door open, not one of you. It would be terribly unfair if the school had to close because of his carelessness.'

'The school close?' The girl looked panic stricken. 'Don't say that, it's the first proper job I've had since I left school two years ago.'

'That's why Mrs Kershaw is so wrong to avoid the press. Given the right publicity, nobody will hold the school responsible.'

'And you could do that? Give us the right publicity?'

'Of course, it's what I'm trained to do. And you could help, if you provide me with the right information.'

'What do you want to know?'

The girl's naiveté was almost shocking.

'Why don't I buy us a snack in the café by the station,' Kate offered.

Seated in the café, the girl, whose name was Sharon Mills, began to relax. 'Which paper do you write for?' she asked.

'*The Flag.*' Remembering Winston's reaction, Kate wondered if it were wise to be so truthful.

The girl was enthusiastic. 'My Mum buys that one. What a coincidence.'

Sharon was completely loyal to her employer, describing her in glowing terms.

'The children love her, and she's so good with them.'

'Is she a good employer?'

'The best.' Sharon's admiration was blatant. 'She's much more than a fully qualified nursery teacher, you know. She's clever. She has a proper university degree as well as social work qualifications.'

Kate's ears pricked at this last piece of intelligence. 'So, Mrs Kershaw used to be a social worker?'

'That's right. Up until three years ago she worked for Wandsworth Social Services. It was after there was all that fuss over the little girl that she resigned and started-up the nursery school.'

It needed only the smallest prompt to turn Sharon into a mine of information. The 'little girl' in question had been part of Caroline Kershaw's personal case load. She had also been on the *at risk* register. The child's mother had a live-in boyfriend. High on drugs, he had swung the little mite by her feet and cracked her head open on a bedroom wall.

'There was a huge fuss about it: a court case, an official inquiry, and it was in all the papers. It wasn't Mrs Kershaw's fault, but the newspapers were horrible and blamed her. They made her life a misery,' Sharon concluded.

It was the lead Kate was looking for. It would be a simple matter to go back through the archives to find the press coverage.

When they entered the cafe, the girl had been suspicious of Kate's motives. By the time she had finished her first cake she was won over and they had become confederates. Kate insisted on buying her a second cream cake and left her munching happily, convinced she had performed an excellent public relations service for her employer.

Kate was reassured: rusty she might be but she had

lost none of her old interviewing skills. People complained about invasion of privacy, but then made it ridiculously easy for journalists like herself to intrude into their lives. Ambition and professional pride stilled any uneasiness about the unethical methods she had employed.

Chapter 4

Though Kate had only vague recollections of the Wandsworth child killing, it was not difficult to get at the facts. The unwary Sharon had provided an essentially accurate account: Tammy, the three year old daughter of single parent Maureen Willet, had been brutally murdered by the latest of her mother's live-in lovers. Tammy had been on the *at risk* register and Caroline Kershaw, as Senior Child Care Officer for the Borough of Wandsworth, was officially responsible for her welfare.

The social worker tried, many times, to visit the child. Not once did she succeed in entering the council flat that was the Willet's home. Tammy Willet was but one problem child of many and Mrs Kershaw was burdened with a case load of unmanageable proportions.

Despite the pressures on her time, Caroline Kershaw was a meticulous record-keeper. Concerned for Tammy's welfare, she alerted her superiors to the situation by sending them a memo for every abortive visit to the Willet flat. In the light of this evidence, the official enquiry exonerated her from all blame. Criticism was levelled, not at the conscientious social worker in the field, but at the desk-bound man at the top. The Director of Wandsworth's Social Services was reprimanded for procedural failure in the handling of the case and encouraged into early retirement.

The killing was a particularly nasty case of child abuse. The post-mortem revealed earlier, multiple injuries: long-healed fractures of ribs and fingers and lesser hair-line fractures to the skull. Some of these injuries dated back to the early months of the little girl's life. Medical evidence proved that most had been suffered before the advent of the killer into her mother's life.

Every paper in the land, including the Sundays, had given the case coverage. It had hit the headlines more than once. The initial story was carried at the time of Tammy's death. Later, the findings of the official enquiry into the failure of the Social Services was given front page treatment. The lengthy trial of Patric Feeney and the child's mother provided prime copy for days.

Feeney was charged with manslaughter, and Willet with aiding and abetting. Both were found guilty and received eighteen months imprisonment. The press crusaded against the leniency of the sentence. Kate was in agreement – eighteen months, less remission, seemed a small price to pay for a child's life.

Virtually every news report on the case included a photograph of Caroline Kershaw. It was noticeable that the same photograph was not used twice. Press photographers must have been pursuing the woman for months, and Kate, appreciative of the woman's beauty, could understand why they had done so. Their subject was strikingly photogenic – her fine bone structure was reminiscent of the young Grace Kelly's and three years ago she had worn her pale blonde hair in a tumbling looseness that was very fetching. More than this, she had a stately demeanour and a classically tragic air. This was a look accentuated in the later photographs, when the strain of her ordeal was clearly written on her fine-drawn features. As long as the case was in the public domain, so was Caroline Kershaw. Her complaint of being hounded was fully justified. However, Kate, as an ambitious journalist, was rarely stirred to sympathy over the plight of the beautiful.

For Kate, the notoriety of the Willet case was manna from heaven. Toby's death outside the nursery school became secondary. The Caroline Kershaw story was of far greater significance. Both child victims would be fully exploited, of course. The alliterative and rhyming nature of the victims' names would be played upon in her snappy write-up. Even the freaky coincidence of the victims being the same age was helpful. Kate was about to turn an unfortunate street accident into a tabloid sensation.

Her coverage extended to three separate articles. Less advertisements, these ran to a front page lead-in and a double-page spread. The first columns were an account of the road accident and its fatal consequences for both little Toby Edmunds and the Reverend Stephen Langton. Though she drew upon Irene's eye-witness account of Toby's death, she kept faith with the Blakeneys and did not name her source. Having no such obligation towards Caroline Kershaw, she gave her a mauling.

Kate emphasised the nursery school's negligence. There were ample grounds for criticising its lack of security. Not only were decorators working on the premises but the hyperactive Toby was known to have a tendency to wander. Tucked away at the bottom of a page was the sob-stuff – a tribute to little Toby Edmunds and his mother whose recent miscarriage was much dwelt upon. Most of the pages, amounting to two-thirds of the column inches, were given up to an examination of who was to blame for

Toby's death. Caroline Kershaw's unfortunate history as a social worker was revisited in some detail and her picture, recovered from a competitor's archives, was prominent. The latter items, with their human interest slant, were exclusive to *The Flag*.

NURSERY SCHOOL HORROR was the first of Kate's triple headlines. YOUNG MOTHER'S DOUBLE TRAGEDY, was the second. The most sensational announced: THE KERSHAW CURSE, followed with a sub-heading pastiche of Oscar Wilde, *To Lose One Three Year Old Child May Be Regarded As A Misfortune, To Lose Two Looks Like Carelessness*. The story had legs, and ran for a second day as an investigative piece entitled, HOW SAFE ARE OUR NURSERY SCHOOLS? And Kate was author of them all.

Colson was impressed. He summoned her to his office.

'Brilliant stuff, Katie. You stole a march on the competition and left them at the starting post. I've had a word with the finance department – how does an extra five grand on your salary sound?'

Her starting salary at *The Flag* had been non-negotiable and was little more than she had earned on *The Advertiser*. That Colson should voluntarily give her a boost up the income ladder was as welcome as it was unexpected.

'You're giving me a pay rise?'

'The paper likes to reward talent, that way we get to keep it. How about meeting me for a celebratory drink tonight?'

To socialise with the home-news editor in a public place was infinitely preferable to being cornered in the privacy of his office. She accepted coolly.

Kevin's was not the only invitation she received that day. Jack Brymer called by her desk.

'I'd like to take the rising star out for lunch. Can you get away?'

A growing professional vanity prevented Kate from reading any sarcasm into Jack's shining attribution. After all, she had progressed from provincial columnist to celebrity reporter in a few short weeks. Those provincial associations already seemed a lifetime away.

Predictably, Jack's offer of lunch turned out to be of the liquid variety. This time he was gracious enough to ask her to name her poison.

Returning from the massive mahogany bar with their drinks, he asked, 'Did you get your rise?'

'How do you know about that?'

He grinned. 'It was me who told Kev you were being head-hunted. I knew he would take the bait.'

'Head-hunted? But I've not been approached.'

'So?' Jack tapped his nose.

'You made it up?'

'Not made-up, more like anticipated. Another scoop like the Kershaw exposé and you'll have all the other tabloids chasing your tail. A word of advice from an old-timer: Kev will try to get you to agree to a long term contract.' He sipped his beer. 'Don't sign-up for longer than six months.'

'I may be naive, but isn't that the sort of job security I should welcome?' she asked.

'It would be selling yourself too cheaply. Stay independent; that way you'll be able to squeeze another rise out of him the next time you turn in something good.'

It made her uncomfortable to know that Jack was her benefactor. It placed her under an obligation to him that she did not relish. Her close encounter with Colson led her to believe that *The Flag's* chief crime reporter might make similar demands. Whilst Jack was younger and probably the better man, his thinning hair, shabby, unshaven appearance and habit of chain-smoking made him an unappealing potential sexual partner. However, Jack gave no hint of any carnal expectations and parted from her with a casual indifference that made her feel guilty about misjudging him.

In the evening she found herself in the same city pub, with the more presentable Kevin. His script was much as Jack had predicted. He raised the subject of her conditions of employment as if it were of no particular relevance.

'You're working for us on a month-by-month basis at the moment, aren't you?'

As it was he who had signed her up in the first place, he was fully aware of the terms of her contract.

'That's right.'

'Doesn't give you much security, does it? Tell you what I'll do. You're a bright girl, you've proved you can deliver what our readers like. I'll get Personnel to draw up a two year deal.'

'Thank you, Kevin, but I prefer not to be tied for so long.' Now she was grateful to Jack for briefing her.

'It would be worth another two grand.'

'On top of the rise you gave me today?'

'Of course.'

'Sorry, the answer is still no.'

He looked dumbfounded. 'We'll keep your contract to a year then, shall we?'

Eventually, they settled for a six month contract and an additional three thousand on her salary.

'You're a tough negotiator, for a little lady from the provinces.' He sounded admiring rather than complaining. 'If you don't want another drink, I'll take you home.'

'To meet your wife?'

He was not in the least disconcerted. 'I meant to your place, not mine.'

'Thanks for the offer, but that won't be necessary. I know the way.'

He reached out, claiming her hand and whispered in her ear, 'I can show you more than the way home, Kate. I'll take you on the path to paradise.'

This arrogant sentiment sounded like one of his own headlines and warranted about the same accuracy rating. During their office encounter, he had provided no such angel delights.

'Mr Colson, you're a married man and I'm not available.' The tone was teasing, the message was not.

'What's this, playing hard to get for a second time this evening?'

'I'm not playing and this is something that's not open for negotiation.'

She rose to go. 'Goodnight Kevin, see you tomorrow.'

He had too great a sense of his own dignity to chase after her. Kate preferred to believe that he let her go without hindrance because of his growing respect for her as a journalist.

Chapter 5

The problem with meteoric success, in any walk of life, is that it creates expectations. As *The Flag's* newest whiz-kid, Kate needed to build on her professional reputation by following the Kershaw exclusive with something of equal impact. The stories she was assigned were the stuff of passing interest, lacking the ingredients for an extended investigation. Everything she covered appeared in similar format in their competitors' pages, and further scoops eluded her.

There was an additional frustration. In her previous employment she had cultivated what she liked to think of as her own inimitable voice. Now she was obliged to employ the simplified vocabulary, snappy phrases and sensation-mongering demanded by *The Flag's* house style. Colson reprimanded staff who adopted a more responsible or serious approach, reminding them, 'Our readers don't want to be challenged by any of that intellectual crap.'

Absorbed in the daily seeking-out of new dramas, Kate forgot her encounter with the Blakeneys. The elderly Wimbledon cripple and her young, black companion might have passed from her mind as if they never existed, but a discovery, made in her jacket pocket, resurrected them – the printed card, advertising The Spice Mill at Richmond. At first it was an effort to recall how she had come by it.

Then she remembered Winston Blakeney's invitation.

Though she was hazy about the details, Winston had mentioned specific evenings when he would be at the club. The only certainty was that Friday was one of those days. Whether or not he had meant the following Friday, which was now many weeks gone, or any Friday she could only guess. Lacking any other engagement and being at a loose end, she decided to find out.

Although only a recent immigrant to the metropolis, Kate knew London well. It had been her old student stomping-ground. She was most at home in the more central parts, defined by Shepherd's Bush in the west, Poplar in the east and Camden Town and Battersea, north and south respectively. Richmond was comparatively unknown territory. Once, one sunny afternoon she had lain with her boyfriend on the grass of Richmond Park, but she could not recall going to Richmond itself.

Before seeking out the club she explored, walking first by a grey Thames and then climbing the terraced gardens, where she admired the view from Richmond Hill. An evening shower sent her scurrying for cover in the town where she discovered the location she sought. The Spice Mill was sited between the riverside and the fine Georgian and Queen Anne architecture of the Green. It was an exclusivity that allayed any fears that the club might be a somewhat sleazy establishment.

Remembering Winston's instruction, she identified herself as his guest. The doorman's friendly response and the swiftness of her admission confirmed that her host was in residence. Her image of the apron-wearing Winston conjured a fleeting expectation that he might be found serving behind the bar, but the barman was slight, white and very much a chirpy native Londoner.

The arrangement of busy tables around the minuscule dance floor, suggested that the club was used less for dancing than as a drinking and eating establishment. A board above the bar advertised a different national food theme for every night of the week. Today's offerings of meze, dolmades, keftedes and souvlaka, proclaimed that Friday was Greek night and a majority of the clientele were already eating.

A pianist was playing a pleasant, jazzy arrangement of a Cole Porter number and, as Kate ordered from the bar, a female vocalist struck up. It was a youthful voice but with a timing and intonation reminiscent of Ella Fitzgerald. However, the singer's physical resemblance to that doyenne of singers stopped at her colour: the young vocalist was enviably slim, with a sexy beauty that made her stylish and polished performance all the more unexpected. Such talent coupled with physical allure was a rare combination. Not until the end of the number, when the pianist rose to share the applause, did Kate realise that it had been Win Blakeney at the keyboard.

It was a charismatic Winston who compered their repertoire. His flawless patter sparkled with humour. The girl went on to sing a couple of Rodgers and Hart numbers and the Beatles' *Yesterday*. Her vocal renderings were interspersed with instrumental virtuosity from Winston. He played some Gershwin, a jazz piano classic and adaptations of recent pop music. The pair performed with great verve and energy and from the noisy appreciation that followed every number, it was obvious that they enjoyed quite a fan-club.

Abandoning the bar, Kate moved nearer to the

floor-show. As the performers joined hands to take a final bow, she attempted to catch the pianist's eye. When Winston glanced in her direction she treated him to her sunniest smile, but he gave not a flicker of recognition. Choosing to believe that she had gone unnoticed, rather than unrecognised or snubbed, she scribbled a note. A waiter obligingly turned messenger and delivered it back-stage for her, but brought no reply.

Winston and his vocalist reappeared to entertain with the second half of their programme. The duo rendered further famous numbers with an aplomb that belied their tender years. A virtuoso solo won Winston generous applause, mid-performance. Kate was puzzled that, in acknowledging the audience's appreciation, he made no attempt to seek out the sender of the note. She began to wonder if the slight was deliberate.

The entertainers left the floor for a second time. Deciding that she had suffered the discourtesy long enough, Kate chose to leave too.

At the exit of the crowded club, Winston intercepted her. 'Well, well, Miss Kate Rider. I didn't expect to see you here.'

There was no pleasure in the greeting. His tone was icy, in marked contrast to the intimacy of its stage warmth. She responded in kind, turning her genuine enthusiasm into deliberate condescension.

'I wouldn't have guessed you were an entertainer and so very professional.' Almost as an afterthought she added, 'Your vocalist gave a fantastic performance, and the Errol Garner number you played was very close to the original. You're quite the accomplished pianist.'

His lip curled, but he inclined his head in acknowledgement. 'As a journalist, you've been putting up something of an accomplished performance yourself.'

It fed her pride to know that he had read her Kershaw coup, but she opted for modesty. 'I thought you didn't approve of the rag I work for.'

'I don't, and neither do I approve of what you did to Caroline Kershaw.'

So that was it. 'I reported what happened, that's all.'

'Is that what you believe?' His tone was incredulous now. 'You resurrected that poor woman's blameless past and made her sound like a threat to children. You destroyed her health, reputation and business.'

'I don't understand. What do you mean?'

'Don't tell me that the hot-shot journalist doesn't know that the nursery school has closed its doors.'

There was such contempt in his voice that she found herself shaking. 'I had no idea. If what you say is true, then I'm sorry. But it will reopen. Memories are short, all this will blow over.'

'You descend like a vulture, take your pound of flesh and you think life will go on as before?'

The evening had been spent enjoying his music, admiring not only his talent but him, and all that time he had been harbouring this low opinion of her. She had heard quite enough of his censure. Controlling her emotions, she made a prim request for her regards to be passed to Mrs Blakeney. This was followed by a speedy exit, out into the Richmond night.

Kate's enquiries confirmed the closure of The Cedars' Nursery School. Following the publicity, Mrs Kershaw had been taken ill and so many children had been withdrawn from the school that its operation was no longer viable. Though always on the look-out for follow-up stories, this was one that she preferred to leave unreported.

Whether Caroline Kershaw's illness had occurred before or after the school's closure was unclear. Whatever the sequence, Kate's own role was not a pleasant one to contemplate. For her own advancement, she had tarnished a woman's reputation, perhaps undeservedly. In the light of the evidence, she was forced to admit that the judgmental criticism heaped upon her by Win Blakeney was not without justification.

In her previous cosy existence on the *Tamar Advertiser,* Kate's revelations had been mostly of a promotional kind. By contrast, her exposé of Caroline Kershaw had been destructive and unforgiving. Not only had the publicity cost the woman her business but it had robbed Sharon, and the other nursery assistants, of their jobs. Unwilling to be reminded of this treachery, Kate consigned her souvenir edition of the offending 'Kershaw Curse' article, to the anonymity of a bottom drawer.

Hiding the evidence did nothing to restore her peace of mind. Over another lunch-time drink with Jack, she attempted to exorcise her guilt.

'Have you ever written anything that you came to regret?' she asked.

'Frequently.' As if guessing why she was sounding him out, he continued, 'And when I do, it's usually because I haven't been sufficiently ruthless in the first instance.'

'But has what you have written ever damaged anyone, someone who probably didn't deserve it?'

'What's this inquisition about?'

When she told him, he scoffed at her shame.

'It's no good being thin-skinned about the

Kershaw woman, or anything else in this business. Journalists are red in tooth and claw. We're bound to maul a few innocents along the way.'

'And that doesn't matter?'

'You mustn't let it matter. It comes with the job.'

His wildlife metaphor reminded her too much of Winston's vulture accusation. It was not the advice that she wanted to hear as it gave no opportunity for further confession.

The recollection of Winston's reprimand made her distinctly uncomfortable. She could not explain why his good opinion was so important, she only knew she craved it. She began to brood over strategies to force him to revise his estimation of her.

Though far from an expert on the music scene, she was sure that Winston, and his young Ella were special. Apart from their musical abilities, they looked highly presentable: Win was handsome, with a personable charm and lively humour, and his companion was physically and vocally stunning. The duo deserved more recognition than could be given by their partisan following at The Spice Mill. Lesser talents played at far grander venues. All that was needed to launch them to stardom was the right publicity. Kate, with the awesome power of the Press behind her, knew that she could arrange that. Perhaps, at the same time, she might earn Win's goodwill.

Larry Fines, *The Flag's* music critic, was gay, charming and an utter eccentric. He was especially courteous towards women. When Kate asked if he would be good enough to provide a second and expert opinion on an unknown musical duo, discovered in an obscure night-spot, Larry was only too happy to oblige.

Unable to presume on Winston's hospitality, they

used their press-cards to get into the club. Larry, an exhibitionist to the core, insisted on establishing himself on a front table so that he might both see and be seen. Kate caught Winston's attention as soon as he came onto the floor. This time, he gave her a cryptic acknowledgement with his eyebrows.

That Win and Lena were brilliant was confirmed; Larry told her so. He was all for ringing back to base to bring in a back-up photographer. Kate cautioned him against doing this.

'Win has some funny ideas about newspapers. We'll do better to consult him first.'

This they did in the first interval when Winston came, unbidden, to their table.

'Hello Kate, what are you doing here again? I thought I'd said enough to chase you away for good.'

His tone was almost apologetic, as if he regretted his former rudeness. She made no reference to that encounter, but hastened to introduce *The Flag's* music critic. Larry Fines had been poached from a well-known musical weekly, and Winston recognised his name.

'If we'd known you were in our audience, Mr Fines, we would have chosen the programme more carefully.'

Fines was effusive. 'Call me Larry, please. I'm glad you didn't, the programme is a delight as it stands. It's been a pleasure listening. You and that little girl are something out of the ordinary. It's a long time since I've reviewed anything that sounds and looks as good as you two.'

Even in the club's subdued lighting it was possible to detect the flush that diffused Winston's dark skin.

Larry laid a friendly hand on his arm. 'If you're agreeable, I'd like to come back with a photographer and do an interview.'

Winston threw Kate a bewildered look. 'Is this your doing?'

'Yes, do you mind?'

'Mind? No, I'm grateful.' He turned his attention to Larry. 'We'll be playing here again on Thursday and it would be great to talk to you then. The publicity could be useful, we're not finding it easy getting other bookings. Most clubs consider our repertoire a bit too traditional for their clientele.'

'You're refreshingly modest, Winston. The numbers may be classics, but your arrangements are original.' Larry referred to his diary and confirmed the suitability of Thursday evening. 'I'd like to think that *The Flag* could give your career the kick-start it deserves. Who knows, I might be able to wangle a recording contract. How would you feel about that?'

'Discs? This isn't some sort of joke, is it?'

'Why should I joke – you sound fantastic and look terrific.' Larry's eyes lingered on Winston's well-developed physique. 'It should be the easiest bit of marketing I've ever done.'

Having arranged the publicity shoot, Larry excused himself – his boyfriend was expecting him. Having no such ties, Kate stuck around.

After the show, Win brought his vocalist to her table to be introduced. Lena proved surprisingly shy for one so totally at home performing before an audience. Kate wasn't sure why, but the girl seemed intimidated by her. News of the forthcoming interview with *The Flag's* illustrious music guru made her positively nervous.

'You must promise to do the talking, Win,' she insisted. 'I wouldn't know what to say.'

Win was very gallant, assuring her that a single photograph of her would do more for their careers than a thousand of his words.

One of the club's regular employees came to collect Lena for what was her customary lift home. She took her leave of them both. Winston saluted with a peck to her cheek and a brotherly pat on the bottom. The singer left unwillingly, giving him a tortured glance. Kate sensed that she was the cause of the anxiety. Lena was obviously reticent about leaving her man with another woman.

The club was emptying. They stayed on at the bar, balancing on stools, drinking coffee.

'I don't want to pre-empt Larry's interview, but how long have you two been performing together?'

'A little over four months. Before that I was a one man show, playing one gig a week here. A regular act quit, and the manager wanted me to fill their spot. The proviso was that I brought in a female vocalist. I advertised in magazines and local papers, the response was amazing. Lena was one of a dozen applicants.'

'So the press does have its uses.'

He ignored the dig. 'Most weren't at all suitable. Some couldn't even sing in key, and those that could were mostly old enough to be my mother.'

'Lena doesn't fit either of those categories. What a find you must have thought her.'

'She didn't seem so exceptional, at first. She doesn't read music, and her repertoire was limited to recent chart stuff, not my style at all. It seemed a hopeless alliance until Ma came up with the solution. You could say that between us, we brainwashed her. Lena came to Wimbledon and we saturated her with my type of music. Ma played her Ella and it was like a revelation. Lena has a good ear and a brilliant memory. She came to us knowing only the things in the charts, but within a month she had mastered the vocal side of my repertoire and we were adding to it.'

'Sounds like a second musical version of Pygmalion.'

'With Ma as Professor Higgins.'

They both laughed. There was a warmth between them now and though the club was closing, Kate was loath to go. When Winston offered a lift home, she accepted with alacrity.

While he was occupied with driving the car, she thought it safe to risk a more personal question.

'Is Irene your adoptive mother?'

'Why do you ask?'

She felt a barrier going up, and hastened to assure him, 'It wasn't a professional enquiry, just personal curiosity, I give you my word.'

'She's my grandmother. It was my mother she adopted.'

'Your mother? Does she still live with you?'

'No, she's dead. Killed in the car smash that crippled Ma.'

'I'm so sorry, I didn't mean to pry.'

'It was shattering at the time, but it happened years ago. Life has to go on.'

'What an awful thing – it must have been quite terrible for you.' Coming from someone whose business thrived on tragedy and misfortune, her sympathy sounded superficial, even false.

'When it happened, I opted out of my education to be with Ma. She needed me.'

Such unselfishness was foreign to Kate. 'You gave up your future to become her nurse?'

'Hardly that.' Her suggestion obviously amused him. 'Ma is a wealthy woman, well able to afford professional nursing care. She paid for me to continue my music tuition privately, there was no sacrifice. I stayed at home to be company for her while she adjusted to existence in a wheelchair. I owed her that, she had done so much for us.'

'For you and your mother?'

'Yes, my mother wasn't a child but a pregnant eighteen-year-old when Ma took her in. There aren't many women around who would do that.'

'It's certainly unusual. I would love to hear about it.' She wondered if he would consider this an impertinence, but he seemed not to mind.

'My natural grandmother cleaned Ma's house. In the school holidays she used to take her little girl along to help. Marsha, my mother, was a bright little thing who gave Ma a lot of pleasure. She left school to become a student nurse at a teaching hospital.

'And then?' Kate prompted as they pulled up at traffic lights.

'And then, in her first term, a handsome Nigerian doctor seduced her. He disappeared back to West Africa when he made her pregnant. My natural grandmother was involved with a new man, and a pregnant daughter was cramping her style. Ma had been recently widowed and didn't hesitate – she welcomed the mother-to-be into her home. Though the adoption was never formalised my mother changed her name to Blakeney before my birth.'

'A daughter and grandson as a job-lot. What a bargain.'

'I'm not sure about the bargain bit, but she's always treated me more like a son than a grandson.'

They pulled away from the intersection and Kate continued her questioning, 'What does Ma think about your career as a club musician?'

'She doesn't mind as long as I'm happy and make a success of it. Though she still regrets what she calls the sacrifice of my serious musical studies.'

'That's understandable.'

'But unjustified. Giving up music college was not

the unselfish act it sounds. I owed it to Ma. You see, it was Marsha, my mother who crashed the car, and the accident was her fault. She was killed. Ma was condemned to life in a wheelchair. Not that Ma held my mother responsible, she's far too generous for that.'

Kate wished that there had been a grandmother in her life like Irene Blakeney. She reached towards the steering wheel and squeezed Win's forearm.

'She's going to be so proud of you when you become a superstar.'

'A superstar?' he chuckled. 'That's a very attractive proposition, though not very likely. This is a highly competitive business.'

'And what does Ma think about Lena?'

'Lena? She's quite fond of her, but that's Ma's nature.'

'You make a handsome couple.' She was trying to discover the legitimacy of Lena's possessive glances.

'What are you suggesting?'

'It looks as if you have a perfect partnership in every sense.'

He laughed. 'We aren't lovers if that's what you're hinting at. Lena's just out of school.'

'I apologise for the misunderstanding, but she's hardly a baby.'

'Lena may be eighteen but her mother treats her as an infant.'

'She's a lovely girl, I can't believe you don't fancy her.' Her tone was teasing.

'Of course I fancy her, but I've given my word I won't take advantage. Diana, her mother, wanted her to go to university. Like a lot of girls with good voices, Lena was stage struck. It was her idea to have a year out to try to break into show business. Her mother went along with it because she thought a year of disappointment would clear it out of Lena's system. Diana is some sort of higher grade executive in the Civil Service. As a single parent, it's been a struggle to get where she is. She wants better for her daughter and sees education as the key. She's frightened I might get in the way of her ambitions.'

'And doesn't Lena get any say in all this?'

'You wouldn't think so. Before Diana agreed to us teaming up professionally, she extracted both my promise and Ma's that I would behave myself. Can you believe it, my grandmother having to stand surety for my honourable behaviour?'

'Poor Lena.'

'Lena isn't the one who was made to promise,' he complained.

'Such temptation must be very hard to resist.'

'Isn't that the nature of temptation?'

From Kensington she gave directions to her Holland Park address. When they arrived outside the flat, she offered a peck on the cheek. With the smallest of manoeuvres he received it on his lips and responded with a more full-blooded version of his own.

'Do I get an invitation to come in?'

His boldness surprised her, there had been no preliminaries, not even a minor flirtation.

'Sorry, Win, but aren't you confusing me with Lena?'

He pretended to be examining the skin on the back of her hand, which he was grasping tightly. 'Not a likely mistake, there seems to be some difference in pigmentation.'

'Then I wouldn't make a very satisfactory substitute, would I?' Her tone was bright yet inside she was disturbed.

'If I expected that, it would be an insult. You're too

gorgeous a talent to be sitting on the substitutes' bench.'

Not only was he handsome, he was likeable and intelligent. She was sorely tempted. Outside of work, her new life in London was proving lonely. It would be good to feel those strong arms around her. He was nuzzling at her neck and she indulged him because it felt so very nice. When his hand travelled to a more intimate place, she broke away.

'Come on, Kate, we'd be good together, I can feel it.'

'Not so long ago, you didn't approve of me at all,' she reminded.

'Untrue, it's your profession I don't approve. That hasn't changed.'

'But that is me, Winston, it's my life. I couldn't give myself to a man who despises what I do.'

'So I don't get to come in?'

'No, you don't.'

He gave a rueful grin. 'I'm disappointed. You shouldn't smile the way you do if you don't mean it.'

'What has my smile got to do with this?'

'Everything – it says *welcome* in a most engaging manner. I genuinely thought I would find the door open.'

She would have loved to hear more of his pretty speeches. In a way it was a disappointment that he made no further effort to achieve her surrender.

Imagining Win's dark, dangerous energy between her sheets, between her thighs, were arousing thoughts that made sleep elusive. Her rejection of him had little to do with her career, nothing to do with Lena and everything to do with her white middle-class neighbours. If they had observed the young negro, Rastafarian locks and all, leaving her flat in the morning, she would never have lived it down. Notwithstanding all her London experience, it was something of a shock to realise that she was still conditioned by the narrow provincialism of her upbringing.

Chapter 6

Caroline Kershaw had committed suicide. The announcement was telephoned through to *The Flag's* news-desk by a freelance newsman who just happened to live in the dead woman's road.

After overdosing on a handful of her prescribed sleeping tablets, the distraught woman had gassed herself. The news numbed Kate. To her it felt more like murder than suicide, and in her guilt-ravaged state she felt personally responsible.

Colson, with no regard for her feelings, expected her to cover the tragedy.

'You're the obvious girl for the job. Reporting on the inquest will be an opportunity to resurrect your earlier stuff. After all, our intelligent readership will need to be reminded who the corpse is.'

His insensitivity stunned Kate. Her imagination was already working overtime. She visualised Caroline swallowing the pills, one at a time; she saw her removing the oven shelves, switching-off the electricity supply to the cooker's automatic ignition system, and turning the gas regulator to full. And finally, she saw the beautiful, tragic head inserted into that poisonous place.

'I'm sorry, Kevin,' she blurted. 'There's no way I can handle this one.'

Colson snorted his disbelief. 'What's the matter, woman, are you going soft?'

Her protest, that the dead deserved to be left in peace, met with a further snort of derision and a lecture on professionalism. 'A true reporter never turns down the chance of a story. In this business you have to learn to stay detached.'

'I can't do it. Don't try to make me, Kevin. You'd be wasting your time.'

'You keep disappointing me, Kate, it's really too bad.'

In the context of their discussion, his oblique reference to her refusal to have sex with him disgusted her.

In the days leading to the inquest, her headline, 'The Kershaw Curse,' returned to haunt her. Recovering the offending article from her word-processor, she re-read what she had written and felt ashamed of the way she had distorted the facts.

The nursery school death had been an accident. Carelessness had been a contributory factor, but others were at fault, not the woman she had blamed. Previously, as a social worker, Caroline Kershaw had been a conscientious contributor to a difficult profession. There was no doubt that she had done her best to protect a child who was at risk. It had not been Caroline, but the system, that had failed the little girl.

For the sake of an exclusive, Kate had persecuted a blameless woman, a decent woman, one who had warranted support not exposure.

Returning home that evening, she retrieved her hard-copy of the same article. The bijou flat did not possess a fireplace, so she made the stainless steel sink her incinerator. She fanned the flames until all that was left of her first scoop was damp, grey ash. The ritual burning proved a pointless gesture. Purging by fire provided no solace, for she knew every word of her exposé by heart. For a long while she stood at the sink, head bowed, mourning her victim.

Jack Brymer had been out of town on one of his fraud-busting assignments. On his return, he stopped by her desk.

'What's up?' he enquired. 'You look terrible?'

'Thanks, Jack. That's just the sort of confidence booster a girl needs.'

'So, what's the problem?'

He was the only person in whom she could confide. 'It's the Kershaw business. I can't rid my mind of what I did to that poor woman.'

'When's the inquest?'

'Today.'

'You'll feel better when it's out of the way.' At least he had the decency to show some compassion. 'You're not covering it for the paper, are you?'

She shook her head. 'I couldn't, Charlie's taken it on. Kevin considers it unprofessional of me to be so lily-livered.'

'Don't let Kev get to you. Look, I'm busy now but intend to knock off at seven. I'll collect you then and we can go for a drink.'

Though not sharing Jack's belief in the restorative power of alcohol, Kate willingly accepted the invitation.

He was punctual, for which Kate was grateful. She was desperate for any form of diversion. On the walk to the pub he held her arm protectively and before ordering accompanied her to a table in a secluded corner. It was an unexpected attentiveness and out of character.

Returning with their drinks he slopped beer in her lap, but typically failed to notice.

'What was the outcome of the Kershaw inquest?' he asked.

In her bag was a copy of Charlie's unedited report. It made unpleasant reading. She handed it to him.

Caroline Kershaw had written a suicide note to her husband. Charlie's report included the full text:

My dearest Michael,

The newspapers have destroyed my chance of making a fresh start. I haven't the strength to face a future where I will be remembered as the woman responsible for the deaths of two children.

I love you, and know the pain this will cause but I am a very unlucky person. You are better off without me. Try to find happiness.

Forgive me.

Caroline.

The coroner had been critical of the press coverage. Outside the court, the husband had made a statement to the press in which he blamed vindictive and inaccurate reporting for disturbing the balance of his wife's mind. More specifically, he named *The Flag* as the prime offender.

Jack patted her hand. 'Don't take it personally, you were only doing your job.'

Kate wished she could believe him.

The criticisms reported by Charlie did not feature in *The Flag's* coverage. The published report was much more selective and included no mention of its own star-billing.

Newspapers dislike criticism of their practices. It was Colson's hope that, in the interest of press freedom, other editors would operate a similar censorship. However, in this instance, the paper singled out for blame was a newcomer that had become rather too successful in the circulation battle. Two rival tabloids took up cudgels. Self-righteously they condemned *The Flag's* methods. Both splashed photographs of the grieving Michael Kershaw on their next day's front pages. Both the husband's statement and the coroner's were reported in full and Kate Rider's name was sprinkled as liberally as *The Flag's*.

Despite the widely-held belief that 'no publicity is bad publicity,' the competitors' coverage displeased Colson as much as it upset Kate. She was summoned to his presence.

'Looks as though you took this one a little too far, my lovely,' he complained.

She bridled. It was all very well for him to be wise after the event. At the time, he had been delighted with her exposé.

'You don't need to tell me that, I can't sleep, thinking about it.' Kate was too guilt-ridden to defend herself.

'What you should be thinking about is how we turn this to our advantage. Or, at the very least, how we effect a damage-limitation exercise.'

'Nothing can bring her back.'

'I'm not concerned with the woman. It's the damage to *The Flag's* reputation that bothers me. Much of that is down to the blasted widower. Apparently he's considering a complaint to the Press Commission. We need to do something to shut him up.'

Kate's loyalty to her paper was overridden by sympathy for the grieving husband. She felt utterly miserable.

'I would apologise if I thought he would listen.'

'You'll do no such thing,' Colson bullied. 'An

admission that we were in the wrong would be tantamount to inviting a huge claim for damages. Though I wonder . . .' An unpleasant smile spread over his even features. 'Tell me, what's the best form of defence?'

'Attack, you mean?' The response was listless. Kate had never felt less aggressive.

'Precisely. We need to show Joe Public that the loving husband isn't to be trusted.'

'The man is grieving for his wife. We should leave him alone.'

'On the contrary, Kate, we must be very nice to him. Correction: *you* must be.'

She didn't bother to ask why, she knew he would explain.

'We'll set a trap, and you, my darling, will be the bait. Kershaw must be persuaded to join you for dinner. The restaurant will be conveniently intimate. There will be a discreet photographer on hand to record your tête-à-tête.'

Colson's deviousness was beyond Kate. 'How will that help?' she asked.

'Oh, it will help a lot. It shouldn't be too difficult to capture the widower smiling into the eyes of the woman accused of driving his wife to suicide. What a front page splash *that* will make. The caption will write itself.'

'It's a crazy idea!' Kate was incredulous. 'This is a man who blames me for the death of his wife. In the first place he'll never agree to see me.'

'You underestimate yourself, my dear. You have sensational tits, a delightful arse, good legs and a very sweet, kissable face. Do you need reminding that it was you who got us into this mess and that it's down to you to get us out?'

'By fair means or foul, it would seem,' she snorted.

Colson ignored the disapproval in her tone. 'Now you're talking sense. Set up a meeting with Kershaw. I'll brief you on the when and where. You'll be sympathetic and so obliging that you'll have him salivating. Bob Spackman can get the shots, he's our best. Our target won't even know he's on camera. It's perfect.'

From the age of sixteen, Kate had wanted to be a journalist. She had regarded her appointment on the *Tamar Advertiser* as a stepping stone to her real goal - fame on one of the nationals. Now she was expected to work as an escort.

Colson's plan to entrap Michael Kershaw broke every code of moral decency. Kate could not believe what was being asked of her.

'Even if he agreed to meet me, I couldn't do this to him,' she argued.

Such protests were ignored.

'You seem to forget you're an employee, under contract,' her editor snapped. 'If you want to keep your job, you'll do as you're told. Liaise with Bob Spackman and make sure he gets his photo-opportunity. He'll tell you where to take Kershaw.'

'Then what am I supposed to do?'

'When the details are sorted, you telephone the protesting widower and arrange your date.'

'Don't you think he may take some persuading?'

'Of course he will,' Colson growled. 'So you'd better get your script straight in advance. Act devastated, show concern, pile on the sweetness and sympathy.'

'There's to be no sexual seduction, then?' she asked sarcastically.

'Keep that for the restaurant. You're a clever girl Kate, words are your forte. He'll agree to meet you.'

He telephoned Spackman. 'I've a nice little

assignment that's right up your street, Bob. We need some intimate shots of one of my girls and an unsuspecting mug. She's on her way to see you now. She'll fill you in with the details.'

He waved Kate on her way. 'Room 211, floor below. Spackman's expecting you.'

She went, wretchedly and unwillingly.

The photographer looked more like a successful, middle-aged banker than one of the paparazzi. She relayed Colson's instructions without enthusiasm.

Spackman detected that her heart wasn't in it. 'It's a pity you don't have more relish for this assignment, darling. There's more scope for intimacy in the bedroom than in a restaurant. Still, we'll have to do the best we can with what we've got.'

'We haven't got anything yet.' She tried appealing to his common sense. 'He's identified me as being responsible for his wife's death. Is it likely he'll agree to meet me?'

'Don't go wasting my time by being negative. I'll book you a discreet little table for two in *The Lantern*, Jermyn Lane, for tomorrow evening. It's overlooked by a most convenient, lens-sized aperture, situated in the manager's office.'

Kate was incredulous. 'It sounds like a setting in a spy novel. I thought the Cold War was over.'

'You'd be surprised. It's a facility much in demand. And not just by compliant spouses anxious to provide evidence for an easy divorce.'

'Is there much call for that sort of thing, these days?'

'Not a lot. It's mainly used for more subtle affairs. That little snoop hole has exposed an MP on the make, a naughty judge with a penchant for rent boys, and a corrupt police inspector.'

'How were you able to do that?' Kate was genuinely curious.

'All set up. Just like the sting we're going to pull on Mr Self-Righteous-Kershaw.'

Chapter 7

Larry Fines was as good as his word. His flattering article, accompanied by a photographic spread, created both public and media interest in the young black artists. The Spice Mill was inundated with would-be-managers and talent scouts, come to view Win and Lena's double act. Their overtures were wasted. Thanks to Larry, the artists had already acquired a high-profile agent who managed half-a-dozen big show-business names.

Within a week this impresario had landed them Saturday night bookings at an exclusive West End establishment and Sunday engagements in the best night-club in Manchester. More significantly, they were to be auditioned for television. If successful they would become the regular musical spot in a new, alternative comedy series. Win and Lena wondered if the big-time had finally arrived.

While they were playing the Manchester gig their agent called.

'Good news. The audition was successful. The Granada producer wants to engage you for two spots in each show. Recording will start in three weeks.'

It was the break they had been waiting for.

Lena took to the stage that night with a new confidence. Her voice was at its silky best, her phrasing immaculate. Dressed in a new, tightly fitting, off-the-shoulder gown, she dripped sex-appeal. She and Win had been apprehensive about appearing before Northern audiences, but the club's clientele was appreciative from the start. A group of over-attentive business men called Lena's name, and invited her to join them after the show. She blew them kisses, but when she left the floor she was clinging to Win's arm. It was a public demonstration of where her allegiance lay.

Their hotel was located only a few hundred yards from the club and, after the gig, Winston ordered a celebratory surprise to be sent up. Their rooms were inter-connecting, and as he hung his jacket, he heard the champagne being delivered to Lena's room. He knocked and joined her.

Lena stood by the ice-bucket, eyes shining. She managed to look desirable and vulnerable at the same time. Smiling at him, she indicated the champagne.

'The waiter said it came from you.'

He sang her words back at her.

She giggled. 'You make us rehearse so much that I'm even speaking in song lyrics.'

'Don't complain. All that rehearsing has paid off. It's not every week we break into television.'

'And what better way to celebrate. You'd better come in and open it.' She smiled her encouragement and raised one of the glasses.

Because of his promise to her mother, he concentrated hard on opening the wine and avoided looking at the bed. They toasted each other and clinked glasses. Lena said the bubbles tickled her nose. He wished it were he, tickling that cute little protuberance.

'The audience was rapturous over your performance tonight, and no wonder, you look incredibly beautiful.' It was a novelty for him to be sweet-talking and to mean every word.

She glowed with pleasure at his praise. 'It was all adrenalin. I was so excited about the TV contract.'

Tossing back the champagne, she held out her glass for more. Once again they chinked vessels.

'To us, to our future.' He felt very old and very sentimental and wondered if she noticed the dampness in his eyes. As long as she continued to look up into his face, the bulge at his crotch was safe from detection. His chest tightened with unrequited longing. He knew only one thing – that he wanted this girl. Desire was no novelty; what was different was the way he wanted her.

She had taken a step towards him, her breasts were brushing his shirt. When she offered her lips, his kiss was both gentle and tender. Passion was not permitted, he reminded himself. But Lena had taken charge. The kiss went on – and on. Their mouths opened. His tongue had been under control until hers darted in.

Blindly they discarded the champagne flutes they were holding, and, with lips glued, manoeuvred towards the bed. Win's promises to Lena's mother were forgotten. He was kissing her lovely neck, her shoulders, the curvature of her breasts. She held his face in her hands, not to hinder but to aid and abet. Her cute nose was buried in his hair.

'We shouldn't be crushing my gown, it's part of the props,' she whispered.

Sharing her concern, he assisted her out of the glittering fabric. She arched her back so that he could release her brassiere. Underneath she was so lovely that for a long moment he was mesmerised, incapable of action.

Diana had told Ma that her daughter was a virgin.

Winston had been made to promise he would never violate her chastity. Discovering her with his eyes, lips and fingers would have to suffice. What they were doing was already delightful. Win accepted that only an ungrateful man would have felt peevish at the restriction on penetration, and he was not in the least ungrateful. In fact, he was a happy man, delirious at his good fortune. He intended to exploit the situation, if not to the full then at least to good measure.

Lena's fingers measured the magnificence of his erection. 'Do you have any condoms?' she asked coyly.

Her directness shocked and made him instantly forgetful of Diana and the promises she had extracted.

The realisation that he had not prepared himself for this eventuality made him feel like a schoolboy who had failed the most significant examination of his life. He groaned his apology, 'Sorry, no condoms.'

'It doesn't matter,' she said with a self-conscious giggle. 'I bought us some, from a dispensing machine in the club's ladies.'

'You did?' He was too surprised to say more.

'I hid them in your jacket pocket. You were supposed to find them and guess that I'd put them there.'

'Oh, Lena.'

Her grip tightened, moving rhythmically in an unnecessary encouragement.

'My jacket's only next door, why don't you come and pick my pocket?' he invited.

Unwilling for their flesh to be separated, she led him by his penis into the other room. Had her mother witnessed this abandon, she might have doubted the truthfulness of her daughter's claim to innocence. Win tried not to think too much about the honour that was being conferred upon him lest the awesome responsibility of taking her virginity cramp his technique. He was not a hypocrite; it would have been unnatural to feel guilt about making love with the woman he loved – and he was in no doubt about the depth of his feelings.

Back in London, there were confessions to be made. Ma would be understanding, but securing Diana's forgiveness would be quite another matter.

Win pounced on Irene in his usual manner, spinning her in the wheelchair before claiming her for a hug and kiss.

'Well, did you take the untamed North by storm?'

'Lena did, you should have seen her. She performed like a true artist. I count myself lucky. She's a fantastic girl, Ma.'

'You sound like a proud and possessive father.'

'Possessive yes, but father is a generation off the mark.'

Irene gave him her full scrutiny. 'Has something happened?'

He laughed. 'You're an old witch, how did you know?' He was thinking only of his triumph with Lena, the success of the television contract was quite forgotten.

'The spring in your step, the expression on that beautiful, open face that tells me you've been lapping cream.'

He knelt to put their eyes on a level. She held his hands encouragingly.

'I think I love her, Ma,' he said soberly.

'Think? Does that mean you're not sure?'

'How do I know, I've never been in love before. I

only know that she's beautiful, adorable and I want to be around her for the rest of my life.'

'Hmm, the way you describe your condition, it does indeed sound remarkably like love.'

'You don't mind?'

'Mind, why should I? Lena is a delightful girl.'

'She makes me very happy, Ma.'

'I'm glad, because happiness is all I've ever wanted for you.'

They embraced.

Basking in Ma's congratulations, it was a while before he remembered the enormous obstacle yet to be surmounted.

'What do I tell Diana? She won't be as happy with our news as you are. I gave her my word to behave and, the first time I get Lena away from home, I break it. She'll never trust me again.'

'Diana could be difficult. Wouldn't it be better if Lena told her mother?'

'No, I want Diana to know that I accept the responsibility for what's happened. I made Lena promise she wouldn't say anything.'

'That's very honourable of you. It might be best to enlighten her here, where she's more likely to behave herself. Invite your love and her mother to dinner. We'll ply Diana with food and wine so that you can make your confession when she's in soporific mood. What excuse can we give for our dinner party?'

He remembered his other news. 'We don't need to manufacture anything. I almost forgot; you know that television audition we did last week? Well, they want us for a six programme contract.'

Irene's eyes twinkled with pleasure. 'Oh, Winston, everything is coming to you at once. I don't mind sharing you with Lena, but I might have to share you with the rest of the world when you're famous.'

'I love the vote of confidence, but it's *if*, not *when*.'

'Nonsense. I've known since the day you were born that you would make something of your life. It's beginning to happen as I knew it would. Now go and make that phone call to your love. I want to see if Lena's eyes are as brilliant as yours.'

Lena answered. It was only a hour since he had dropped her off at her home, yet just hearing her speak aroused him. Diana was not yet back from the office but the new, confident Lena accepted the invitation on her mother's behalf.

Over dinner, Diana casually mentioned Kate. 'Did you know that your reporter friend has been starring in the news rather than writing it?'

'Kate Rider?' Winston asked. 'What has she been up to?'

'Some aggressive reporting. The Flag's competitors are blaming Kate for your nursery school proprietor's suicide.'

The Blakeneys had been unaware of Caroline Kershaw's suicide but learning of it were saddened. It came as no surprise that her widower held *The Flag* responsible and that Kate's aggressive reporting had been cited by the other tabloids.

Though shocked at the young woman's death, Irene still found sympathy for Kate.

'The girl was only doing her job. I imagine she will be devastated over what has happened.'

Winston was more critical. 'Kate's an intelligent woman but she's chosen a dirty profession. The rules of normal decency don't apply in tabloid journalism. She has to take some responsibility.'

Lena looked at her lover gratefully. She was uncertain as to his precise relationship with the attractive and clever reporter. Not only had Kate flirted and laughed with him, she had taken too much interest in their future to be a mere casual acquaintance. Lena had suffered agonies wondering about the night Larry Fines had first come to the club and Win had driven Kate Rider home. Before Manchester, she would have condemned the reporter too, now she could afford to be magnanimous.

'She can't be all bad,' she demurred. 'She went out of her way to promote us. We owe her a lot.'

'She's not bad, only misguided,' Win judged.

He was simultaneously too happy about Lena and too preoccupied with his forthcoming negotiations with her mother to dwell on Kate Rider's problems.

Irene manipulated Diana just as she had promised. She sat close to her at dinner and recharged her glass at every opportunity. As Diana relaxed, Winston saw, for the first time, the strong physical resemblance between mother and daughter. At forty, Diana was in her prime. She had kept her figure, and the symmetry of her fine bone structure made her features beautiful. But there was a hardness about her too. She had a way of looking down her nose at Winston that made him feel inadequate. He imagined that most men would regard her as a bit of a ball-cruncher. Lena believed her mother to have been celibate since before her birth, which Win found not at all surprising.

Winston postponed his disclosure. How could he tell an over-protective mother, who valued chastity, that he had carnal knowledge of the daughter she believed pure? It was Irene who initiated the confession.

'Winston and Lena have something to tell you, Diana.'

His sweetheart's mother stiffened visibly. Winston cleared his throat and sought Lena's hand under the table.

'We didn't set out to make it happen, and I know it's not what you wanted, but we've fallen in love. We want to be together, and we hope you will give us your blessing, Diana.'

Diana dabbed her lips with her napkin and studied him coldly.

'You gave me your word, you promised,' she accused. 'I should have known you weren't to be trusted.' She appealed to her daughter, 'Please tell me you haven't slept with him, Lena.'

Lena was silent. She clung to Win's arm as if he were about to float away.

His heart was pounding but he tried to remain dignified. 'I feel bad about letting you down, Diana, but I couldn't help myself. I know the only way to make amends is by making Lena happy, and I intend to do that.'

'You can never make amends. You've seduced my daughter when you gave your solemn promise that you would look after her. You're no good.' She turned towards her daughter. 'Oh, Lena, you little fool.'

'No, Mother, you're the fool. For all those months while Win was behaving so correctly towards me, I was miserable. I loved him from the start and couldn't bear to be treated like a little sister. Win didn't seduce me, it was the other way around.'

Diana shook her head in disbelief. 'You expect me to believe that?'

'It's true. I threw myself at him. If he'd rejected me, I would have been wretched.'

'*You* seduced *him*?' Diana was scornful, 'You little

innocent. He's seven years older than you in years, and decades older in experience.'

'Mother, stop it, I love him. It doesn't matter what you think. You can't stop us from being together. It's what we both want.'

'Love him? You've been brain-washed by the lyrics of all those sentimental love songs he's taught you. When he's tired of your body, then see how much he loves you.'

Lena began to sob, her head buried in Win's chest.

His face clouded. 'I don't mind your anger being directed at me, but I won't let you upset Lena. Your experience may have made you cynical where love is concerned, but it gives you no right to transfer your bitterness to us.'

Irene intervened, 'That's enough, Winston, don't say anything you may later regret. Why don't you take Lena to your room and run over your new number? There are things Diana and I need to discuss.'

Diana moved towards her daughter, intending to physically restrain her from going anywhere near Winston's room. The expression on Lena's face deterred her. Instead, she turned her ire onto Irene. 'How can you - you're encouraging them?'

The lovers, exploiting this diversion, fled the room.

'Lena is not a child,' Irene chided, as the door slammed behind the couple. 'She's about to become a financially independent young woman. If you don't accept that fact then you will lose her altogether.'

Diana crumpled into a chair. 'How can you understand when you've never had a daughter or even a child of your own?'

If the remark was intended to hurt, it failed.

'But I do – Winston's my child. I held his mother's

hand throughout her labour, and I held her baby before she did. I've always been *Ma* to Winston. Like Lena, he never knew his father, but perhaps was more fortunate in that he grew up knowing the love of two mothers.'

She manoeuvred her wheelchair closer to Diana before continuing. 'You have a very low opinion of my boy, one that he doesn't deserve. When he was a little fellow he was often naughty. All his life he has been high spirited, but I can honestly say I have never known him to be dishonest or do a single mean thing. And I'm proud of the man he has grown into. When he says that he and Lena have found something special, I believe him. He can make Lena happy, I'm sure of that.'

'You don't understand. He's wrong for her.'

'What makes you say that?'

Diana was quite prepared to justify herself. 'He's a musician, what stability can he offer? Lena is a clever girl, she should go to university, mix with professional people.'

'You would rather she associated with doctors and lawyers than with my son?'

'Frankly, yes.'

'I don't think you quite appreciate Winston's position. If he and Lena do make a stable relationship, he will be able to provide your daughter with more financial security than ninety percent of this country's professional men.'

'What do you mean?'

Irene hesitated. 'I didn't intend making this disclosure, and I do so only in the strictest confidence. You must promise not to repeat what I am about to tell you.'

Diana nodded her agreement

'Not to anyone, you understand. Not even Lena?'

'You have my word.'

'Thank you. You may be aware that when my husband died, he left me a very wealthy woman. So wealthy, in fact, that my income exceeds even my most extravagant needs. I still have a financial interest in the shipping line he founded, and the shrewd investments he made in his lifetime have continued to grow. In real terms, my fortune is larger now than it was when I was widowed, twenty seven years ago.'

She had Diana's complete attention now.

'Apart from some legacies I intend to make to my employees and favourite charities, Winston will be my sole beneficiary. He knows that I have provided for him in my will, but has no idea to what extent. When I go, Winston will be a wealthy man. He will have a fortune large enough to make him completely independent of paid employment. Not that I expect him to be idle, he is too ambitious for that. He has the intelligence and charisma to do anything he wants and it's my belief that he is destined to achieve something in life.' She paused, as if challenging Diana to deny this estimation of her beloved son, then went on, 'Who knows, perhaps he will become a famous song writer, or he might enter politics and become this country's first black Prime minister.'

Diana was visibly impressed. Recovering her equilibrium, she asked, 'And this house, will it be his?'

'Naturally. It has always been his home, so I hope he'll want to stay on here.'

'And you really think he's serious about loving Lena?'

'He told me this morning that he wanted to spend the rest of his life with her.'

Lost in their private thoughts, both women fell quiet. Diana raised her eyes to the ceiling.

'I don't hear the piano, what can they be doing up there?'

Irene chuckled. 'Diana, you will have to learn to let go. What they are up to is entirely their business.'

Chapter 8

Kate reasoned that the best way of protecting Michael Kershaw was to turn double agent. She would pretend to go along with Colson's invidious scheme, but at the same time would look for an opportunity to warn his victim.

With Spackman listening in on an extension, she rang the widower's home number but there was no reply. Following instructions, she tried his office and was put through. She was aware that Spackman would tell tales to Colson if she failed to sound convincing.

The first part was easy, for her regret was sincere enough. 'Mr Kershaw, you don't know me, though you know of me. If I give you my name you'll probably hang up, but I beg you, please listen to what I have to say.'

'Are you the press?'

'Yes, but I don't want an interview, only to apologise.'

'Who are you?'

'Kate Rider of *The Flag*.'

She expected him to slam down the receiver, as she hoped he would. Instead, he said dully, 'You have a nerve.'

'Please listen. I read the statement you made after the inquest. If I could turn the clock back I would. I'm truly sorry about the pressures my article caused your wife.'

'Perhaps the experience will make you think twice before you embark on another character assassination.'

His sounded tired rather than bitter, resigned rather than angry.

'I don't intend to write anything as uncharitable or irresponsible again,' she assured him.

'What are you telling me – that my wife didn't die in vain because you have been taught a lesson? Is that supposed to console me?' His voice was rising as some spark of anger ignited within.

'No, and I'm sorry if it sounds that way. I want you to know that I haven't gone unpunished, that I will have to live with this for the rest of my life.'

'I see, so it's the knowledge that *you* are suffering too, that's supposed to make me feel better?'

'I hoped it might give you some consolation.'

'Ah, I'm beginning to understand. You offer restitution by punishing yourself and expect my forgiveness in return.'

'I'm not asking for your charity. I don't expect it.'

'So why are you calling?'

She couldn't believe it, he was playing into *The Flag's* hands. Spackman jabbed her in the ribs, mouthing silently, 'Get on with it.'

She did as she was told. 'I need to talk to you, but it's difficult to find the right words over the telephone. Could we meet?'

'To what purpose?' A note of suspicion had entered his voice.

'Not to put things right. I realise that it's too late for that, but, at least to put things straight. It's an impertinent thing to ask, but I'd like to meet you. I'll be at The Lantern in Jermyn Lane, at 9 o'clock this evening. It would mean a lot, if you would agree to come.'

There was a silence at the other end of the line, she willed his refusal.

'I'll think about it.'

And that was all, he had hung-up.

Spackman was delighted. 'Brilliant! He's hooked. I must say, the catch in your voice was most convincing.'

'All he said was that he would think about it. He may not turn up.'

'Of course he'll be there. You've intrigued him. He wants to find out what sort of woman you are.' Spackman leered. 'I wonder, will he want to punish you or give himself a treat?'

He saw her expression and misinterpreted it. 'Don't worry, you'll be in a public restaurant, he can't do you any harm there. Whether there'll be opportunity for the other is entirely up to you, but you'll need to play your part to the full.'

'What's that supposed to mean?'

'Give me something worth shooting. Don't waste an opportunity. Top-up his glass while it's still in his hand. If he puts his mitts on the table, you cover them with yours. Make sure you look into his eyes with all the sincerity you can muster. A mouth on mouth job might be expecting too much, but, while you're offering sympathy, try to get close enough to brush his cheek with your lips. If he's sucker enough to make a pass in public, then give him every encouragement to make a fool of himself.'

He looked disparagingly at her trouser-suit. 'Forget the power-dressing this evening. Wear something low-cut. I can make it look as if he's ogling your boobs even if he's only contemplating the meat on his plate. Keep in mind that the camera is trained on you, but, whatever you do, don't look for my snoop hole.'

Kate felt sick to the pit of her stomach. Bob Spackman had made it sound as if she were a film starlet under direction. But it was real-life, and Michael Kershaw was unwittingly playing the male lead.

Her apology to Kershaw had been genuine, and amazingly he had heard her out. Before the call, she had comforted herself with the certainty that he would refuse to meet her, even hang up on her. But he hadn't refused, he was actually considering it.

Even if it put her job at risk, she could not let Colson's ruse go any further. There was only one way to protect Michael Kershaw: she must find a way to warn him off.

To minimise the risk of discovery, she had intended calling him from a public telephone, but once in the street she headed for the tube station. Michael Kershaw's place of work was only two stops away. The sincerity of her intentions would be more convincing if they met face to face.

Reaching his office, she considered her next move. By a stroke of good fortune, Michael Kershaw chose that moment to leave the building. He was instantly recognisable from the post-inquest photographs that the other tabloids had run: a strikingly attractive man, strong featured and almost as blond as his dead wife. He made an urbane figure as he stood at the kerb, clutching a furled black umbrella, waiting for a taxi.

Her approach was tentative. 'Excuse me, Mr Kershaw, may I speak with you?'

A pair of extremely blue eyes met her own. 'Kate Rider?'

His recognition surprised her. 'How did you know it was me?'

'Your voice; it's only minutes since you were talking to me on the telephone. What are you doing here? What is all this about?'

She felt that he had every right to be irritated. 'Is there somewhere we could go to talk?'

For a moment she thought he was going to refuse, but he pandered to her, as if to a small child.

'Will the Embankment Gardens be private enough?'

It was an autumnal afternoon, but the sun still shone with some strength. Colourful flower beds combined with the backcloth of a cloudless sky to give the riverside gardens the appearance of high summer.

He indicated a bench that was just being vacated. 'Shall we sit down?'

Grateful for the undeserved gallantry, she felt an urge to protect him. She came straight to the point. 'The phone call I made earlier – it was made under duress.'

Her statement was obviously unexpected. 'You were forced to apologise?'

'No, my apology was genuine enough, but the invitation is not what it seems. You mustn't go to the restaurant this evening.'

He was waiting for more, but to tell the truth was dangerous. It would provide him with an excellent case to take to the Press Complaints Commission.

'Please, just stay away. That's all I can tell you.'

'I'm sorry, Kate Rider, but that's simply not good enough. I agreed to listen, and I think I deserve an explanation.'

After the suffering she had visited upon him, she owed him some explanation. Reluctantly she said, 'There will be a hidden camera at the restaurant. My paper wants photographs of you.'

'Photographs? I don't understand.'

Suddenly, it didn't matter that she was putting her career on the line. 'Compromising photographs. Of us together.' She found herself blushing. 'Photographs to discredit you.'

'What am I expected to do in a public restaurant that could be in the least compromising?'

The steel in the blue eyes softened. He was smiling, not taking her seriously.

'My editor can be vindictive. He's seething over the way our competitors capitalised on the statement you gave to the press. His idea is to produce evidence of us being cosy together. That will be enough to debunk any official complaints you might make against *The Flag*.'

'The tabloids' coverage was as unwelcome as it was hypocritical. As you can imagine, I'm not pleased at becoming a pawn in a dirty circulation battle.'

She was encouraged by his understanding. 'You're right about the hypocrisy. Their piety was entirely false. They attacked *The Flag* in the hope that the adverse publicity would win back readers who have changed allegiance.'

'But if *The Flag* publishes pictures of me having an intimate dinner with the journalist held responsible for my wife's death, the world will judge me the hypocrite, is that it?'

'Something like that.' She flushed with shame.

'Why are you telling me this?' The voice was gentle.

'I've caused you enough pain. I've no desire to tarnish your reputation as well.'

'When did you change your mind?'

'Change my mind?' She didn't understand the question.

'It was only half an hour ago that you rang to set up the dinner date.'

'I told you – the call was made under duress. It was being monitored. My choice was simple: to call you, or lose my job.'

'And this evening, you'll go to restaurant, as arranged?'

'I have to be seen to be obeying orders.'

'I'm not convinced that a photograph of us together in a public restaurant would really be so compromising.'

Blood again suffused her cheeks. 'I was supposed to make sure that it was.'

'You were under orders to seduce me?'

She nodded wretchedly.

'Do you often play the vamp in the line of duty?'

'Never before!'

Her indignation amused him. 'I'm sorry, I shouldn't tease. And I'm grateful that you've spared me the embarrassment of being front page news again tomorrow.'

His body language said the interview was over. They rose from the seat together. Smiling pleasantly, he offered a handshake.

'This business has been upsetting for you, I can see that. Don't dwell on what happened. Multiple factors drove Caroline to suicide. The blame isn't exclusively yours, and it was unjust of me to suggest that it was. As for my threat of going to the Press Complaints Commission, that was made in the stress of the moment. You can tell your editor that I'm not after his blood. I much prefer to avoid further publicity.'

In the circumstances, his willingness to consider her feelings was selfless, to say the least. She was too choked with mixed emotions to reply. The last thing she had expected was for him to be so forgiving, and it served to make her feel more wretched. Tearful, she bit her lip.

'Hey, come on, we can't have that.' He produced a handkerchief to wipe away an escaped tear.

'I'm sorry, I'm not usually so emotional. It's because you've been so understanding.'

'There's been enough pain, Kate. I don't want to make more, not for anyone.'

His use of her name twisted her emotions still more.

As they parted, he gave her the briefest of hugs. She understood that the gesture was intended as a mark of solidarity, yet his touch disturbed rather than comforted.

If circumstances had been different it would have been pleasurable to have returned the embrace. Michael Kershaw was precisely the type of man whose attentions she would have liked to encourage.

Chapter 9

Kate's appearance at The Lantern was dutifully spectacular. As prescribed, her neckline was revealing and her uplift impressive. Even under the subdued lighting of an alcove, her brighter-than-usual lipstick and dramatically-applied make-up were stunning. Her appearance, and unaccompanied status, drew lascivious glances from three Japanese businessmen sitting at a nearby table. She sipped an aperitif, uncomfortable that her solitary presence should be attracting such unlooked-for attention.

She played her allotted part well. When the street door opened she looked-up expectantly, ever-alert for the companion who would not appear. Having scanned the newcomers, her expression readjusted to register disappointment. She imagined Bob Spackman's increasing impatience at his abortive watch. The temptation to look for his snoop hole was difficult to control.

After waiting for what she estimated to be an appropriate length of time, she summoned a waiter. 'I'm sorry, my companion doesn't seem to be coming. I'd like to order, now, please.'

She saw no reason to forgo the meal. After all, it was on expenses. However, when the food came she spent more time rearranging it on her plate than directing it towards her mouth.

Satisfied that her lone repast had lasted long

enough, she waved away the dessert trolley and requested the bill. While thus preoccupied she failed to notice Kevin's arrival until he pounced on her.

'Well, Kershaw has missed an opportunity,' he sneered.

She twisted round, eyes widening.

'Kevin, what are you doing here?'

'I thought I'd just check that you were doing your duty,' he replied dryly.

To her chagrin, he seated himself beside her.

'I'm about to leave; he didn't show up.' She tried to sound regretful.

'There now, what a surprise.'

'I told you he wouldn't come.'

'So you did, what a clever girl you are. Never mind, the evening's young, and Kershaw's loss is my gain.'

Ignoring her protest that she had already wined and dined, he intercepted a passing waiter and ordered cognac and coffee.

'Perhaps Bob Spackman would like to join us,' she suggested, not relishing Kevin's company. 'He deserves some recompense for a fruitless evening.'

'Spackman's not here.'

'He might have let me know, then I could have left with him.'

'You misunderstand; Bob hasn't been here at all this evening.'

She stared at him. 'Hasn't been here? What do you mean? It was Bob who arranged this fiasco.'

'Correction, this fiasco is all down to you, my scheming little minx.'

She was indignant, 'You didn't think my Kershaw pieces were a fiasco when you published them.'

'That's not what I meant.'

'It's late and you're talking nonsense. I'd like to go home.'

'I'll take you home, after the brandy.' He trapped her hand under the table. 'That's a most revealing dress you're almost wearing. I feel the stirrings of a very pleasant memory.'

She wanted to walk out, but his order for cognac and coffee had delayed the arrival of the bill. To divert him she switched back to talking shop.

'Why didn't Bob show? Did something more important come up?'

'I gave him the evening off. He'd already earned his bread today, for some excellent work he did earlier.'

'Then why didn't you tell me?'

'I thought I would give you a nice surprise and come along and join you myself.'

'But what if Michael Kershaw had been here?'

'Save the games for the bedroom, Kate.' He ogled her unpleasantly. 'I think you owe me some restitution for failing to deliver Kershaw this evening, don't you?'

So he knew. What was less easy to understand was that he didn't seem to care. Her heart pounded.

'My partner is waiting for me at home,' she lied.

The self-satisfied expression slipped to reveal one of annoyance. 'Perfidious *and* unavailable. Can you give me one good reason why I shouldn't fire you?'

She was shaking. 'Yes, I'm a damned good journalist.'

'Correction, you aren't good, you're disloyal. But don't worry, I'm not getting rid of you just yet. Go home to the boyfriend. I'll pick up the tab here.'

As she rose he gave her a stinging slap on the

buttocks. The oriental gentlemen, who had been watching her so closely all evening, followed these proceedings and her stumbling exit with an expression of speculative interest.

After her mutinous dereliction of duty, she believed it more than likely that Colson would carry out his veiled threat and sack her. Only days earlier, she had been smelling success, now she was up to her neck in something rather foul. It was a miserable change of fortune.

In joining *The Flag*, she had been so confident; so sure that she was on the verge of a successful journalistic career. Her first and only scoop had been exhilarating, but the thrill had turned bitter and her former elation become just an embarrassing memory. She could not forget that others had paid dearly for her fleeting triumph.

In Plymouth, on *The Advertiser*, she had been the golden girl, the apple of the avuncular editor's eye. She had been so impatient to turn her back on all that. How naive she had been. For the first time, she cursed her move to London.

The chorus of whistles and congratulations that greeted her entry into the telephone- warbling newsroom the following morning was as bemusing as it was unexpected. Enlightenment was swift. A grinning Charlie spread two copies of The Flag's latest edition across her desk, allowing her to take in the front and inside pages simultaneously.

The front-page photograph was of her and Michael Kershaw, captured together as they sat on the bench in the Embankment Gardens. The caption shouted: *Mike's Tête à Tête With Kate. More revealing pictures – pages 2/3*. The inside pages carried an out-of-order, photographic sequence of the two of them standing before the same bench. In the first, Michael Kershaw was wiping a tear from her cheek, in the second, he was embracing her and, in the last, his finger lifted her chin. It looked for all the world as if they were about to kiss. It was this last picture that, apparently, justified the headline, KISS ME KATE, that sprawled in inch-high letters across the photo-spread.

The photographs were of a grainy quality, confirming the use of a telephoto lens. Spackman had invaded their privacy. He had followed from the office, seen her intercepting Michael, and tracked them to the Embankment Gardens.

Incredulous, she read the accompanying text. It described Michael's attentions as "love-making," and went on to ask: *Can this really be widower, Michael Kershaw, on the eve of his wife's funeral? The same Mr Kershaw who, two days ago, castigated* The Flag, *blaming this paper for his wife's suicide?*

Sickened, she read on.

The late Mrs Kershaw ran the Wimbledon nursery school, the scene of toddler Toby Edmunds' recent death. A Flag *exclusive exposed worrying lapses of security at the school, and revealed how Mrs Kershaw, in her previous occupation as a social worker, was implicated in the death of another child.*

Michael Kershaw was captured on camera yesterday, and the lovely lady on the receiving end of his seduction routine is none other than Flag *reporter, Kate Rider, the journalist responsible for our exclusive coverage of his wife's unfortunate past.*

To the "grieving" widower, and those rival newspapers who condemned our earlier coverage, we send this message: The Flag *will not be silenced by hypocritical carping. We are here to inform our readers. We will give them the facts – it is for them to decide.*

Colson, oozing smugness, came out of his office to stand by her side.

'Very accommodating of you, Kate. Kershaw certainly seems to be enjoying the consolation you offered.'

Unintentionally, she had played into their hands. She had given them all they had wanted. Michael Kershaw would see her warning about the restaurant as a double bluff, designed to win his trust in order to disgrace him.

'You had no right!' she fumed.

'No right? Aren't you forgetting that you agreed to this? We changed the venue that's all.'

'He was so understanding, and you've made him look a scoundrel.'

'Correction, Kate, you've done that.'

'But this report is a complete distortion of what actually happened.'

'How can that be? It's all on film and everyone knows the camera never lies.'

He picked up the offending page, and admired it at arm's length. 'Quit complaining, darling. I ought to sack you for breach of discipline, but Bob has saved your bacon by coming up with this stuff. I'm going to be magnanimous, I'll give you another chance. But get this into your lovely head – another show of disloyalty and you're out.'

Kate was not sure that she wanted his reprieve. Certainly, a dressing-down in front of the whole office was not her idea of magnanimity.

Michael had shown tolerance, compassion and forgiveness. It was so unjust that this libellous photo-spread was to be his reward. With a sinking heart, she realised that he would judge her as being totally unprincipled. A suitable employee for a disreputable tabloid. Not for the first time was she filled with an aching nostalgia for the wholesome values of *The Tamar Advertiser*. But the greater pain was the certain knowledge that Michael Kershaw would despise her.

Chapter 10

Robin Rider belonged to the same Masonic lodge as Phil Kitto, the editor of *The Tamar Advertiser*. When his newly graduated daughter had found the competitive world of the media difficult to break into, Robin's influence had secured her job with Kitto. To her credit, Kate had proved herself an exceptionally able junior reporter. Both father and editor had cause to be proud of her.

It had been her mother's death and her father's indecently swift remarriage, that had brought about a radical change in their previously good relationship. The bride-to-be was her mother's closest friend, Ellen McIntosh. Kate was stunned by her father's haste. It felt like an act of gross disloyalty to her mother's memory. She had even attempted to persuade him not to take such a precipitous step.

Hurt by his daughter's resentment, Robin had attempted an explanation.

'You shouldn't be surprised, after all Ellen and Bill McIntosh, were our oldest friends,' he reminded. 'When Bill's heart attack left Ellen a widow, it was your mother who encouraged me to go round to Ellen's to help out.'

Kate refused to believe that it had been her mother's intention to initiate a romance between her husband and her best friend.

'Ellen was very good to your mother, we have a lot to thank her for.'

It was an appeal to his daughter's sense of gratitude, and it was a point that she had to concede. When her mother had been diagnosed as having an inoperable liver cancer, it was Ellen who turned Samaritan. Not herself, the absent daughter. Ellen had even moved into to the Rider home to nurse her dying friend.

Robin had been too honest to pretend a platonic relationship. He admitted to his daughter that he had been attracted to Ellen for many years. Out of respect for the dying woman, Ellen had put up a token and temporary resistance. But as Robin confessed to his daughter, 'There are some things that can't be repressed. Your mother never knew, we were always discreet. We would never have hurt her, we were both too fond of her to do that.'

Kate had long suspected that Ellen had been her father's mistress. With the physical side of his marriage over, it was hardly surprising that he turned to the other woman for solace. Though she had been able to forgive his adultery, his confession did nothing to ease her acceptance of his hasty remarriage. Ellen stepped easily into her mother's shoes, and the cosiness of the two middle-aged lovebirds made Kate feel excluded. Jealousy was born.

The rivalry was all the more personal because Kate felt that she had been replaced in her father's affections. The additional cause of her bitterness was Ellen's extended family. She had two sons, a daughter and numerous grandchildren. The stepfamily were soon monopolising her father's time. To complete her sense of rejection the Rider home was sold, and Robin moved into the bosom of Ellen's family.

When father and daughter had their first quarrel, words were said that could not be forgotten. Kate never saw her father without members of Ellen's clan being present. As he grew ever more engrossed in his step-family, his daughter's visits became more infrequent. By the time of her removal to London, they were close to being estranged.

Kate had last spoken to her father just after her Kershaw scoop had hit the streets. She had been proud of her columns, with their by-lines, and had phoned him to share her success. Pleased to hear from her, he had been generous in his congratulations.

Robin initiated their next call. The tone was quite different.

'What's happening, Kate? We couldn't believe it when we saw those intimate shots of you and that Kershaw chap in this morning's *Flag*.' He sounded anxious and reproving. 'Is there something going on between you?'

'Ignore it, Dad. It's just a lot of tabloid twaddle that doesn't mean anything.'

'Then what possessed you to take part in such scurrilous stuff. What do you think you're playing at?'

A misplaced pride would not permit her to admit that the photographs had been taken without her knowledge and published without her permission.

'Playing? It's not a game, Dad. It's work.'

Her father would not be palmed-off so easily. 'Kershaw blamed your paper for his wife's suicide, and it was you who wrote the offending articles.'

As if she needed reminding.

'So how in the devil,' Robin continued, 'did you

come to be in his arms, on the eve of the poor woman's funeral?'

She was too old for him to be coming the heavy father.

'It wasn't what it seemed,' she protested. 'I was offering sympathy, that's all.'

'A strange sympathy. By publishing those photographs, your paper has made the man look a total reprobate. I simply don't understand. What made you do that to him?'

She bristled at the unwarranted and extended criticism. 'Look, Dad, *The Flag* isn't *The Advertiser*. I'm not running my own show up here. I have to do what my editor tells me.'

'I don't like the sound of that, Kate. Are you saying that you have to prostitute yourself and fabricate your stories?'

He was far too close to the mark. 'Of course not, but I'm expected to comply with *The Flag's* way of doing things.'

'Then I'm sorry to hear it. No career justifies breaking the bounds of decency, and that's what's happened here. Haven't you considered your own reputation? Who will trust you after this? Phil Kitto will be disappointed in you. He would never allow such mud-slinging to appear in *The Advertiser*.'

Robin was unable to understand that, as a minion of *The Flag*, his daughter was expected to abandon her own mores and conduct her professional life on her paper's terms.

Once she had been the apple of her father's eye. An only child she was more used to basking in parental admiration than suffering admonishment. Now Robin had joined the swelling ranks of her critics, and his defamatory assessment was a bitter pill to swallow. His judgmental telephone call in her hour of need left her feeling isolated and miserable.

The only thing left to sustain her was her career, and that was in tatters. To revive it meant submitting to whatever Colson demanded of her. She had chosen an occupation that offered freedom of expression, but in the freedom lay servitude. She had become a slave to the media machine.

She took her misery to the bustle of the office, where Charlie offered platitudes.

'Cheer up, things could be worse,' was one of them.

Boldly, she adopted a cheery face but things, indeed, did become worse. Not just worse but more awful by an order of magnitude.

Later, as she attempted to leave the building, she was accosted by a barrage of reporters and photographers. They brandished microphones in her face, and bombarded her with questions.

'What's your relationship with Kershaw, Kate?'

'How long have you been lovers?'

'Did his wife know about you?'

'Was it your affair or the article that drove Caroline to suicide?'

She thought she must be going mad. In terms of public interest, she was a nonentity, so was Michael Kershaw, yet they were being hounded like celebrities. It didn't make sense.

It turned out that the excessive interest was down to Colson. He had sold Bob Spackman's exclusives to their competitors. A similar pair of pictures appeared in every tabloid: Spackman's shot of Kershaw embracing Kate, coupled with one of the widower taken more recently. The latter showed a mourning Michael Kershaw at his wife's grave-side. All the captions, of which *Goodbye Caroline, Hello Kate* and *Out With the Old, On With the New* were samples, were similarly offensive. The juxtaposition of the photographs suggested that the embrace was conducted at the graveside. One caption actually ran, *Hot Stuff at the Funeral – Before the Wife is Cold.*

Being on the receiving end of press intrusion was a novel experience for Kate, and one she could have done without. She sought sanctuary in the privacy of Jack Brymer's office. In any other matter he would have been sympathetic. But he was a newspaperman to the core, and in this instance he considered her fuss to be unprofessional.

'To be candid, Kate, you're far too sensitive. In this job we have to grow a thick skins. I agree Colson's played it dirty, but it's been a slow-news-week. He has to get something on the gossip front to fill his pages.'

'But he didn't have to sell Spackman's pictures to the other tabloids. Why is he doing this to me?'

'Kev's just a big kid, and he's showing off. You won't give him what he wants so he has to prove he can control you.'

'He's persecuting Michael Kershaw just to get back at me?' Kate could not believe the smallness of the man.

'I'm no psychoanalyst, but that would be my interpretation. Look, stop worrying. As soon as there's a real scandal to chase you and Kershaw will be of no further interest. Keep your fingers crossed that a vicar admits making a bevy of parishioners pregnant, or a politician advocating family values is discovered inside his researcher's knickers. That will take you off the agenda.'

'But the damage is done. What about our reputations?' She was remembering her father's telephone call.

Jack gave her an affectionate squeeze. 'What an

old-fashioned girl you are, Kate. Don't you see, your reputation is enhanced? There's nothing to boost a career like infamy. Kate Rider is a name that will ring a bell with every editor in the land. And don't worry, they're unlikely to remember the context.'

'And what about Michael Kershaw?'

'What is this? Are you trying to pull that guy?'

Kate tossed her head. 'Of course not!'

'Good, I was beginning to feel jealous.'

It was the first time he had admitted such a personal interest. She submitted to a tobacco-scented embrace, but pulled away before he could kiss her.

'I'm your friend, Kate. It's not very flattering when you flinch away like that. Especially when I was about to ask you out to dinner tonight.'

Not wanting to hurt his feelings, she tried to let him down lightly. 'I'm sorry, Jack. Right now I don't feel like putting in any public appearances.'

'Suits me. How about I collect a take-away, and you come round to my flat?'

'I'd be poor company. I'm getting a taste of what it must have been like for Caroline Kershaw and I don't much like it.'

'There's one big difference, you aren't suicidal. The Kershaw woman was disturbed. You have to stop carrying the burden of her death, it wasn't your fault.'

'I was her chief persecutor. I can't forget that I invaded her privacy when I had no right to do so.'

'The only privacy a reporter should acknowledge is the legitimate activity that goes on behind closed bedroom curtains. Everything else is in the public domain. You didn't pry into Kershaw's private life but into her professional one. As a journalist that's what you're paid to do.'

But this tenet was anathema to Kate. She was coming to realise that her ambition had limits after all.

Chapter 11

Kate had to call Michael Kershaw's home number several times before he answered. The four syllables of his name, pronounced in that resonant voice, made her pulse race. Identifying herself was an embarrassment.

'Mr Kershaw, it's Kate Rider.'

She was conscious of her name falling between them coarse as an obscenity. He replaced the receiver with no further acknowledgement.

The need to speak to him, to explain, gnawed at her like a pain. An hour later, she rang again. Avoiding any salutation, her apology tumbled out. He was obliged to hear at least the first few words before he rang off.

Next day, when she tried to call again, she failed to obtain even a ringing tone. Enquiring of the operator, she was told that the number was unallocated. Michael Kershaw had transferred to ex-directory.

Jack's wisdom had been that it would all blow over. His advice was to forget everything, and let things run their course. Kate could not do this. She took to loitering outside the glass tower that housed the offices of *Campbell, Kershaw and Mather*.

On the third day of her vigil, she saw the architect leaving his premises. He was in company and what she had to say was too private for a third party to hear. She attempted to withdraw, but before she could melt into the crowd, he spotted her. His expression signalled something stronger than displeasure. Though she understood his repugnance, she could not bear it. It increased her need to explain. He had to be told of her own unwitting part in the unwelcome publicity.

Their next meeting was unplanned, their paths crossing accidentally on the street. This time he was alone, and she did not hesitate to intercept him. His reaction was one of incredulity.

'If you don't stop this harassment, I'll take out an injunction against you and your damned paper,' he warned, before brushing her aside.

She kept pace with him, determined to say her piece. 'This has nothing to do with my paper. Please, give me a chance to explain. I have to talk to you, and my reasons are entirely personal.'

His long stride rapidly closed the distance to his office, but she stayed at his shoulder, trotting, pleading for his attention.

'I know how it must look, but I had no idea those pictures were being taken. When I warned you against going to the restaurant, I was genuinely trying to save you from embarrassment. I'm distraught about what my paper has done to us both. Please believe me.'

He paused briefly and looked into her face. 'Not half so distraught as me. You scheming little bitch, you actually had me feeling sorry for you. Keep away from me in future or I might not be responsible for my actions. Understand?'

His facial muscles were taut, his blue eyes glacial. She shrunk from him as though she had been struck. Then he was gone, his proud figure swallowed by the darkened glass doors of the office block.

The message was unambiguous: he had given his

absolution once, he would not give it a second time. She could not work for *The Flag* and expect to gain the respect of a man like Michael Kershaw.

In an attempt to forget her predicament, Kate occupied herself with the work that she had been neglecting. Apart from a minimum number of hours necessary for the body's maintenance, her days and nights, became dedicated to the paper she had grown to hate. Hard work was the only way she knew to blank-out her past mistakes and she toiled at the office long after the paper had been put to bed. These quiet hours were the best time for conducting research. She accessed the archives and surfed the Internet, sifting for ideas for her latest story.

Her latest coverage was of a Rottweiler mauling: a young bride hideously mutilated on her honeymoon. Her emotive account had aroused the readers' sympathetic indignation and stimulated a flood of letters. She followed the story with two feature articles. The first was a criticism of the Government's reactive legislation that had been singularly ineffective in controlling dangerous breeds. This was supplemented by a moving investigation, extending to a double page-spread, based on interviews with the victims of past attacks. Years and plastic-surgery later, the scars were still vivid and lives still blighted as a result of these ferocious encounters.

Kate excelled at the human interest bits, Colson told her so. He seemed to have forgotten her misdemeanour over Kershaw and was cloying in his admiration. She was good at her job; the subject of her sacking was off the agenda.

When working late, she frequently took a last tube home. She felt no fear at being out late and alone on the London streets, and was careless of her safety. Though trained in observation, the unkempt fellow, sitting opposite her on the tube, did not merit her attention. Her mind was filled with her latest assignment to the exclusion of all else. She was oblivious of the eyes fixed intently upon her. That both the eyes and their owner followed her when she disembarked, also went unnoticed.

It was a half-mile walk from the tube station to her front door. On that walk, she became conscious of a following footfall that seemed to be keeping exact step with her own. Without looking round, she quickened her pace. When the lumbering echo did the same, she was sure she was being followed.

The relief of reaching the dark porch of home was considerable. She had her keys ready and almost fell through the front door. She thought the 'Goodnight Kate,' that followed her into the communal hall must have been imagined.

Three nights later, riding an equally late tube-train, she had the uneasy sensation that she was being watched. Casually, she glanced along the advertisements opposite. As she read them, she occasionally dropped her focus onto her fellow passengers. There were four of them. Opposite sat a teenage couple who were far too interested in exploring each other under their jackets to even notice her. To their right was a young man with thinning hair, intent on the map of the underground system above her head. Next to the map-reader, slumped an overweight business man who appeared to be sleeping. Her neck prickled and instinct carried her observation into the other half of the carriage. Beyond the unoccupied seats was a large, unshaven man in sweater and jeans. She was certain that he averted his gaze as she glanced in his direction.

When her stop came, she was already on her feet by the automatic doors. She watched her suspect from the corner of her eye. When he made no move to follow, she scolded herself for her foolishness.

The creaking of the escalator disguised other movements, and the powerful shoulder barge, that almost knocked her off her feet, was completely unexpected. The perpetrator neither stopped nor apologised, but hurried on, taking the steps two at a time. Though her only view was of his back, she saw enough to confirm his identity: it was the unshaven man from her carriage.

The bulky figure continued on, through the ticket barrier and out into the night. He had not once looked back. Recalling her stalker of a previous night, she felt uneasy. This man would pound the pavement with the same heavy tread.

Common sense urged that she take a cab home from the station, but it was a warning she did not heed. Her stride purposeful, she passed through the station entrance. Traffic was still heavy on the street outside. There were a few pedestrians on the pavements, but none resembled the hefty individual who had barged into her. Relieved, she broke cover into a light drizzle and walked briskly in the direction of home, mildly berating herself for having trusted the weather forecast and leaving her umbrella at the office.

The first few hundred yards of the route took her along the still busy main road. Before taking the right turn into a quieter residential street, she paused to examine the way she had come. She was satisfied that she had not been followed. Except for an elderly man walking a dog, the glistening side-street pavement was deserted. Relaxing, she fell into a more comfortable stride. Fifty yards on, she made another right turn into her own tree-lined avenue.

He came at her from behind the trunk of one of the

massive plane trees that lined the pavement. A self-defence programme she had taken years ago had advocated screaming. She could manage no more than a whimper.

A hand found her breast and squeezed. She swung the briefcase she was carrying, catching him across the ear. The resultant howl was more of anger than of pain. Then she was running. Heart thumping, she reached her own door. Though her door-key was to hand she trembled so much that she could not insert it in the lock. With every fumbling moment, she expected to feel again the pressure of those huge hands.

Once inside she flung the door shut with such force that the wall seemed to shudder. The comforting click of the lock told her she was safe. She pressed her ear to the door but could hear nothing.

Her flat was on the first floor. Entering it, she groped her way through the darkness, to the window that overlooked the front of the building. Screened by a curtain, she peered out. The avenue appeared deserted. Growing bolder, she opened the window and leaned out to view the garden below. There was no one in sight.

Once the curtains were drawn closed she put on the light. In the familiar surroundings her fear subsided to be replaced by a sense of triumph. It was no mean feat to fight off an attacker, eight inches taller and twice her weight. The experience gave her an idea. She began to plan a new article in her head. Tomorrow, she would write about stalking: do a post mortem on the new legislation, dig up past cases, and arrange some interviews with victims.

It was later, when she lay in bed reliving the experience, that the worry began, for it had been no casual attack. Outside, with the street light shining in her eyes, she had not seen his face clearly, but there was no mistaking that bulk. He was definitely the man from the underground, the man who had bumped into her on the escalator. That he knew where she lived suggested he was the same man who had followed her earlier that week.

The danger was real. Precautions would have to be taken: she must remain alert at all times and late-night walks from the tube station were a definite no-no.

An idea for a new assignment always made the adrenalin flow, but tonight it flowed because she was afraid. Yet even as she quaked inside, she was too self-reliant, too stubborn to consider involving the police.

Chapter 12

Kate was speaking on the phone, when Charlie signalled that there was a call for her on his line. 'For you – says it's important.'

She terminated her conversation and reached across the desk to use her colleague's phone.

'Kate Rider speaking. How can I help you?'

There was no response. The line was not dead; she could hear a hum. 'Caller, are you still there? I'm sorry, I can hear nothing at this end, I'm ringing off.'

'Don't do that.'

It was a man's voice. The words very carefully enunciated. Her immediate thought was that the voice was being disguised.

'Who is that?' she demanded

'An admirer.'

She was uneasy. 'What do you want?'

'I have something for you.'

'Information?' It was not unusual for informants to wish to remain anonymous.

'Better than that.'

Kate was tiring of the game. 'What do you mean?'

'Meet me and I'll show you.'

'Who gave you my name?'

Her question was ignored.

'I'll be waiting for you in Villiers Street, at the entrance to the Embankment Gardens, eight sharp, OK?'

The careful accent slipped, she thought she detected Liverpudlian.

'I can't agree to meet you, not unless I know what this is about.'

'You'll regret it if you don't come.'

The words were harmless enough but the tone wasn't. She scribbled large on her desk pad, CAN WE GET THIS CALL TRACED? and held it up to attract Charlie's attention.

'Can't you give me some idea why you want to see me?'

There was a pause. 'You could be in danger.' The Liverpool twang was more noticeable. 'I'm the only one who can protect you.'

Charlie was through to the switchboard. He gave her the thumbs up, followed by a rolling index finger to convey that she should keep the caller talking.

Kate tried to oblige. 'Why do I need protection?'

'Meet me tonight and you'll find out. Be sure to come alone. What I have is private, it's only for you.'

The line clicked, he was gone.

'Damn, I couldn't hold him,' she complained to Charlie.

'Not long enough to get a trace, I'm afraid,' he said with a shrug. 'What was it all about?'

'Someone arranging a rendezvous for this evening. It was a bit threatening. If I'm to keep the appointment, I'll need back-up. Are you game to come along?'

'Sorry, prior engagement. Anyway, if it's a nutter, you should stay away.'

Charlie was probably right about it being a nutcase. Recent publicity had made her name public property.

She made no conscious decision on whether to keep the appointment. But, engrossed in her writing, she was unaware of the passage of time. When she remembered, it was too late, and her curiosity about the anonymous caller had faded. When she next heard the voice, next morning, it came directly to her own extension.

The careful enunciation and slightly nasal tone were immediately recognisable.

'You should have come. I'm very angry.'

'Tell me who you are ?' Kate insisted.

'I can't do that. You will have to be punished now, and it's your own fault.'

Charlie was right, it was a nutter. She decided to play along. 'I thought you were going to protect me.'

'It's too late for that now, you should have come.'

There was a click on the line as the call was terminated. Kate cursed. The caller made her uneasy. It might have been wiser to agree to a meeting, so that he could be trapped. Fleetingly she considered whether the caller and her stalker might be one and the same. It was an idea she preferred to dismiss for the connection with her attacker made the call even more sinister.

Charlie was out of the office, and she made no mention of this second call to anyone else. This sort of harassment went with the job. It did not occur to her that she might be caught up in something too serious to be handled alone.

Hurrying out of *The Flag* premises a few days later, Kate saw her stalker again. She was about to push through the revolving doors when she recognised his bulky figure loitering outside. His face was turned away, but she was in no doubt that it was the same man.

The man's attention had been momentarily diverted from the building by a fracas going on across the street and he appeared not to have seen her. Slinking back into the concealing depths of the foyer, Kate's immediate thought was to enlist the help of Jack Brymer. She called his number via the reception desk and was rewarded by his grating tones.

'It's Kate. I'm in reception. I need your help, urgently.'

He responded immediately, entering the foyer with a grin of pleasure. 'It's good to be needed by a beautiful girl. Where's the fire?'

She kept her explanation brief. 'There's a man outside who's been following me. He may also be the person responsible for a couple of threatening phone calls I've received in the office. It's a chance to confront him, but I need some moral support.'

There was no hesitation from Jack. 'Let's get the bastard.'

The 'bastard' was still standing on the same piece of pavement, but was now part of a small crowd. What had been a minor traffic skirmish between a taxi driver and a private motorist had developed into full-blown road rage, and passers-by had gathered to watch. Two policeman were endeavouring to calm the protagonists.

Kate pointed. 'That's him, the big, unshaven fellow.'

'That big brute? It's not moral support you want, darling, it's a professional minder.'

Despite his words, Jack advanced, dragging Kate along by the hand.

Before they reached their quarry, he spotted them. Ignoring the moving traffic, he dived into the road. The crossing he negotiated was near suicidal. Brakes were hit, tyres screeched, and bonnets salaamed the tarmac. Glass tinkled as headlights butted a fender.

But the man's life appeared to be charmed. He reached the opposite pavement unscathed. Pursuit was pointless, and Kate and Jack could do no more than stand and watch as he disappeared into a side street.

'Bloody maniac,' Jack snorted. Motorists were seconding this opinion on car-horns.

Naturally, Jack demanded the full story. He steered her into the nearest pub to lubricate her vocal chords. She gave him chapter and verse, concluding, 'Why me?'

'He fancies you? Seriously though, I don't like the sound of it. The big guy who stalked you is almost certainly your anonymous caller too. Perhaps he recognised you from the Kershaw shots.'

'I'd thought of that. Those pictures were taken in the Embankment Gardens, and that was where he wanted to meet me. But it doesn't explain why he's persecuting me. What can he want?'

'Kate, can you really be so innocent? The pervert's already made a grab for your tits. It's my guess he's made you the centre-piece of his desire, and who can blame him for that. Unfortunately, unlike the rest of us, he seems intent on acting out his fantasies. Whether you're willing or not.'

It was the second time Jack had made an oblique reference to his interest in her. It was an admiration she would have much preferred to go unexpressed.

'You really think I'm at risk?'

'What I think doesn't matter. You're scared, I can see that. I don't like the idea of you being alone in that flat. Why don't you come and stay at my place for a bit?'

She tried to make light of his invitation, 'And how many bedrooms do you have, Jack.'

'One, but there's a perfectly good settee in the

lounge that doubles as a bed. I wouldn't pester you. Not unless you wanted me to,' he added hopefully.

'It's a bit premature to be looking for a bodyguard, but thanks just the same.'

'Then you'd better report your stalker to the police. You're unlikely to be his first victim, and the chances are he'll be known to them. An ugly bastard like that is pretty distinctive, and between us we can provide a good description.'

'An *ugly* bastard who is *pretty* distinctive? You're beginning to talk in *Flag* oxymoron journalese,' she teased.

'And you are talking as if you're not taking this seriously,' he reprimanded.

'I don't want a fuss, and I certainly don't want to be bothered with police questioning. Now the brute has seen I have a protector, the chances are he'll leave me alone.'

Jack didn't argue, partly because he didn't want to frighten her, but mostly because her description of him as her protector gave him cause for hope.

Win Blakeney's professional career had taken off. After just three television appearances, the photogenic duo were the toast of the music business. Their first single, a tuneful and evocative number that began with the line, *I've seen the birds fly across the great December sky, it's getting colder,* had rocketed into the best sellers. Recreated as Black Ivory, the pair were busy recording an album which included mostly original material, written by Winston. As soon as this was complete they were to embark on a lengthy, cross-continental, American tour.

These high-profile activities had put an end to appearances at The Spice Mill, but it was at that low-profile Richmond club that their farewell party was to be held. The printed invitation, for Kate Rider and partner, arrived in the office post. It gave Kate pleasure to be numbered among Win's friends and supporters.

So strict had become Kate's working regime that her leisure was non-existent. She had almost forgotten how to indulge in a purely social activity. There was no partner in her life, and she felt no inclination to take Jack along to Win's party. In fact, she preferred to go alone.

In vulnerable moments, she remembered the advances the young musician had made. Conjuring up his handsome face and winning smile made her regret her hasty rejection. The party invitation suggested his continuing interest, and she was flattered. It did not occur to her that the invitation might be merely a gesture of gratitude for the part she had played in promoting his career.

That Win's interest was a thing of the past, soon became apparent. At the party, he and Lena entertained their guests with a floor show. It was obvious from the first number that the professional relationship had blossomed into something more. On the previous occasions when Kate had seen them perform, Lena had delivered her songs from a fairly static position, at the remote end of the grand piano. Now, beginning with Cole Porter's *I've Got You Under My Skin,* Lena sang for Win. Moving gracefully, she stroked his cheek, wound an arm about his chest and brushed the back of his neck with her pert little breasts. It was stylishly erotic, and Kate was mesmerised by the confidence of the girl. The audience, seduced by actions as much as by her husky voice, hooted their approval. It was such a loaded performance that it eclipsed Win's virtuosity at the piano.

Lena was talented and stunning, and Kate was embarrassed by the expectations she had harboured. With the enthusiastic charms of this dusky beauty so obviously available, Win could have no interest in her pale self. However, he did pay her the courtesy of his attention. In acknowledgement of her unaccompanied status, he arranged for her to be seated in the midst of a party of his and Lena's friends. When the hosts circulated among their guests, Win came first to her table. After accepting the warmth of his friends' congratulations, he drew up a chair next to her.

'I'm happy that everything is working out for you,' she told him. 'I can't open a magazine without coming across an article about you two.'

'You seem to be getting a lot of publicity yourself. Why are you doing it , Kate?'

It was the same question that her father had asked. She hadn't expected that she would need to defend herself this evening.

'I wasn't party to the taking of those photographs. They were taken and published without my knowledge.'

'I'm pleased to hear that. The publicity must have made Michael Kershaw pretty pissed off. Ma was disappointed because she thought better of you.'

'Then please tell her it wasn't my doing. I wouldn't have gone anywhere near Michael Kershaw had I known that a photographer was on my tail.'

Her distress was obvious, and he reached out to squeeze her hand consolingly. 'I'm sorry if we misjudged you and I apologise for raising the subject. I brought you here to thank you, not to interrogate.' Wishing to change the subject, his eyes roved the club. Locating Lena, he asked, 'What did you think of my partner?'

'She's very lovely and incredibly talented. You're both very lucky to have found each other.'

'I'm the luckier one. You know, she never ceases to surprise me. She's writing the lyrics to our new songs now. I need only play a tune, suggest what I have in mind to go with it, and she comes up with the right words. It's not Moon/June slop either, it's real poetry.'

The pride in his voice was unmistakable.

'You're so obviously compatible. The whole audience felt that.' She spoke with real sincerity.

'I'm crazy about her.'

His eyes were following Lena on the other side of the room. The love that Kate saw in them was touching, but it made her suddenly sad. No man had ever looked at her in that way.

In the friendly atmosphere, people kept recharging her glass. It made it extremely difficult to estimate the alcohol consumed. She was unaware of her inebriated condition until the party broke-up and she stepped into the chill air outside the club. She walked unsteadily, more than a little drunk. She cursed her lack of judgement.

A mini-cab pulled into the kerb and she swayed her way towards it.

'Collins?' the driver asked.

'No, Rider.'

'Then I'm not for you, sweetheart, more's the pity.'

Kate relinquished the cab to its rightful passengers and continued to wait. Most of the clubbers had left, when another taxi pulled into the kerb. Before she could claim it, a heavy hand fell on her arm and a stubbled face bent to her own. There was the stale smell of hops, then four whispered words before she was pushed unceremoniously against the car. Her attacker made off.

The cab driver got out swearing. 'You all right, love?' he asked anxiously.

'I think so. Are you the cab for Rider?'

'That's right, love, hop in.'

She climbed unsteadily into the back. The shock had sobered her. What her assailant had whispered was, 'Beware the Kershaw Curse.'

Chapter 13

Kate sat perched on the corner of Jack's untidy desk. He swivelled his chair, creating an angle between them that made his ogling of her thighs less obvious. It was an unnecessary subterfuge. She was too much engrossed in telling of her Richmond encounter to care about his surreptitious lusting.

'It's possible Michael Kershaw is paying him to frighten you,' Jack suggested when she had finished.

Kate protested, 'I can't believe that of him. I'm sure he isn't the vindictive sort.'

Jack shrugged. 'You've spoken to Kershaw, I haven't.'

Kate began to wonder. 'He certainly thinks I connived over those photographs that Colson splashed over the front page.'

The display of affection recorded in those photographs still rankled with Jack. There was some satisfaction in thinking that Kershaw was responsible for her on-going persecution. But Jack was a good newsman, with a nose for the truth.

'If he resents you enough, it could be pay-back time. Though, somehow, I share your view that Kershaw isn't behind this business. The more likely scenario is that your Sumo stalker saw you in the tube and recognised you from those photographs.'

'And his use of my phrase?'

'*The Kershaw Curse* was a catchy headline. It's a nice

alliterative phrase, and easy to remember. That's why you coined it in the first place. And it was picked up and used by two of the other tabloids, don't forget.'

'So you think he was simply quoting what he'd read?'

'He's probably kept those cuttings, and re-reads them every time he comes after you.' He exhaled, adding to the tobacco fug.

'And when will he tire of his enthusiasm, do you think?'

'My chief worry,' Jack admitted, 'is that he doesn't seem to be tiring at all. If he keeps this up, you could be hurt.'

Kate accepted that she must confront the situation. 'What should I do about it?'

'I've a pal on the force, name of Nick, who owes me a few favours. He's got access to a register of sex offenders. Why don't I give him a call? Your guy is distinctive; if he's offended before, we'll find him easily enough.'

He moved to pick up the phone but she stayed his hand.

'But what if Michael Kershaw *is* at the root of this?'

'Then we need to find out, and put a stop to his nasty tricks.'

'No, Jack.'

'What d'you mean "No"?'

'He's a decent man. If he has organised this, then he's unwell.'

'So?'

'If he's ill, I'm the cause.'

'Why are you being so paranoid about Kershaw?' Jack snapped. 'The chances are the big guy pestering you is a loner. No more than a head-case out to hurt you. You need protection, and that's a job for the police.'

'I won't risk bringing any more trouble to Michael Kershaw. I've done enough harm to him already. Please, you must promise that you won't go to the police, behind my back.'

'It's bloody madness to be so stubborn. You're putting yourself at unnecessary risk.'

'I'll be careful. I promise.'

'Careful! Like you were last night? That guy must have followed you to Richmond. You're a journalist, trained to be observant, yet you didn't notice him. He's clever, Kate. He's outwitting you every time. How am I going to feel when you end up raped, murdered, and dumped in a skip?'

She understood that he was only being brutal because he cared.

'So far he's frightened me, that's all. He hasn't been particularly violent.'

'You're kidding yourself. Last night there were too many people around for him to do any more than frighten you. When he had you alone he grabbed your boobs, didn't he? That's sexual assault. Have you forgotten that you had to fight him off? Next time you may not be so lucky.'

Despite the strength of his argument, she would not be swayed. 'I won't involve the police; not while there's an outside chance that Michael Kershaw is implicated.'

That she was prepared to endanger herself to protect Kershaw was a bitter pill for Jack to swallow. He tried another tack. 'If Kershaw is involved, then I agree he's unwell. He needs psychiatric help.'

But Kate remained adamant. She did not want the law involved.

'Have it your way, but on your head be it,' he warned, thinking her a bloody-minded little idiot.

The next few days were peaceful, with neither sight nor sound of her persecutor. Nevertheless, she heeded Jack's advice and remained extra vigilant.

The Richmond experience had taught her caution. Then the stalker had waited around for hours, until her emergence from The Spice Mill. In all likelihood he had been on the same train to Richmond and must have tailed her as she toured the town. Jack was right, she had been a fool not to notice she was being followed. She disciplined herself to be more observant.

From the taxi, the avenue looked reassuringly deserted. She paid her fare and climbed the steps to the front door, her keys in her hand. Behind her, she heard her cab accelerating away.

Suddenly a massive paw clamped bruisingly over her mouth.

'Quiet or I'll slit your throat,' he hissed.

Screaming was out of the question anyway with his hand wrapped around her jaw. The light of a street lamp glittered on the broad blade of a knife and cold steel pressed lightly against her throat.

She had written about the raw terror of others: a mother battering the dog whose jaws were fixed on her child's head; the sub-postmistress, gun-whipped by a raider; a couple tortured to disclose the whereabouts of a home safe that didn't exist. Now she was experiencing that terror herself.

'Get the door open. You're inviting me in.'

Her brain raced. Several lights were on in the house, but how could she raise the alarm with the knife held to her throat? Self-preservation gave her cunning. She signalled to him to let her speak. He nicked her under the chin with the point of the blade.

'That's just a warning. I'll go for your windpipe if you try anything.'

She felt a warmth on her neck, and realised it was the flow of her own blood. He loosened his fingers but did not remove his hand from her mouth. It was unpleasant moving her lips against the flesh of his fingers. Her senses were overwhelmed by the taste as well as the smell of him. Once inside she would stand no chance. At least out here her predicament might be noticed.

'I can't take you inside. My flat-mate is there,' she bluffed.

If he knew her flat was on the first floor, then she was lost, for that floor was in total darkness.

He believed her. 'I didn't know you shared. You're no good to me here.'

Desperate to gain some time, she suggested, 'Can't we go to your place?'

'Too far. There's gardens off the next road – we'll go there.'

The gardens were several minutes walk away, she did not want to think beyond that. All that mattered was that she had gained some precious time in which to engineer an escape.

He pressed his mouth to her ear to whisper. She felt the dampness of his breath.

'I'm taking my hand from your mouth, but you're not to call out, understand?'

She nodded, very carefully, for his knife was still at her throat.

As they walked, his left arm encircled her. He freed two buttons, and his right hand, holding the knife, slipped under her coat. The blade was pressed beneath her breast.

'Keep moving, unless you want a mastectomy,' he commanded.

She walked, but slowly. Her legs scarcely felt part of her body.

On the opposite pavement, an elderly couple were making their way home. The hand under her coat tensed. If he panicked she was done for.

'It's all right, they're not looking at us,' she reassured. And if they had looked, what would they have seen but two lovers taking a walk? The knife was concealed under the coat. There was nothing to indicate she was being abducted.

They turned the corner, and she could see the trees that fringed the gardens. The garden's ornate gates were locked at dusk, but that wouldn't save her. He would make her climb over the railings. It wasn't difficult, she had seen children doing it. But, while Neanderthal was climbing, the knife could not be the threat it was now. She decided that would be the moment to make her bid for freedom and survival.

A car turned into the road behind them, the full beam of the headlights cast their shadows onto the wall they were passing. The approaching vehicle seemed to be travelling very slowly but Kate could think of no safe way to attract the driver's attention. Suddenly the motor roared and their shadows were no longer on the wall but on the ground before them. The car had mounted the pavement and was bearing down on them.

Her abductor released her, throwing himself into the road. As he did so, the knife snagged on her coat and clattered to the ground. Kate flattened herself against the wall as the vehicle came to a juddering halt, two of its wheels on the pavement, two in the road. Someone got out of the car. Disorientated, she didn't know whether to run or stay.

'Kate, has he hurt you?'

It was Jack's voice. She sank to her knees in relief.

'What has the bastard done?'

He was kneeling too, holding her in his arms

'Nothing serious. I'm OK, really, it's just the shock.' The miracle of his rescue struck home. 'But how did you come to be here?'

'I was looking after you, you lunatic.'

As he lifted her to her feet he noticed the dark stain on her jacket.

'Shit, you're bleeding, he's knifed you.'

'He cut me under the chin. It's not hurting, so it can't be much.'

Jack was on his mobile phone, calling for police and ambulance.

'Did the car hit him?' she asked.

'No, damn it, though that's what I intended. He's scarpered. I doubt if the police will pick him up tonight.'

'How did you know I was in trouble, I don't understand?'

'I've been keeping an eye on your place for the last few nights. He was hanging about here yesterday, but spotted me watching him. I tried to follow, but he lost me.'

'But why didn't you warn me?'

'I should've, I'm sorry. But I had the idea that it would make a better story for your feature article if we gave this particular stalker his freedom for a bit longer before handing him over to the boys in blue.'

Kate sighed despairingly. 'Oh, Jack.'

'It was a bad piece of misjudgement on my part. Tonight I followed your cab, and parked just down the road. I thought you were safely indoors, and was about to drive away when I saw him. I thought he was holding a gun to you, I didn't know what to do.' He kicked the knife where it lay. 'I know it was taking a risk but I thought I could protect you.'

'You did protect me,' she contradicted. 'You couldn't have done better.'

'I don't know about that. I've never been so scared. If it had been a gun, with the safety catch off, anything I tried might have ended in you being shot. Driving at him was a risk. He might have thrown you into the path of the car. Christ, I could have got you killed.' His voice was unsteady with emotion.

'You did the right thing, Jack. He was taking me into the gardens. I don't think I would have come out of there alive. You saved my life.'

He held her protectively. 'You can present the bravery medal later. For now, just try to relax. Come and sit in the car, the police and medics won't be long.' He was trembling too.

In the car, he pressed a handkerchief to her neck wound, though the bleeding was already stemmed. Growing bolder, he kissed her forehead, then her cheek. These attentions were irritating, but, conscious of how much she owed him, she did not resist.

Chapter 14

Jack insisted on accompanying her to the hospital. After a long wait for a medical check, two stitches were inserted in her neck-wound.

The police took only the briefest statement. Jack's ginger- headed friend, Inspector Diss, felt that there was not much they could do that night as her attacker would most certainly have gone to ground. He instructed her to go home and rest. A more detailed interview was arranged for the next morning, when they were to report to Paddington Green Police Station. The object of that visit would be to produce a photo-fit of the assailant.

'I'd put money on them picking him up in the next forty-eight hours,' Jack comforted.

Kate was less confident. 'How can you be so sure?'

'Between us, we can give a full description. The photo-fit should be as good as a photograph. Besides, the police found a good set of prints on the knife. And you heard what Nick Diss said, your attacker will almost certainly be known to them.'

Jack drove her back to the flat. Quite naturally, he came inside to ensure that everything was secure. Exhausted, she longed for him to go, but he made no move to do so.

'You've been a good friend to me tonight, Jack.' There was an emphasis on *friend* that he was not slow in picking up.

'I hoped you might see me as rather more than that.'

She was acutely aware that he had saved her life and didn't want to appear ungrateful. 'Of course you're more than a friend, you're my hero.' She patted his hand affectionately. He covered hers with his own.

'There's something I want to say, Kate. I was shit-scared for you this evening. It's made me realise how much you mean to me . . .'

'Jack, please.'

He ignored the protest. 'I haven't had a relationship with a woman since my marriage break-up four years ago. I haven't wanted one. You could say that a failed marriage has made me a bit of a misogynist. I've a tendency to blame the whole of womankind for what my wife did to me. But that day we met – d'you remember, we went up in the lift together?'

She nodded resignedly. She was not in the mood to listen to these sentimental reminiscences.

'You were a new girl. I could feel your excitement like something tangible. Shit that I was, I wanted to spoil it all. Put the frighteners on you. But I found I couldn't. From the first, I felt protective towards you.'

'And you have protected me.' She tried to be supportive without giving encouragement.

'When I thought you and Colson had . . . you know, I was so jealous I wanted to break his bloody neck. I don't just want you, Kate, I respect you. Both as a woman and a journalist.'

She was thankful he made no mention of love.

'That's very flattering, Jack. I respect you too, but just now all I can think about is getting some sleep. You can leave me. I'll be fine and I'll see you in the morning.'

'Of course, kid. I'm sorry, you must be shattered

after all that's happened. I'll pick you up at ten-thirty for our appointment with Nick.'

His lips brushed her cheek but made no attempt to find her mouth.

Before he left, there was a promise she needed to extract from him. 'Jack, there is something else.'

'What is it? Just say the word.' He was embarrassingly eager, like a dog awaiting his mistresses command. All he lacked was a lolling tongue.

'Can we keep what has happened out of the paper? I don't want any more publicity, it brings too many problems.'

'Sure, if that's what you want. But it will have to come out when the guy's brought to trial.'

'That I can cope with, but not now, please.'

'Of course not, I understand. Goodnight, sweetheart.'

'Goodnight, Jack.'

His compliance made her feel so mean.

At Paddington Green Police Station, they were told that no match had yet been made with the fingerprints found on the knife. The photo-fit took priority, and Kate shivered as her tormentor's face took shape before her.

'It's uncanny, it's almost as if he posed for it.' She shuddered.

Inspector Nick Diss sought confirmation from Jack, who agreed.

'Spot on, I'd say. Add six-four and two-forty pounds, and you have him to a T.'

'Good. We'll get these out and circulated within the hour. Anything else you remember?' he asked Kate.

'I was too concerned with survival to notice much last night. But if he's the same one who made the calls, then I think he's disguising a Liverpool accent.'

Diss looked sharply at Jack, but spoke to Kate, 'Are you telling me that last night's assault wasn't your first contact with the attacker?'

The revelation that the same man had followed her home more than two weeks earlier and had been troublesome ever since, did not please the Inspector. He turned his spleen onto Jack.

'You knew what was going on? Why the hell didn't you call us in earlier?'

The Flag's chief crime reporter made a sheepish apology.

Diss remained incredulous. 'God damn it, Jack, what were you thinking about? You could have got the girl killed.'

'I warned her of the risk, but what's the good of arguing with a woman. We never win.'

'But what possessed you to keep quiet? Did you have a reason?'

Kate and Jack were both silent.

'I get it, you thought you'd sew it up without us, and turn it into your next exclusive. I can picture the headline: *Flag Reporters Bust Sex Attacker, Policeman Plod Grateful*. Was that it?'

Jack shifted uncomfortably. 'It wasn't like that, Nick.'

'So what was it like? I'd really like to know.'

'Tell him what you suspected, Kate. It has to come out now.'

It seemed that she had no alternative. 'I was trying to protect a third party. I see now how silly and unnecessary that was. That person can't have had anything to do with this. He might have wanted me frightened, but he wouldn't have condoned violence.'

'Will one of you please tell me who this mysterious *he* is?'

Jack picked up the story. 'When the stalker pounced on Kate in Richmond, he used an expression from one of her own headlines: *The Kershaw Curse*. Kate upset a bloke called Kershaw because of an exposé she did on his wife. It seemed possible he was hiring the big guy to frighten her.'

'Kershaw? Wasn't that the nursery school business involving a dead kid?'

'That's the one. The sequel was that Kershaw's wife topped herself.'

Kate winced inwardly at Jack's choice of words.

Diss looked at her, acknowledging her infamy. 'Of course, I should have recognised you.'

'This is silly,' she protested. 'Michael Kershaw can't have had any connection with that dreadful man.'

'If we bring him in for questioning, we'll find out.' Diss reached for a telephone.

'No, you mustn't,' Kate objected.

The Inspector raised an eyebrow. 'If he can give us a lead on the assailant, then we must.'

She appealed to Jack. 'Tell him, this is crazy. We can't subject Michael Kershaw to any more.'

Jack shrugged. 'There's a dangerous lunatic on the loose. You might not be the only one at risk.'

'In which case this can have nothing at all to do with Michael Kershaw. He needn't be bothered.'

Diss tried to soothe her fear. 'Contrary to public opinion, we're not always heavy handed. I'll handle Kershaw sensitively, don't worry.'

Kate felt as sick as she had when the point of the blade had entered her neck. 'I'm making no accusation against Michael Kershaw. You said yourself that the police hunt will pick-up my attacker so there's no purpose in questioning him.'

Jack intervened. 'Kate feels protective towards Kershaw because of the unwelcome publicity her coverage generated. The chap has had a hard time of it lately. Can't you wait until our knife-man surfaces? You'll soon find out if he is a lone operator or not. As for Kershaw, he won't be going anywhere. He's the partner in a firm of award-winning city architects.'

'OK, we'll play it your way,' Diss conceded with obvious reluctance. 'But if we don't get results in a couple of days I'll have to check him out.'

He looked again at the photo-fit likeness. 'Don't worry, Miss Rider, despite your reticence in coming forward, we'll get your attacker.'

Kate shook the policeman's hand. To Jack she said, 'Thanks for that. I couldn't have Michael Kershaw thinking I was persecuting him again.'

Kate's clue as to her stalker's accent proved critical in identifying him. He was identified as one Jordan Dawes, well known to the Liverpool force as a persistent sex offender. He had never served a prison sentence, but had spent long periods in mental institutions. His latest release had been some eight months previous, since when he had disappeared from his usual Liverpool haunts. Investigations into his background revealed that, as a youth, he had spent three years living with an aunt in the Notting Hill area of London. This was where the hunt for him was now centred. The failure of the police to pick him up suggested that their quarry had gone to ground.

Colson summoned Kate to his office. 'Why are you wearing that scarf?' he demanded as she entered.

Her first thought was that Jack had betrayed her, but she brazened it out. 'Because it's fashionable.'

'For some, perhaps, but you're at your best showing some cleavage. Perhaps that's what attracted your stalker.'

Her eyes flashed. 'Who told you about that?'

'I've just had the solicitor acting for Michael Kershaw on the phone. He claims that you were assaulted and wounded several days ago. Apparently his client has been questioned by the police in connection with the attack.'

A wave of sickness engulfed her as Colson droned on.

'Kershaw refutes any allegation that he rented a thug to sort you out. He's threatening to sue the paper if we so much as print a word of it. Well, I'm waiting. What do you have to say for yourself?'

'I made no such allegation. If the police talked to Michael Kershaw, it's because my attacker used his name. That's the only connection.'

'What do you mean, *used his name*?' Despite the legal warning it was obvious that Colson was smelling a story.

'He borrowed one of my headlines, and threatened me with *The Kershaw Curse*. Michael Kershaw isn't involved, and I specifically asked the police to leave him alone. They know who my assailant is, but have failed to pick him up. Questioning Michael Kershaw is a purely diversionary activity.'

Colson was not impressed. 'Why,' he asked, 'hasn't *The Flag* received your exclusive on this?'

'My attacker is a fruit-cake. He's been in and out of mental institutions all his adult life. It won't help him if he receives newspaper coverage.'

She paused to remove her scarf. Raising her chin, she revealed the stitches. 'This is what publishing those pictures did for me. I hope you're proud of yourself, Kevin.'

There was some satisfaction: the scar, so near her windpipe, flustered him.

'You're not trying to shift the blame for that onto me, surely?'

'I don't want the publicity either. I'm a reporter, my job is to write the headlines, not star in them.'

The editor in Colson asserted itself. 'That's rubbish, you love publicity. You're anxious enough to get a by-line. If I remember correctly, didn't you have your own photo-headed column in *The Tamar Apocrypha*.'

This mis-naming of her former employer was the height of hypocrisy. It was pointless to protest that her *Advertiser* picture was something quite different. Anyway, wasn't her editor right? No journalist could decry publicity, it was their bread and butter.

She tried an appeal. 'Please, Kevin, surely we don't have to go public on this until my attacker is caught. I'm already working on a general piece about stalkers. If you want, I'll include my own experience, but under a pseudonym. We mustn't make any connection with Michael Kershaw. Not with his solicitor breathing down our necks.'

Colson was pacified. 'That's the kind of professionalism I've come to expect from you, Kate,' he patronised.

'And Kershaw?'

'We don't mention him. I prefer not to provide lawyers with ammunition. It tends to come expensive.'

Her attacker was spotted by a cruising patrol car. He had given himself up without a fight. It was discovered that, after coming to London, Jordan Dawes had held down a labouring job on a building site in Acton. The stalking of Kate coincided with his being laid-off.

The walls of Dawes' rented room in Shepherd's Bush were decorated with cuttings from the tabloids. The displays included *The Kershaw Curse* article and related pictures. The majority of the pin-ups depicted a well-known television actress, to whom Kate bore more than a passing resemblance. All the cuttings were annotated with obscenities or explicit sexual comment.

Dawes denied injuring Kate or intending her any harm. His defence was that he loved her. His history ruled out any connection whatsoever with Michael Kershaw. He was remanded, pending further psychological reports. Nick Diss was of the opinion that he would be found unfit to plead.

'With his history, he'll be back in the loony bin. Perhaps the trick cyclists won't be so ready to let him out, next time.'

This was welcome news to Kate, as she had no wish to feature as star witness at his trial.

Jack persuaded Colson that Kate needed a holiday. It was November, and his intention was to take her away for a week in the sun. He favoured Madeira. Islands were more romantic than continents, at least that was his view ever since his disastrous honeymoon in Canada. Despite this forward planning, caution persuaded him not to book before consulting her.

'You deserve a break, and it will do you good to get away,' he suggested. 'What do you say to taking a trip to Madeira, my dear?'

What could she say? She opted for a professional excuse. 'I'm in the middle of researching my stalking piece. I can't possibly drop it. There are people I've arranged to interview.' This was part-truth, though she had already accumulated most of the material.

'Even Kevin admits you're looking peaky, and he's hardly hot on staff welfare. If he's prepared to put your stalking article on hold, then so should you. You work too hard, Kate, a change will do you good.'

'You're a fine one to talk. If anyone is the workaholic around here, it's you.'

Jack was not prepared to be so easily thwarted in his designs. 'Untrue. I'm prepared to take a week off, and you're not. I rest my case.'

To agree to go on holiday with him would be tantamount to accepting him as her lover, and this she was not prepared to do. At the same time she did not want to lose his friendship, he was useful to her professionally. Someone who knew as much about the business as Jack undoubtedly did was someone worth cultivating.

The pressure-of-work excuse had not worked so she tried another. 'It's not just my article, I'm committed to spending some time with my father. He hasn't been well lately. If I take time off, then I must go down to Plymouth to see him.'

'You can go to Plymouth any weekend,' he countered. 'You don't need to take time off for that.'

'He's my father, Jack, and he needs me.' Faking sincerity had always been her forte.

'Do you suppose I don't need you?'

He looked so miserable that, for one crazy moment, she considered giving in to him. Inspiration saved her, and she offered him a face-saver.

'I can't give you what you want, Jack. Your divorce is long behind you, but my failed relationship is more recent. I'm not ready to make a commitment with another man.'

'Well, it's something of a relief to hear that there has been a failed relationship. Your lack of boyfriends was beginning to worry me.'

'What are you insinuating?'

'Tasteless joke, sorry. OK, Kate, I accept your father's prior claim, but my offer of a holiday still stands. When you're ready, I'll be waiting. You're the only woman who has meant anything to me for an awful long time.'

A small part of her was sorry that she could not grant his wish.

Chapter 15

Her spur-of-the-moment excuse did more than help avoid Jack's island idyll. It served as a reminder of daughterly duty and promoted a desire to blot out past unpleasantness. Her invention became reality. To be more accurate, part-reality, for her father, far from being ill, was in the best of health. This she discovered when she telephoned to arrange a visit.

Within hours of arriving at her stepmother's Plymouth home, she saw that nothing had changed. She was still the outsider. In part, this was her own doing. Her father encouraged her to talk about her journalistic escapades, but these she had come away to escape. The stalker experience, in particular, was something she wanted to conceal. The evidence of the assault was disguised by carefully applied make-up.

Quizzed on her new life, her responses were vague and non-committal. Conversation soon turned to the apparently more interesting doings of her step-mother's family. Old jealousies revived. Unwilling to play second fiddle to Ellen's gene-pool, Kate cut short her stay. The reunion had lasted less than forty-eight hours.

It was a surprising relief to be back in London. She needed some time to herself and as Jack and the rest of the office believed her to be away for the whole week, she could count on being left in a splendid isolation. Before she had chance to unpack, the door-bell rang, shattering this illusion.

Her caller was the last person in the world she expected to see. Since she had known him, his strong, sensitive features had always looked strained; now they were positively haggard. His eyes were encircled with dark rings, his cheeks were drawn. He looked a sick man.

There was no greeting. 'I received your letter,' he told her.

After finding out about the police dragging him into the Dawes investigation, she had sent a personal apology. She repeated the sentiments expressed in her letter.

'I asked the police not to involve you. I'm truly sorry that they did.'

'I need to talk to you.'

In the past it had been she who needed to talk to him. Her pulse quickened.

'It's a matter of life and death,' he insisted.

She held the door wide, inviting him to enter.

'I'd rather not come in. My car is parked outside, we can talk there.'

It was a cool night, and he waited while she collected a jacket.

His vehicle surprised her. It was not the predictable BMW or Audi, but a four-wheel-drive Japanese model. Courteously, he opened the passenger door. She climbed up into the cab. Taking his place next to her, he started the engine.

'Strap in,' he ordered.

She was confused. 'Where are we going? I thought you wanted to talk.'

'We can do that later.' He did not speak again but concentrated on his driving.

A light drizzle began to fall, and the intermittent wipers swept just a little too slowly. Beads of water pock-marked the windscreen turning the headlights of oncoming traffic into a dazzling blur.

She knew the route he was taking. They were on the Great West Road heading for the M4 motorway.

'Please, Michael, I'd like to know where we are going.'

'Sit tight, and you'll find out.'

The road lighting illuminated the hands holding the steering wheel. They gripped so tightly that the knuckles were white. He was not at all like the man she had sat with in the Embankment Gardens. She was sure he was ill.

Once on the motorway, the needle crept to ninety. At the junction with the M25 they turned off, east-bound. She did not speak again until he took the slip road for the M3. She moderated her voice to disguise her anxiety, 'I'm beginning to think you're abducting me.'

'I am.'

She attempted a laugh. 'I won't fetch much of a ransom, if that's what you have in mind.'

'It's not.'

She did not ask the obvious question. She had a feeling that she would not like the answer. A service area was signposted.

'Why don't we pull off here,' she suggested. 'We could both do with a cup of tea.'

He was unresponsive, so she asked, 'Are we going to Southampton?'

In reply he took the inside lane to join the A303. It was a road she knew well, a favoured route from London to the West Country.

The weather had closed in, the drizzle becoming fog. It was a relief when he reduced speed. Some miles on, he braked without warning, and they swung into a deserted lay-by. Though it was invisible, she knew they were near the ancient monument of Stonehenge.

The motor was left running. For the first time on the journey, he turned his face to hers. It was too dark to see his expression. He groped into the glove-pocket and took something from it. Spurred by memories of the knife attack, she deftly released her seat belt, and wrenched at the door handle. It was an abortive bid for freedom. She was locked in.

As she struggled with the door, something cold was clipped around her right wrist. Then, while her numbed brain was still registering this development, her left wrist was encircled too. She was handcuffed. He came at her again, this time to tape her mouth. She fought, bringing up her knees, obstructing her face with her chains. It was a spirited resistance, but he was determined and it was soon overcome.

He let himself out of the car and came around to the passenger side.

'Get out,' he ordered.

Her desire to leave the car evaporated. Discoveries of bodies in lay-bys were an all too common occurrence in her line of work. She shrank away from him, but he grabbed her ankles. In kicking out, she lost a shoe. Trapping her feet, he applied the sticky tape to bind her legs together. She rained blows upon his head, battering him with the handcuffs. He seemed oblivious of the attack. With her ankles secured, she was slung unceremoniously over his shoulder, and deposited in the back of the vehicle.

She was conscious of his heavy breathing as he fiddled with the handcuffs in the dark. When a wrist was released, he rolled her over and, wrenching her arms behind her, restored the restraints. He sat astride her torso, his weight restricting her breathing. She thought his intentions were sexual, but he moved away without touching her.

The texture of wool touched her cheek, as a blanket was drawn over her head. Her mind ran riot with tabloid stories of concealed bodies.

There was a shift of the suspension as he climbed out of the vehicle. Open doors were slammed shut. The driver's door creaked, and the suspension rocked again as he climbed back behind the wheel. A final door-slamming and then they were moving again, speeding westward.

It was stuffy under the concealing blanket, and an unpleasant sensation to be able to breathe only through her nose. She shifted her weight to find the most comfortable position. Despite the discomfort, she grew surprisingly calm. She kept telling herself that Michael Kershaw was neither a sex maniac nor a killer.

Time passed and she lost track of it, even half-dozing. Eventually the car slowed. She wondered if this meant the fog was thicker or if they were now travelling on minor roads. They stopped and her abductor got out. She heard the sound of creaking hinges from beyond the bonnet. The vehicle moved a few yards and stopped again. The distinctive, gate-hinge sounds were repeated, coming from behind, this time. Kate worked out that they had left the public road and were on private land. The jolting of the vehicle confirmed this. They were either travelling off-road or along a very rutted track.

They stopped yet again, and this time he killed the engine. Still he did not speak. She strained her ears to every new sound. His footsteps receded, and she was left alone for several minutes. When he returned, the blanket was pulled from her head to be replaced by a softer material that felt like a pillowcase. Even in the dark, she was not to be permitted a view of her surroundings. Through the weave of the pillowcase she could see artificial light. He manhandled her from the vehicle. Then she was picked up and carried, bridal fashion, across a threshold.

The chair in which she was deposited hemmed her in with wooden arms and a high back. He said not a word, though she could hear him, busily tearing material into strips.

Cutting through the tape, he freed her legs. When he grasped an ankle and attempted to secure it to the chair leg, her co-operation ceased. She kicked out but, with her arms still pinioned behind her back, it was a token resistance. With strips of fabric, he attached her ankles to the chair legs. It was a restriction that left her sitting in knock-kneed discomfort. Using one hand to restrain her, he fed the handcuffs around the ladder-back of the chair and re-locked them on her wrists. Then he removed the pillowcase.

She blinked in the light, taking in her surroundings. She was in a small, low- ceilinged room with whitewashed, stone walls. There was one internal door and a single window, firmly shuttered on the outside. The floor was stone, its large, worn flags partly covered with a square of garish carpet. The room's other furniture comprised a two-seater settee and matching easy chair in a William Morris fabric, a substantial oak dresser, and a utility coffee table. A radio-cassette player stood on the latter. Opposite the door, an open fireplace with empty grate yawned blackly.

'This will hurt,' he warned, preparing to tear the tape from her mouth.

She flinched, anticipating the depilatory effect. As

her lips were freed, she cried out. Her eyes watered. It was a struggle to speak. When she did, all she could manage was an indignant, 'Why?'

'If you have to ask that, then it's obvious you have no remorse.'

'I do have remorse. I never intended to involve you, not in any of it.'

'And what about my wife, was she fair game?'

'She shouldn't have been.'

'The murder of the little girl in Wandsworth made her ill. You dug it up. She went through it, all over again.'

'I was wrong to do that. I regret what happened, believe me.'

'Caroline loved children. It would have been difficult enough for her to come to terms with Toby's death, without you persecuting her for it. Have you any idea how you made her feel when you printed those things in that filthy rag of yours?'

Kate had no answer for him. She knew only too well what she had done to his wife.

'I'll tell you what you did. You made it impossible for her to eat or sleep. She wasn't asthmatic, yet she had panic attacks that left her unable to breathe. Your sordid scoop was paid for with her life. But you didn't care about that did you? Even when my wife was dead, you couldn't leave us alone. What were you trying to do – finish me off too?'

She had no quarrel with his version of events, but attempted to defend herself.

'It wasn't like that, you mustn't think it was.'

'Shut-up. I didn't bring you here to listen to your excuses. *The Kershaw Curse* was your invention, but I'm going to turn it into a reality. I want you to know what it was like for Caroline. You made her suffer and I intend to make you suffer. You'll find out what it feels like to be pushed so far that you wish you were dead.'

He moved round behind her. The rags made an effective gag. He pulled them tight so that they bit into the sides of her mouth, forcing it open. The written word was her livelihood. Her ability as a wordsmith was her best means of defence, but his gagging robbed her of the power of speech. She was incapable of defending herself and could only wait to discover the nature of the suffering he had devised. The uncertainty did not last long.

'You may be here for some time, so I've prepared a little light entertainment.'

He removed a recording tape from his pocket and inserted it into the cassette player. Plugging in a headset, he attached the phones to her ears.

'Are you sitting comfortably?' It was black humour, his eyes had a cold, glazed look.

Turning the up the volume, he switched on. Her head exploded with the Morse-like bars from Beethoven's Fifth, which very abruptly metamorphosed into to a cacophony of heavy metal. She stiffened as stabs of real pain skewered her ear drums. A duet of soprano screeching followed, wailing like cats and then a marching band's rendering of Colonel Bogey slowed into the Death March. The sequence was repeated every few minutes. Interspersed between each repetition was a shrill whistle that acted as a fanfare for his own voice declaiming, 'The Kershaw Curse'.

There was a moment of blessed relief when he removed the earphones to speak to her. His words offered no comfort.

'Entertaining mix, don't you think? All but the special effects were taken from radio transmissions. I'll leave you to enjoy it.'

The earphones were replaced, the light switched off, and she was left alone. Alone except for the unbearable nightmare of sound that invaded her head.

How long would it take for the sonic battering to drive her insane? Almost immediately she comforted herself with the thought that the tape was finite. The relief of silence would surely come. She gave up an earnest prayer that the tape was standard length. If so, her ordeal would last for only thirty minutes.

The tape ended, but her rejoicing was interrupted by a clicking in her head. The player possessed the same facility as car tape-decks: its head automatically playing the reverse side. A further burst of Beethoven blasted her eardrums, confirming that both sides of the home-made recording were identical. The full horror struck her.

There was to be no end. When the tape stopped, there would be only the briefest intermission, and the robot machine would begin playing it again.

She could expect no relief until Michael Kershaw took pity on her, and, for all she knew, she might already be abandoned. Had he driven away, she would not have heard. Panicking, she threw her head from side to side. Like a stag trying to dispose of its old antlers, she rubbed the ear-phones on the chair-back. They were easily dislodged, though it was harder to work the head-set away from her ears. It slipped down her neck, to be supported by her shoulders. Further wriggling made it drop between her back and the chair. There its fall was arrested by the obstacle of her arms. It was the best she could do. She could still hear it, but it no longer played inside her head.

She concentrated on other things in an attempt

to ignore it. Mostly, she thought about Michael Kershaw. It was impossible to hate him. He was ill and she had driven him to this. If she hated anyone it was herself.

Chapter 16

Beyond the tinny insistence of the earphones, the house was silent. Kate's anxiety took a new direction. If he had abandoned her, then how long could she hope to survive? Though she wore a jacket, her clothing was light. After the heated car, the room struck chill.

No liquid had passed her lips since the drink bought from the train buffet-car. The coffee she had made on arrival back at the flat had been barely touched, because of the interruption by her kidnapper. Already thirst was becoming a major discomfort. She attempted to swallow, but her tongue got in the way. Her mouth was too dry to create saliva. To die of hypothermia would be bad, but death from thirst would be worse.

Though Michael Kershaw had made no direct death threat, he had done so by implication. His declared intention was to make her suffer as Caroline had done. He would push her until she no longer valued her life. To be in extremity through dehydration might well be the point at which oblivion would be welcomed. The sound of creaking boards above her head indicated a footfall on the first floor. The realisation that he had not left her to die, brought a sobbing relief.

Once the paramount fear was removed, she became aware of new and more immediate discomforts.

The dull ache that gnawed at her restricted limbs gradually became more intense, until it was developing into full-blown pain. She concentrated on exercising every part of her person that was not restrained. She wriggled fingers and toes, made circular movements with her neck, hunched and then dropped her shoulders, tightened then relaxing the muscles in her buttocks. In her nervous and dehydrated state it was an exhausting exercise, whenever she stopped it brought unbearable pain to her limbs and spine.

The agony was easier when her mind was occupied. She diverted herself with the huge mental effort of keeping track of time. It had been after 9 p.m. when the Plymouth train arrived at Paddington Station, and somewhere around 10 p.m. when she got back to the flat. She wasn't sure how long the car journey had lasted. It had taken an hour to reach the lay-by near Stonehenge, that was the last time she had been able to see her watch. Once under the blanket, the passage of time had been more difficult to judge. What had felt like many hours might have been fewer. Even if he had continued driving westward to Land's End the journey could not have taken longer than five or six hours.

Now the cassette player substituted as her clock. Each turn of the tape represented thirty minutes. She struggled to recall how many intermissions there had been and assessed that her torture had lasted for at least three hours. If these calculations were correct it should already be dawn. Her eyes sought for confirmation in the darkness. She had been wrong in thinking that no daylight was likely to penetrate her shuttered prison: a broken, grey light filtered through the slats. With the new dawning came renewed hope.

He was moving again, at first above her head and then on the stairs. Domestic sounds came from an adjoining room. The shrill whistle of a kettle reminded her of the tape's cacophony, but its more pleasant association increased her longing for a drink. The tape continued to run, playing out its muted performance through the ear-phones lodged in the small of her back. She wondered how he would deal with the modification she had made to her night-long misery.

The door opened with no sound of a turning lock. The knowledge that the door had not been secured somehow lifted her spirits. Blinking in the artificial light, she saw that he was carrying a steaming cup. She swallowed in expectation, her tongue feeling like a foreign body in the dryness of her mouth.

He stared at the dislodged the head-phones. 'You shouldn't have done that.' His voice sounded brittle, unrecognisable.

He left the room, leaving the steaming brew in view. When he returned, it was to bring more of the material that gagged and bound her. He held the cotton strip taut, like a garrotte, between his two hands. Moving behind the chair, he placed it over her head and around her neck. This then was the end. He intended to throttle her. Straining against her bonds, she threw her head from side to side. Not yet had he reduced her to Caroline's state. She still valued her life.

The fabric was drawn tight across her throat, but not tight enough to restrict her breathing. His intention was restraint, not suffocation. He tied her by the neck, to the chair's high back. It was sweet relief, not to be strangled. Sweet but brief, for having tested the knots, he replaced the head-phones. Once again,

Colonel Bogey mocked inside her head. Her life was spared, but in all other respects things were worse. There was to be no drink. Her movement was more severely restricted. And the tape from hell made an all-out assault on her bruised brain.

If the previous hours had been torture, the next were more agonising than anything she could have imagined. Though she could no longer feel her legs, a burning rod had replaced her spine. Her shoulders were bearing an invisible and crushing weight. She tried to brainwash herself into believing that she was merely restrained, in a sitting position, in a chair, but her brain would not be fooled. She knew that she was being crushed against burning coals, her arms were being pulled from their sockets, and a mechanical hammer was striking rhythmically at her temples. She hoped that the hammer would soon crack open her skull, for then the terrible noises trapped inside might escape.

The Inquisitor appeared. He was bearing a tray that bore torture implements. Fear caused her bladder to fail, she felt a trickle, and then a spreading warmth. She saw that the inquisitor was only Michael Kershaw, and that he had brought her food and drink.

Although the headphones were removed, the sounds in her head seemed to continue as loudly as before. The suffocating material was loosened and removed, leaving her mouth still fixed in the lines of the unnatural grin that the gag had induced. Wrists and ankles were unshackled, but they no longer seemed to belong to her. When she tried to move them, they would not obey her command.

She was unable to hold the mug he gave her, and some of the contents spilt into her lap. The hot fluid soaked through her clothing, scalding her thigh. It would disguise the spreading stain of the urine. Though it could not disguise its smell.

Reclaiming the mug, he held it to her lips. She drank greedily, relishing the sweet, black fluid. The circulation began to return to her limbs, making her cry out.

'Get on your feet. Walk about.' he commanded.

Wanting to please him, she tried to obey, but her legs gave no support. She stumbled and fell. Looking down, she saw that her ankles were enormous.

'My legs are swollen,' she pointed out. She couldn't bear him to think these ugly appendages were part of her usual appearance. Even in her present pitiful state the old vanities persisted.

Pulled to her feet and half supported, she was frog-marched around the room.

'Slap your arms, like this.' He demonstrated.

She did as she was bid.

He showed her other exercises. The circumstances were so strange, she wanted to giggle. He was behaving as if he were her fitness instructor in a gymnasium. Gradually the pins and needles relented, though the swelling persisted.

He indicated the bowl on the tray. 'Do you want to eat?'

She nodded, and took up the spoon. The bowl contained soup poured over a slice of brown bread. She ate slowly, her stomach protesting from the long neglect. Her last meal had been lunch with her parents, days ago. No, not days; she fought to bring her thought processes back under control. It had been yesterday. A lifetime away, yet less than twenty-four hours earlier.

'You're taking too long,' he complained.

She finished the meal hurriedly, frightened that he might deprive her of what was left.

Forced back into the chair, she held onto his arm and pleaded. 'No more, please, I can't stand it.'

He seemed not to have heard her, already he was reaching for the handcuffs.

'I need the lavatory. Please, it's urgent,' she begged.

It was not an exaggeration. The warmth of the fluids, combined with the exercise, had initiated a movement in her bowels. A movement that she feared she couldn't master.

'You're staying here,' he told her. 'I want you to know what it was like for Caroline. The day before she took her life, she lost control of both her bladder and bowels. That's what your reporting did to her.'

His pronunciation of *reporting* turned the word into an obscenity.

Binding her wrists with rags, he secured them to the arms of the chair. His intention was to attach the redundant cuffs to her ankles, but the apertures were too small to go round those puffed and swollen extremities. He employed more strips of rag to tie her legs together. Her lower body was no longer attached to the chair. She wanted to thank him, but before she could speak he gagged her again. The rest was as before: her head was restrained by the tie around her neck, and the brain-screws were fitted to her ears.

'See these?' In the palm of his hand were two bottles of white tablets. 'When you're ready to take them, let me know.'

He placed the pill bottles in her direct line of sight, on the table, next to the cassette player. She understood what was on offer, the way out he offered was the one that Caroline had taken. Watching her face, his forefinger hovered over the play button on the recording machine. Her mind willed him not to, but he exercised his prerogative and pressed.

The new bondage gave much greater freedom of movement to her lower body. For a while at least, her arms, resting on the broad wooden arms of the chair, felt almost comfortable. If she could bear the other she would be able to tolerate this. In a triumph of mind over matter, she had controlled her bowels, though she could still smell the urine that soaked her underclothes and seeped into her skirt.

She concentrated on blanking out the music from hell and for thirty minutes almost succeeded. Then the robot torturer commenced playing the reverse side. It was the reminder that he could go on for ever and ever. Her bolstered resolve collapsed to nothing.

Without the diversion of physical pain, the hellish music ate into her brain. No thought in creation could lessen its impact. Her mind was wired to a direct route to insanity. To hold out against the torture, she needed the certainty of knowing that in a day, two days even, the tape would stop turning, that there would be an end to her punishment.

She tried to lift her spirit with thoughts of rescue, but she remembered that she was supposed to be on holiday. She would not be missed. Hunting for crumbs of comfort, she imagined that her father, wondering why she hadn't rung, would guess something was wrong. But she remembered how strained her visit had been. Her silence would be interpreted as pique. She was damned to perpetual torment by the noises of perdition. The two bottles that promised oblivion mocked her from their inaccessible position, a few feet away.

The grey light that penetrated the shutters grew dim. Darkness descended. She could not take another night of this. When he came again, she would beg to be given the drugs that would deliver the relief of silence. But, even in these thoughts, a flame of resistance flickered. She intended to cheat him by taking sufficient tablets to guarantee unconsciousness, but insufficient to deliver a more permanent oblivion.

It was a long time before he came to her again. She had quite forgotten her intention to trick him. She wanted the contents of those bottles with a desire that burnt more fiercely than ambition had ever done. Nothing mattered but oblivion. As he loosed the gag, the words tumbled out, 'I'm ready, I'll take them.'

'Not yet, it's too soon. You have to suffer as she did.'

'I am suffering, believe me I am.'

He began to loosen her bonds. The freedom felt unnatural.

'You have ten minutes for exercise, then I'll bring your supper.'

Before withdrawing, he commandeered the pills, putting them in his pocket. For the first time she heard a key turn in the lock.

She did as he bid, walking stiffly around her cell and slapping her arms across her body. Only as the lock sounded again did she realise that he had left her alone with the robot tormentor. It would have been a moment's work to have dashed its devilish mechanism onto the stone flags. Her eyes stung with tears for an opportunity lost. Her blurred vision distorted his face. She did not see the change in his expression.

Chapter 17

Kate was wrong in her reasoning. She *had* been missed. She had forgotten Jack and his persistence. Her refusal to go away with him had been a setback for him, but, having swallowed his disappointment, he became even more determined in his pursuit.

He acknowledged that, for the first time in his life, he was preoccupied with a woman. It had not been like that with Eileen, she had made all the running. The marriage had been a disaster from the start. Her interests were centred on homemaking and he had no intention of wasting his life choosing wallpaper or tinkering with lawn mowers. When he refused to conform Eileen turned bitter. The disadvantages of married life seemed to outweigh the advantages by so vast a margin that he had sworn never again to commit himself to a permanent relationship.

He was still uncertain exactly what it was he wanted from Kate. That he was eager to bed her was undeniable, but he yearned for something beyond that. Life with Kate would be very different from entrapment with Eileen. For a start they were in the same trade, on the same wavelength. They would be able to discuss the business with equal participation. There would be mutual agreement that the job came first. An acceptance that they could not live in each others pockets. Independence would make the occasions of their coming together all the sweeter.

It was not like him to indulge in such fanciful thoughts. They were too unsettling, and he pushed them aside. All he wanted was to sort out where he stood with her. Jack Brymer was not a man to court a woman with pretty speeches or red roses, but he would be active in his pursuit.

The initial of Kate's father's Christian name put him near the end of the Riders listed in the Plymouth telephone directory. Jack had called every one before he found Mrs Rider, Mark Two.

'Yes,' she confirmed, 'you do have the right number. Kate is my step-daughter. But I'm afraid, you're too late. She returned to London by the fast train, this evening. She should be back at her flat by now.'

Jack thanked her, but took this information personally. Kate had turned down a week's foreign holiday with him for a short weekend with her father. If that were a true indication of how much she valued him, then he was wasting his time. Aggrieved, he wished her in hell and spent the next twenty-four hours figuring how to revive what appeared to be a lost cause.

His several attempts to contact Kate by telephone proved fruitless. It occurred to him that she might not be answering in order to conceal her return. On the strength of this reasoning, he paid a Monday evening visit to her flat. The light, shining through the drawn curtains, confirmed his suspicion.

An aggressive ringing of the door-bell brought no more result than his telephone calls. It was not pleasant to be ignored by the woman you were crazy about. As a substitute for showing her two fingers, he tapped out a rhythm on the single-tone bell that he hoped was a recognisable *Colonel Bogey*. After this performance, he adjourned to the nearest pub.

Three pints and several cigarettes later and feeling increasingly maudlin, he returned to Kate's door. The light was still on in her first-floor living room. A more respectful ringing of the bell met with the same lack of response.

The memory of Kate, bleeding from the knife wound made him suddenly anxious. There were lights in both the ground-floor flats. He selected the bell below Kate's and pushed. The door was opened almost immediately, by a middle-aged woman who eyed him suspiciously. Jack turned on a little-practised charm. It was an attribute he seldom needed when dealing with the criminal fraternity.

'Forgive me for troubling you, but I've been ringing Miss Rider's door-bell and can't get an answer. She's the tenant on the floor above you. I think her bell must be out of action.'

'Was it you ringing so persistently, earlier this evening?' the woman demanded, frowning heavily.

'You heard it? Then it must be working.'

'I don't think your Miss Rider is at home. Sounds travel in this building, and I haven't heard anything from upstairs in days.'

Jack adopted his concerned expression, which was rather more convincing than the one supposed to charm.

'Then she must be ill. Her light is on and has been all evening. I'd like to go up and check it out if that's all right.'

The woman hesitated.

'Something may have happened to her,' Jack urged.

'Very well, though I'm not sure the landlord would be happy about me letting in a complete stranger.'

'I'm not a stranger, I work with Kate.' He produced

his press card. 'You can check my identity by ringing my paper, if you like.'

The woman studied the card, then his face, and was apparently satisfied. 'That won't be necessary, you'd better come in.'

He forced himself to hold back and allow her to lead the way. On the first landing, he hammered on the door, calling Kate's name. From the other side came the sound of voices.

'There's something wrong, the light is on, and the radio's playing. Is there anyone in the flats who acts as the key-holder?'

'I don't think so. The landlord has duplicate keys, but he lives in Chelsea. I can give you his telephone number, if that is of help.'

While she was talking, Jack tried the door. He pushed and it opened. For a moment they stood on the outside looking in. The even-tones of a news-reader came from the radio, the room was deserted. Ignoring his chaperone, he dashed through to the bedroom. It too was both empty and tidy. The bed showed no sign of recent occupancy. He checked the abandoned suitcase, it was still packed with Kate's clothes. On a work surface in the tiny kitchen there was an almost-full cup of black coffee. Jack sniffed, it was stone cold, but he detected a trace of Kate's lipstick on the rim. He wondered what had prevented her from drinking it.

The woman came out of the adjoining bathroom. 'Oh dear, where can she be?' she wondered aloud.

It was then he spotted the handbag, thrown into an easy chair. In two strides he was examining it.

'Do you think you should?'

Ignoring the muted protest, he pulled out a wallet and checked its contents: press card, credit cards, money, make-up, everything was intact.

'No woman goes out without her handbag, does she?' he interrogated.

Kate's neighbour attempted to calm his agitation. 'Not unless she's visiting a friend here in the flats.'

'What about the unlocked door?'

'I think you should telephone the police,' she said in reply.

Nick Diss was off duty, but Jack stressed that he needed to speak to him urgently. An obliging desk sergeant promised to pass the message. Too impatient to wait idly for a return call, Jack decided to embark on the search for Kate unaided. The Sumo psychopath was under lock and key, that left Jack with a single lead – Michael Kershaw.

He rang Kate's office number on his mobile.

Charlie answered, 'Jack, you just caught me. I'm out of here in a second.'

'Hold on, pal. There's something you can do for me before you go. I want Michael Kershaw's home address; it'll be on file.'

'All that stuff will still be on Kate's computer. Hang on, I'll take a look.'

He turned up what was wanted and dictated an address in Putney.

'Thanks Charlie, I owe you. By the way, keep this call under your hat will you? I don't want Kev to know what I'm up to.'

'What gives?'

'Tell you when I see you.'

He had already started the engine and was considering the quickest route across the river to Putney.

Kershaw's house was one of a block of four town houses in a tree-lined road of older detached properties. The ground floor was taken up with the entrance and twin garage doors. There were three floors above, including the dormers in the roof. It was just after ten when Jack pulled into the short driveway, and every window was in darkness.

Jack was pondering his next move when a car drove onto the neighbouring property. Its emerging occupants eyed him suspiciously. It was late to be loitering outside an apparently unoccupied house. He got out to speak, and the hack in him took over.

'You Mike's neighbours? That's a bit of luck. I need to get hold of him urgently but he doesn't seem to be at home. Have you any idea where I might find him?'

'You're not a reporter are you?'

Jack gulped inwardly but contrived an offended look.

'Hardly, I'm his cousin. I imagine you've seen enough of reporters around here.'

The couple came towards him He had obviously hit the right note, as the woman at once became most confiding.

'They've given poor Michael such a terrible time. I was quite sure that he was heading for a breakdown. It was a relief to know that he was going away on holiday.'

'That explains why I couldn't get him on the telephone. I'm based in the States, and couldn't get over for the funeral. I'd be sorry to miss him. Do you have any idea where he's gone?'

The man spoke for the first time. 'He said he wanted to get right away, find some wilderness to hide in. He didn't take his own car; he hired one of those Japanese off-road jobs.'

'When was that?'

The informant turned to his wife, 'Middle of last week, wasn't it, old girl?'

'It was Tuesday. Olivia was here when we spoke to him. Olivia is our daughter,' she explained. 'She always visits on Tuesdays.'

'Looks as though I've missed him then. When you next see him, perhaps you'd be good enough to tell him his cousin, Ray, called.'

He reversed off the drive. Illuminated by his headlights, they waved him goodbye.

He was back in the office, looking through Yellow Pages for car-hire firms in the vicinity of Putney, when Nick Diss phoned.

'Got a message that you wanted to speak to me urgently, Sherlock.'

'I do. Kate Rider's been abducted.'

Nick listened without interruption to Jack's resumé of events, then attempted to quash his theory.

'But Kershaw left London a week ago. Kate has only been missing since last night. I fail to see the connection.'

'Who else would have taken her? He holds Kate responsible for his wife's death, it has to be him.'

'You're too close to the girl. You aren't thinking clearly, Jack.'

'But it fits. He had to go first, to set up some place where he could hide her. When everything was arranged he came back and abducted her.'

'Revenge may be sweet, but Kershaw isn't some East End mobster. He's the respected partner in this city's most successful firm of architects. He's not going to risk all that.'

'Damn it, Nick! You're the one who's not thinking straight. His neighbours suggested that the man was close to breakdown. You said yourself that he made a lot of trouble when you pulled him in for questioning on the stalker business. I have a gut feeling about this and it's a bad one. Who knows what he might do, if he's sick in the head.'

'I'd like to help, but I can't instigate a nationwide search on the strength of a gut feeling. Kate's an adult, not an underage kid. More significantly, she's a journalist. What if she's staged this disappearance as a publicity stunt for her next article? Some of your chaps would have their testicles removed for the sake of a good story.'

'That's apocryphal, Nick. And Kate's not like that. She doesn't court publicity. Quite the opposite, she shuns it.'

'So how come she keeps making the front page? She's a pro, like you are, Jack. She's probably out on the job as we talk. Is it likely she's got herself abducted twice in the same month?'

'I wish I could believe you.'

'Let's look at what we've got. She's not at her flat. The door is on the latch and a handbag with some of her possessions has been abandoned. You say she's been gone for twenty-four hours, but you don't know that for sure. There's no justification for posting her as a missing person.'

'Do we wait until we're looking for a body.'

'Look, Jack, you're as good as we are at ferreting out information. See what you can find. If you can come back with something more positive, I'll pull out all the stops I can to help.'

Jack had to be satisfied with that. The most frustrating thing was that there was nothing more he could do until the car-hire firms opened for business on Tuesday morning.

Chapter 18

The night brought stomach cramps. The new pain was almost welcome. It gave Kate something else to focus on, something to divert her from the amplifications that were splitting her brain. She pictured her head as a walnut. The shell that was her skull was being attacked from the inside. When the thunderous vibrations succeeded in cracking it open the battered kernel that was her brain would ooze out. Far gone, she did not notice the grey bars of dawn at the window.

Until he spoke, she was oblivious of his entry. He stood over her, the head-phones in his hand. Yet still the cacophony tortured her brain

He removed the gag. 'What have you done to yourself?'

She couldn't reply, for she didn't understand his question. Kneeling at her feet, he lifted her stained skirt.

'There's a lot of blood.'

He freed her neck from the chair-back. It was an agony to bend, to look.

She saw what he was talking about. 'It's a period,' she croaked. The stomach cramps were explained.

'Do you usually bleed so heavily?'

'No.'

A cup of lukewarm, sweet coffee was placed to her lips. She drank greedily. Sitting upright unsupported was difficult. She fell against him, and he held her while she drank.

'Do you think you can make it upstairs?'

The voice was neutral, no longer threatening, but she lacked the energy to answer. The noise that had kept her awake for two nights and a day began to fade, subsiding to a continuous hissing sound. All she wanted to do was close her eyes and slip away into sleep.

Her torturer would not permit such indulgence. In her zombie state, she was manhandled upstairs and into a small bathroom, where she fell into a heap on the floor. She was conscious of running water thundering into the bath, but it was a sound that came from outside her head, so it soothed her.

She found her tongue, 'Are you going to drown me?'

It was a strange thing, but if that were his intention she didn't really care.

'Drown you?' Her question caused him more distress than she knew.

'No, I'm trying to help. You need to clean-up. Can you undress yourself?'

She couldn't, and stood like a rag-doll as he peeled off her clothes. Standing in only her knickers, she could smell her own blood, menstrual and musky. The thought of her blood on his hands was distasteful to her.

'Let me,' she pleaded.

When she stood naked before him, he lifted her into the bath.

Her flesh was chill and the warmth of the water soothing. He handed her a flannel and soap and she wiped ineffectually. All she wanted to do was sleep. When her head dropped, he shook her awake.

The plug was pulled, and the comforting warmth

gurgled away in its vortex. She wanted to cry at this new deprivation.

The taps had a primitive shower attachment which he used to rinse her body. She thought how strange it was to be opening her legs to this man she hardly knew. He directed the shower head on her vagina, and the water pricked her into life. When he wrapped the soft white towel about her, she wanted to weep at his gentleness.

He left her, wrapped in the towel. She lay on the floor and fell into a doze. His return startled her.

'Can you manage with this?' he asked.

He had made a pad from rags. Taking it, she recognised the material of her bondage. Her thanks were slurred. From the comfort of the towel, she watched as he collected up her soiled clothes and went away.

When he returned, he brought with him a man's shirt, underpants and sweater.

'I'm afraid these will have to do. They're all I have.'

A few minutes before, he had washed every part of her body. Now she was shy of emerging from the concealment of the towel. Sensing her reticence, he gave her the privacy she needed to dress.

The bathroom was an unsuspected heaven, sitting above her recent hell. In his absence, she used the toilet. Despite the misery of the night, what was uppermost in her mind was a sense of satisfaction that she had retained mastery over her bowels. Cautiously, she stood without support. Her legs obeyed and carried her to the sink. Above it, a mirror revealed a hollow-eyed face, framed with lank, damp hair. Studying that unfamiliar reflection, she finger-combed her hair into a semblance of its usual style.

The clothes he provided smelt fresh. Being several sizes too large, the garments covered her down to the knees. She pulled on his Y fronts last of all. There was an indecency about wearing his underpants.

A tube of toothpaste stood on a shelf over the wash-basin. Using a finger, she savoured the refreshing mint taste. He returned to find her cleaning her teeth. She took her time, for she did not want to relinquish this well-lit paradise, where a wall-heater glowed down like the sun.

For a while he was patient, content to watch, but then urged, 'We must go down now.'

'I can't.' She anchored herself by clinging to the basin.

'You must,' he insisted.

'Let me stay here,' she begged. 'Just until I'm stronger. I can't do that again, not yet.'

The muscles of his face were working. She was very afraid she had made him angry again.

'You don't have to do it again. The business with the ligatures and chair is finished.'

She wanted to believe him. 'And the . . . entertainment?' She was proud of her euphemism, it was a small joke that declared her spirit was not broken.

'And the cassette. That's finished too.'

When he offered his hand, she grasped it trustingly. He led her back down the stairs and they re-entered her prison. He noticed that she had begun to shiver, and offered to fetch blankets.

She listened to his footfall on the narrow stairs. He had left her alone and unfettered. It was an opportunity to escape. She pondered too long. He was standing before her again, the blankets in his arms.

'Your ankles aren't so swollen,' he commented.

She contemplated her legs, protruding below the outsize sweater. 'No. They're much better.'

'You should put your feet up. It will help.'

He encouraged her onto the sofa. With the addition of a cushion, he converted the low table into a footstool. Upholstery and cushions. It was the height of luxury, she felt almost decadent.

He wasn't satisfied. 'We need to get your feet higher.'

The easy chair was cannibalised for its seat cushion. He thrust it under her feet.

Previously, he had been a Spanish Inquisitor, making a chair the instrument of her torture. Now he was fussing like a mother hen, attending to her needs. Warm, comfortable and unfettered, she approved the transformation. Her changed circumstances dragged from her a crazy, deranged laugh.

It was a laugh that disturbed him. Without any leave-taking, he went. The key turned in the lock. Looking about, she noticed that the transistor was gone. She lay back and listened to the only noise in the room - the monotonous hissing in her ears, legacy of those interminable hours of non-stop sound. She wondered if permanent damage had been done.

She slept long and deeply, with no awareness of his hourly visits to check her breathing and to adjust her blankets. Yet in her dreams, Michael rescued her from some undefined terror that hovered at the edge of her unconsciousness. When the thing she feared approached, she saw that though it walked in a man's body, its head was a skull. It came closer, and she saw movement in the dark, eye sockets. Instead of eyes it had spools of turning tape. The jaw opened wide, then wider. It was about to devour her head. It was her own cry that woke her.

Starting from the nightmare, she saw that the sunken eyes still looking at her.

She shrank back, quivering. 'Don't touch me, please don't.'

'It's all right,' he comforted. 'You've been asleep, it was a nightmare. I've brought you some food.'

He placed coffee and scrambled egg before her.

'What time of day is it?' she asked.

'Afternoon, you've slept for six hours.'

She felt so much restored, that she dared make demands of him. 'I need to go to the bathroom, and I'll need some more rag to make a fresh pad.'

'I made another while you were sleeping. You'll find it upstairs. Can you manage on your own?'

She wanted no help. Though her legs were unsteady, she was able to walk from the room unaided. He stood at the bottom of the stairs to watch her progress. The hand-rail steadied her, and she was able to hold her head high.

Gaining the bathroom, she boldly threw the bolt on the door. The mirror again reflected a drawn and altered face with dark and sunken eyes. She was struck by their similarity to Michael's.

Dust motes, floating in beams of sunlight, drew her attention to a window. She hadn't noticed it on her previous visit. Praying that Michael would not hear, she opened it. She breathed the fresh air in great gulps.

The cottage was set in a hollow, but from her vantage point on the first floor it was possible to see across an expanse of moor – a wilderness punctuated here and there by granite outcrops. There was no sign of habitation. Familiar scents assailed her nostrils as she took-in the view. The moor stretched towards distant tors, and the contours of the peaks, like the smells, were familiar. Adrenalin flowed. It was Dartmoor; she was almost home.

She leaned from the window, calculating the sheer drop to the cobbles where his vehicle was parked. Escape by this route was impossible, she decided. She reassessed her situation. Her captor had granted her sleep and shown concern for her comfort. If the ordeal really was over, then the need to get away was less urgent. Part of her remained fearful. Perhaps his sudden attentiveness was just part of the softening-up process. When she was at her most vulnerable, he might punish her again.

His voice came up the stairs, making her jump.

'Are you all right?'

'I'm fine. I'll be down in a few minutes.'

Did she imagine the note of concern in his question?

She would not hurry. She used the lavatory, changed the soiled pad, and flannel-washed her body. Feeling much revived, she took another look at the outside world.

Although the cottage was bathed in late autumnal sun, black clouds were gathering ominously on the western horizon. She watched their progress for some time, as if mesmerised. It was a good half-hour before she emerged. She had expected him to shout or rattle at the bolted door to hurry her along, but he did neither. It seemed a benign omen.

None of the Putney-based car-hire companies rented Japanese four-wheel-drives. Jack extended his search further afield. In making his enquiries, he posed as an officer of the Metropolitan Police. He suffered no qualms at impersonating Inspector Nick Diss. It was an identity that opened doors. He soon discovered that, in the previous week, no company south of the river had rented out such a machine. He re-crossed the Thames to repeat the exercise, beginning with car-hire firms within a modest radius of Kershaw's office.

At last he struck lucky.

'Yep, here it is: Kershaw.' The manager stubbed a finger at the data appearing on the computer screen. 'He picked it up a week ago today and paid in advance for three weeks hire. What do you want him for? He's not pulled a job in it, has he?'

'No, nothing like that. His mother is dangerously ill. Don't suppose he gave you any clues as to his destination?'

'I just run the office side, Tony handles the cars. Have a word with him.'

Before setting out that morning, Jack had visited *The Flag's* offices and helped himself to one of Bob Spackman's mug shots of Kershaw. This he showed to Tony.

'Yeah, sure I remember him. He insisted on a big machine with a high ground clearance. Said he'd rented a cottage, well off the road, on Dartmoor.'

'Dartmoor? You're sure about that?'

'Definite. I remember joking with him about it. Told him to watch out for escaped convicts.'

Jack was about to tip his informant when he remembered he was supposed to be a policeman.

Chapter 19

He was waiting for her at the foot of the stairs, all aggression gone. 'Your egg must be cold, I'll scramble some fresh.'

'I can do it.'

There were only the two doors off the entrance passage. One was open with an expanse of worktop showing beyond it. She attempted to pass him but he barred the way.

'I'm sorry. I can't let you can't go in there.'

Their eyes met, she read his confusion and it emboldened her. 'Why not?' she challenged.

He shrugged awkwardly. 'The kitchen windows aren't shuttered.'

Her mouth turned down. It meant that he still considered her a prisoner. Wordlessly, she turned to re-enter her cell.

'Breakfast won't be long,' he promised.

Though he pulled the door closed, he did not lock her in.

The egg, when it came, was hot and the coffee steaming. She ate with relish and told him how good both were. As a journalist she was familiar with all the usual strategies for survival as a hostage. No longer gagged, she intended to practise every ploy.

Her healthy appetite appeared to please him.

'It's good to see you eating so well.'

'I always eat well when I'm staying in the country.'

The irony of her comment made him uncomfortable.

'If I'm to cook a proper meal, I'll need to shop for more provisions.'

'Good. While you're at the shops, perhaps you could buy a few items for me.'

The normality of the request was at odds with the strangeness of their circumstances.

'Of course. I'll buy you clothes and whatever else you need.'

He seemed to be waiting for her to provide a shopping list.

'I'd like a comb or hairbrush, and I need proper sanitary protection. Some appropriate feminine underwear would be nice.'

He looked at her with something akin to embarrassment. 'I'm sorry if my things are uncomfortable to wear.'

His eyes were drawn to her legs, bare under the tail of the borrowed shirt. Instantly embarrassed, he glanced away.

'What size do you take in jeans?'

'I'd prefer some jogging trousers. Size twelve.'

'Fine. I'll get you some.'

'And shoes? One of mine was left behind in the lay-by. I take size five.'

The reminder of the lay-by made him avert his eyes. 'Whatever you want.'

She had him eating out of her hand. However, it was too soon to ask for a ticket home.

'Oh, and if you're offering an extended hospitality, I'll need a toothbrush.'

He was staring at her. 'How can you make so light of all this?'

'I'm coping, not joking. Don't you know the difference?'

'There won't be anything more for you to cope with. It's over.'

She felt herself weakening, but pretended strength. 'Is that a promise?'

'Yes, a promise. I give my word.' He raised his hand, as if about to touch her, but let it drop without making contact. 'I'll have to be off if I'm to catch the shops before they close.'

His remark was incongruous, coming as it did from her gaoler.

She called after him, 'I use tampons.'

'Right.'

It was weird, to be providing such a personal shopping list for the man who had so recently offered her oblivion in the shape of two bottles of small, white pills.

He removed the dirty china and returned, wearing a storm-coat. Almost apologetically, he produced the handcuffs from the pocket. She backed away from him.

'You promised,' she accused.

'Be reasonable. You might be tempted to run away. These are for your own protection. The moor can be treacherous. There are bogs, and there's a storm brewing.'

The suggestion that she was to be manacled for her own safety was a bitter irony.

'I won't be tied to the chair,' she asserted.

'Of course not. I told you, I'm finished with that. It's just your hands. You'll still be able to move about, and I'll release you as soon as I return. I won't be gone long.'

She brought the heels of her hands together and offered her wrists. 'It's a fair cop, Guv.'

The attempt at humour did not soften him. Before she realised what he intended, her arms had been pinioned uncomfortably behind her back and the restraining cuffs positioned and secured. He mumbled, 'I'm sorry,' and left. She heard him lock both doors behind him.

Jack had arranged to meet Nick Diss in the pub. Expecting him to be punctual, he ordered a pint apiece. While waiting for the ginger-haired inspector to put in an appearance, he downed his own and started on the other.

When Diss finally showed up, ten minutes late, Jack didn't waste words in greetings. 'I've found out where Kershaw is hiding.'

He told of the encounter with Kershaw's neighbours, and his successful hunt to track down the hire vehicle.

Diss listened attentively, but instead of offering congratulations voiced an objection. 'If you were about to carry out a kidnapping would you broadcast where you were going? It stinks, Jack. If Kershaw is on Dartmoor, he's there alone. If he has got Kate, Dartmoor is a red-herring.'

'That's what I thought at first, but look at it another way. What if the hide-away only turned into a hide-out later?'

'Go on, I'm listening.'

'According to the neighbours, Kershaw is close to breakdown. He wants to escape the publicity that has been plaguing him. He goes into retreat. The accommodation turns out to be really remote, and the isolation does him no good. He has too much time to brood, to feel sorry for himself. He becomes angry, and his thoughts turn to revenge.'

'And *The Flag* being too impersonal a target, it's Kate Rider he blames.'

'Precisely.' Jack was pleased to have the policeman

on his wavelength. 'Kershaw gets to thinking how sweet it would be to pay her back. His retreat on the moor offers the ideal location for exacting retribution. He fantasises what he might do to her.'

Imagining what the other man's fantasies might be, sweat broke out under Jack's collar. There was an uncomfortable stirring in his loins Aloud, he said, 'Christ, the little fool could have been safe in Madeira with me.'

Diss recognised the expression on Brymer's face. 'Safe? With you ravishing her?'

'Don't be so bloody flippant,' Jack objected.

'Sorry, I didn't mean to be. I know how concerned you are. So, your theory is that he drove back to London to grab her.'

'It all points to that.'

'But it doesn't. There was no sign of any struggle at her flat. Surely she wouldn't have gone with him willingly?'

'She might have done. Remember how protective she was towards him when you wanted to pull him in for questioning? He could easily have tricked her about his intentions.'

'I hate to say this, Jack, but isn't there a possibility that if he is shafting her, he's doing it with her full co-operation?'

'So why did she leave her handbag, all her things?'

For a few moments both men contemplated their glasses.

'So, what do you expect me to do?' Diss asked. 'Dartmoor is a vast National Park. It covers hundreds of square miles, and probably contains dozens of cottages used for holiday lets. It would be like looking for the proverbial needle.'

'There can't be so many cottages that are isolated enough to serve Kershaw's purpose.'

'I suppose we could circulate the Devon and Cornwall Police with the vehicle description and registration,' Diss conceded.

'If he's holed-up somewhere, that won't do much good. What about his credit card? If we knew where he's made purchases, it could pin-point him.'

'Kershaw's not a wanted man. He's already alleged police harassment over the stalker business. If we start asking questions of his bankers it could upset his credit rating. If that happens he'd have every right to take us to the cleaners.'

'Come on, Nick, you have friends in useful places. There must be something you can do.'

The detective inspector was well aware of the many useful tip-offs and unofficial favours done in the opposite direction. 'OK, I'll do what I can. But he's only been gone a week. It's too soon to be tracking him through his flexible friend.'

'So what's the plan?'

'Just leave it with me. But it's no good getting impatient, there won't be instant results. Don't expect anything for twenty-four hours at least.'

Twenty-four hours was a long time, but Brymer had done his best.

Michael had been right about the storm. Shortly after he drove off, Kate heard the first rumblings of thunder. Bursts of white light found the gaps in the shutters, and she amused herself by counting the seconds before the thunder's roll. The interval between flash and rumble was decreasing, for the cottage lay in the path of the storm. All her life she had enjoyed the frenzy of the elements. As a child, she had always watched from her bedroom window, fascinated by the energy of the lightning, and had laughed at her mother's warnings of the risks of being struck. She wished she could do the same here but she was imprisoned downstairs.

A squall hit the cottage, and with it came the rain. Water drove against the shutters and drummed on the roof. It was only late afternoon, but the darkness that had descended made a convincing night. Her pleasure in the pandemonium diminished. She did not want to lose the light. Then came the unmistakable crash of breaking glass.

Heart suddenly thudding, she wondered at the cause. Perhaps a tree had been struck by the lightning, and a falling branch had penetrated a window of the house. In the crescendo of the storm, movement from the other room and the rattle of the door handle were insignificant sounds, yet she heard both. The key scraped in the lock, and she watched, mesmerised, as the door was pushed open. There came a scrabbling sound as hands groped for a switch. The room flooded with a yellow light.

The first thing she noticed was the woolly hat and combat uniform. On his feet he wore stout walking boots. For a crazy moment, she thought he must be a soldier, come to effect a commando-style rescue. His facial expression belied this theory. He was startled to find the room occupied. Clearly he had broken in, and, finding someone at home, was already turning to flee.

'Wait!' she called out. 'Please, I need your help. Don't leave me.'

Uncertain, the interloper stood his ground, water dripping from his clothes and the rucksack on his back.

'I am very sorry,' he said in a faltering English, heavy with German intonations. 'This is a bad mistake. I think the house is empty. I look . . .' He was struggling to find the vocabulary to express himself.

'I look for . . .' He touched the tips of his fingers together, making the shape of a roof. 'You understand?'

'You were looking for shelter,' she interpreted.

He looked relieved. 'Thank you, yes – shel-ter,' he repeated. 'And to sit.' He indicated the sofa.

He took a pace towards her. Despite his height, she saw that he was no more than a youth.

'You must help me,' she enunciated slowly, 'I am being kept here against my will.' She half-turned to reveal the handcuffs 'I am a prisoner.' It was her turn to ask, 'Do you understand?'

He looked confused, but freed himself of the rucksack. Coming closer, he examined her fetters.

'There is a . . . *Schlüssel*?' He made a turning motion with his right hand.

'A key? No. You must get help. I have to go away from here. Now, before he comes back.'

He didn't understand. She wondered if he were an idiot, for a slow grin had spread across his face.

'You make a joke, yes?'

He was an idiot. 'This is not a joke. I have to get away, to escape.'

His eyes travelled the room and alighted on the wooden chair that still bore the evidence of her bondage.

'You and your man, you play.' It was not a question. He sat himself in the wooden chair, and tugged at the rags, grinning again. 'You like to play with me?'

She came to him, appealing, 'This is not a game. I'm in trouble. You must help me.'

When his hand reached out towards her breast, she knew the appeal was wasted. No help would come from this quarter.

She fled through the open doors into the kitchen.

A broken window, left open, swung in the wind. She backed towards it. With her pinioned arms, she attempted to lever herself onto the sill.

The youth pulled her from her perch, and wrestled her back into the shuttered room. His hand travelled to her breast again. She brought up her knee, aiming for his groin but connecting with his thigh. His response was instantaneous – the palm of his hand struck her across the mouth. The force of the blow knocked her off balance and she fell.

Tasting blood, she tried to rise. Her pinioned arms made it too difficult. He stood over her, his boot lifted as though he intended to squash her underfoot like some helpless insect. She instinctively rolled away and the boot missed. He delivered a kick to her torso that was impossible to avoid. As she doubled-up in pain, he forced her onto her back.

He sat astride her. She was defenceless. Nothing in her previous ordeal had prepared her for this.

'Don't hurt me,' she pleaded.

His attempts to uncover her breasts were hindered by Michael's bulky sweater. Because her arms were fettered behind her, it could not be removed. Undeterred, her assailant forced up the garment until it was turned back over her head. He did not unbutton the shirt, but ripped it open. He slobbered over her breasts and his teeth found a nipple. Her cries were muffled by the sweater covering her face.

She hoped her condition might spare her from actual rape, but the combination of male Y-fronts and menstrual blood drove him on. His eager thrusting was of short duration, and he ejaculated inside her, whimpering like a puppy. His whole weight bore down on her, and the sweater was suffocating. It was a relief when he pulled it down to uncover her face.

He grinned, pleased with himself. 'You like fuck?'

His grey eyes were small and peevish in his plump, baby face.

'Yes, I liked it.' She would say anything to pacify him.

'Good. You kiss me, now.'

She was grateful to be subjected to only his lips. When she didn't respond, he became angry and pulled her hair.

She tried to reason with him. 'You got what you wanted. Why are you hurting me?'

'Hurting?' he sneered. 'I not understand hurting.' She saw from the malice in his expression that he knew the meaning of the word only too well. He returned his attention to her breasts, his hurried, shallow breathing announcing a renewed desire.

She made a conscious decision not to oppose him. He was young and fit and had the strength to seriously hurt her. Not until he manipulated her body so that she was lying face down did she offer any opposition, kicking out wildly. In retaliation, he lifted her by the hair then forced her head onto the stone floor. She took the full impact on her left brow. She was barely conscious of his finger nails, gripping like teeth, as he forced her buttocks apart.

Chapter 20

Jack's night was restless. His agony was made all the worse because he could not stop imagining Kate's ordeal. The very act of the abduction proved that Kershaw was unbalanced. In such a confused state of mind he might be capable of anything, even murder. Rather than dwell on that possibility, Jack found himself hoping that Kershaw's motive was purely sexual. It sickened him to think of her being raped, but at least, if she co-operated, she had a chance of survival.

There was no irony in his hope that Kate was giving satisfaction to another man. It was a measure of his concern for her. Several times he resolved to drive down to Devon immediately, but caution stayed him. Dartmoor might indeed be a red-herring. It made more sense to wait to see what Nick came up with in the morning.

Jack knew that to chase Nick Diss would serve no purpose, other than to delay his friend's enquiries. What he hated was the waiting and the feeling of impotence. Usually, he ran his battery shaver over his face twice a day, as by mid-afternoon his chin was darkly shadowed. Today, he decided on a wet-shave with a real razor. It was not just a matter of passing the time, it was an act of faith: in the back of his mind was the conviction that this was the day that they would find Kate – alive. He wanted to look his best.

It was late afternoon before the telephone summons came.

It was Nick. 'Come round to the station. We've got a lead and it fits your hunch.'

'You've news of Kate?'

'Nothing definite. I'll give you the details when you get here.'

His stomach churned and he tasted bile. What Nick had been doing was supposed to be unofficial, not sanctioned by his superiors. Now it had suddenly become police business, to be conducted at the station.

'If she's dead, tell me now,' he demanded.

'Relax. From the look of what we've got, that's most unlikely.'

'Bless your copper-knob for that.' The pun was automatic.

'Save your thanks for when we find her. Just get round here at the double.'

Fifteen minutes later, Jack was shown into the detective inspector's office. He found him poring over an ordnance survey map of Devon.

'So what have you got?'

'Plenty. I circulated Kershaw's description and details of the hire vehicle, to the Devon and Cornwall Police. They've come up trumps. A police constable saw the vehicle in a supermarket car-park in Okehampton yesterday. He even spoke to Kershaw.'

'They've taken him in for questioning?'

'It's not quite so simple. The constable was off-duty. It wasn't until later, when he reported in to his station, that he discovered the significance of his sighting.'

'Hell, what lousy luck.'

'Not at all, it was pure good fortune. By sheer

fluke, the constable who made the sighting is an off-road enthusiast. He's just bought himself a second-hand Shogun. Kershaw's hire vehicle is the latest model. Our lad was giving it an admiring once-over when Kershaw caught him at it.'

'Caught him? You mean our upstanding architect assumed that the copper was about to break-in?'

'That's exactly what he thought. Of course, our off-duty copper immediately identified himself. Apparently goods had been left on display in the unattended vehicle and, to get his own back, the constable gave Kershaw a lecture on tempting honest citizens into committing opportunist car-crime.'

'How did that go down?'

'Not well. Kershaw was so agitated and shifty, that our bright young PC took a good look at him and made a note of the vehicle number. He was also able to provide information on the fascinating shopping that had been left on show.'

Brymer interjected the obvious question. 'What was so bloody fascinating about the man's shopping?'

'I thought you wouldn't let that pass. According to the carrier-bags, he'd been shopping at a place called *Uplifting*.'

'I don't need riddles, what's the significance?'

'Come on Jack, you're supposed to be the word-monger. *Uplifting* is a local shop that specialises in rather intimate undergarments.'

'Women's things, d'you mean?'

'Precisely. Bras, panties, suspender belts, night attire. Whatever turns you on.'

Jack did not look at all turned on by this revelation.

'Are you telling me that while I've been worrying

my guts out, she's willingly modelling undies for Kershaw's delectation?'

'It's one interpretation, but I don't see it that way. Kershaw was on his own when he was seen. If he and the delectable Kate were holed up in a cottage for carnal pleasures, wouldn't they have shopped together for such intimate items?'

'Not if the goodies were intended as a surprise present.' Jack preferred not to dwell on this particular scenario. 'Anyway, as that young copper let him go, where does this get us?'

'He had no reason to hold him. You can't charge a man for being in possession of female undergarments, even if you suspect him of transvestite tendencies.'

'We can rule out the transvestite theory,' Jack growled. 'Where do we go from here?'

'Hang about, there's more. That young constable should go far, he used his loaf. When he found out we were looking for Kershaw, he made some enquiries of his own and came up trumps. The day your girl was abducted, Kershaw bought petrol at a garage near Exeter. On the eastbound side of the A30, to be precise.'

Jack shifted self-consciously. He fervently wished Kate *was* his girl.

'Are you saying he wasn't in London on that day?'

'Just the reverse. He had plenty of time to get there. The petrol was purchased in the morning. It's not conclusive, of course, but if he *were* heading for London, it fits your theory that he drove back to collect her.'

'This sounds too pat to be true. How come the petrol station remembered Kershaw?'

'I asked the same question. Apparently, the proprietor has just bought the place, and it was his first

Sunday opening. Kershaw was the first customer of the day. He bought a full tank for that gas-guzzler he's driving. That's what made the purchase memorable.'

He tried to shake Jack out of his lethargy. 'Come on, cheer-up. I was the doubting Thomas, but I've come round to your way of thinking. Kate *is* down there in deepest Devon, and Kershaw is probably holding her against her will.'

'Damn it, of course he is. So where do we start?'

'That's more like it. Take a look at the map. Kershaw shopped in Okehampton, to the north-west of Dartmoor.' Nick stabbed with a broad finger. 'If Okehampton is his nearest shopping opportunity, it looks very much as if he has gone to ground in this area.'

He pointed again, this time drawing a circle around an area bounded by the high tors in the west, the A382 in the east and the B3212 in the south.

Jack gave his companion a pretend hug. 'Have I told you how much I love you, Diss? We've got him.'

'Not quite. There's still a lot of spade-work to be done, it's a big area. We'll drive down tonight and start checking out the rented accommodation first thing tomorrow.'

'That could take forever. It's Thursday tomorrow and he's been holding her since Sunday. It's too long, and I don't like it. There must be a faster way of finding them.'

'Suggest one.'

Jack returned to the map. 'There's an airport at Exeter. We could hire a chopper or light aircraft, and go up at first light. The Mitsubishi will be easier to spot from the air.'

'Hang on, Jack, an air-search will be expensive. My Super's been helpful – he's given permission for me to go down there and liaise with the local force, but he won't agree to anything that will make bigger demands on his budget.'

'I'll put the air surveillance down to expenses, or pay for it myself if need be.'

'It could be a waste of money. What if the vehicle is parked under cover?'

'OK, so let me do the air-search while you organise the local plods on the ground. I want to find her, Nick. Before that bastard does something we will all live to regret.'

The rain eased as Michael stopped. Opening the gate that guarded the approach to the cottage, he noticed that the track ahead had become a quagmire. The downpour had turned the ruts into boggy rivers. He was grateful to have the extra traction provided by the four-wheel-drive of his hired transport.

The cottage was still ridding itself of rain-water. A drain gurgled, a sagging gutter dripped, and at the north-west corner a water-butt overflowed onto the cobbles. He was anxious to get inside. It had been a spectacular electrical storm, and he was concerned about the effect it might have had on Kate's already ragged nerves.

As soon as he stepped through the door, he saw that something was amiss. He had left the door to the sitting room locked, but now it was ajar. Though he felt apprehensive as he entered, he was not prepared for what he found.

Kate's body was lying on the floor, naked below the waist. There was blood on her face. Michael rushed across to her, strewing plastic carrier-bags in his wake. Dropping to his knees, he turned her gently into a supine position. Her eyes were closed, her lip split, and her brow was swollen to a lump.

God knows what damage was hidden by the sweater. He cradled her, feeling for a pulse and was rewarded by a low moan.

He gulped his relief. 'Thank God.'

'Michael?'

He responded by holding her close. A salt tear fell onto her bloodied lip. He was shaking.

'The key, Michael. Unlock the handcuffs, please.'

He tried to, but his hand shook so violently that he had trouble with the lock.

Free at last, she pulled herself to her knees and clung to him.

He prevented her from rising, holding her gently by the shoulders. 'How could this happen? Who did this to you?'

She didn't want to talk about it. 'Please run me a bath. I have to clean him off me, out of me.'

'You're hurt. We must get you to a doctor.'

For Kate, the need to bathe was overwhelming. 'No. Don't you understand? I have to wash away what he did.'

He did understand, and hated denying her. 'You can't, it would destroy evidence.'

'Evidence?' Her brain was not functioning.

'The police will want a swab,' he explained.

She assumed his concern was self-interest, that he was anxious to preserve the DNA traces to establish his own innocence.

'That won't be necessary. Despite what you think, I'd never make a false accusation against you. You won't be blamed for this.'

'I was thinking of your attacker, not myself. The genetic evidence may be needed to convict him.'

She had undergone abduction, torture, and now rape and assault. Yet, at that moment, she saw him as more vulnerable than herself.

'If we go to the police, they will ask questions of you, too,' she reminded.

'I'm prepared for that. What I've done to you is lunacy. But I'm not mad, and I have to accept responsibility for my actions.'

'The police will arrest you for my abduction. You can't want that.'

'It makes no difference now.'

His suffering was as deep as her own, and her most protective instincts were aroused. She had no wish to see him punished further. 'And what if I choose not to involve the police?'

'You don't have that choice. The police have to be told.'

She shook her head. 'They don't. The decision is mine, not yours.'

Reading his perplexed expression, she took control of the situation. 'If you won't run my bath, then I will.'

Bemused and defeated, he followed her to the bathroom, making no further attempt to interfere.

Though no longer her gaoler, he watched as she prepared her bath. She turned her back on him and, almost wanton about her nudity, undressed. Her body had been too abused for her nakedness to have significance any longer.

For the first time, he saw the claw marks on her buttocks. 'Surely to God, not that too.'

'What is it?' she asked.

'You were . . . sodomised?' He had to struggle to say it.

'No, I was spared that. It was the sound of your car that frightened him away.'

'Thank God.' He moved to embrace her, but stopped as the significance of her words sunk in. 'You mean, he was still in the house as I drove up?'

Instead of answering, she sank gratefully into the comforting embrace of the water, revealing the full extent of the bites to her breasts.

'God damn him, he really hurt you, didn't he?' He turned towards the door.

'Where are you going?' she cried.

He paused his hand on the door knob. 'He can't have got far, I'm going after him.'

'That's crazy, he's dangerous.'

'So am I.'

It was so childish, it made her weary. 'You don't know who he is, and it's dark out there. How can you hope to find him?'

'I don't need to know what he looks like. There won't be anyone else out on the moor in weather like this.'

Her patience snapped. She wanted to bring him to his senses. 'Why are you so keen that he should be found and brought to justice? What he did to me was only a variation on what you've been doing. Except what you did was worse. The rape lasted minutes; you tortured me for hours, days. Is hurting me your prerogative, a pleasure to be denied anyone else?'

He looked stunned. 'What I did was *worse*?'

She would not let him off the hook now. 'Yes, it was.'

He shook his head, denying it. 'I never planned the physical brutality. The threats I made were mostly bluff intended to frighten. I wanted you to suffer mentally but it went too far, it got out of hand.'

Her head ached too much to listen to his defence. 'I'd like some privacy. Please, just do what you have to do and leave me to my bath.'

Looking miserable, he withdrew.

As she lay there, soaking her wounds, she heard the thud of the car door, but there was no sound of an engine. After a decent interval, Michael reappeared. He came, eyes averted, bearing a towel, first-aid box, a packet of tampons and a hang-dog expression.

'The first-aid kit is from the car,' he explained. You need to be careful; a human bite can be more dangerous than a dog's. Will you let me treat your wounds?'

She was non-committal, but allowed him to help her from the bath. It was the second time, in that long and eventful day, he had swathed her in the softness of a towel.

'When you're ready, come to the bedroom. We'll try to patch you up.'

Drying was a painful process. She needed the first-aid he offered.

Wrapped in the damp towel, she joined him in the bedroom On the bed lay dressings, cotton wool and antiseptic cream.

'May I see your injuries?'

She discarded the damp towel, and sat on the bed. He began applying antiseptic to the areas of broken skin, seemingly indifferent to her nakedness. After so much violence the gentleness was comforting.

'There's bruising around your lower ribs. I'm no medical expert but I'd like to check in case anything is broken.' He hesitated. 'It would help if you would lie down.'

She acquiesced, surprising herself by her absolute trust in him. As his hand travelled over her rib-cage, it brushed the underside of her breast.

'How did he do this?'

His fingers explored a badly discoloured area. She flinched.

'My visitor was testing the durability of his climbing boots. Is something broken?'

'I can't feel a break, but your ribs may be cracked. There's a large area of bruising.'

When his ministrations were over, he handed her a carrier-bag. It contained an expensive, cotton-and-lace nightgown.

'I bought you this. The shop assistant said it's made with Honiton Lace.'

'It's pretty.'

This simple response embarrassed them both. Kate slipped into the night-gown and then into the bed. She pulled the covers over her bare shoulders.

'I'd like to rest,' she ventured.

'Kate, I've given only the barest first aid. You ought to be checked over by a doctor.'

'There's no need, I'm feeling better already. I told you, I want to forget what has happened.'

'Forget? How can you forget?' He became very agitated. 'You've been raped and viciously abused. When you've rested, I'll take you to the nearest hospital.'

'I don't need professional medical attention for cuts and bruises.' Her voice was quietly firm and unemotional.

'There may be more serious repercussions.' He could not be more specific, he did not want to scare her.

'There's no treatment for cracked ribs.'

It was bravado. She knew that the repercussions he was referring to were of the kind that did not become apparent until later.

'And if he's infected you with something unpleasant?' he persisted.

'Something tells me he hasn't,' she assured him.

'You don't know what you're saying. How can you take it so calmly?'

She was not exactly calm, but she was trying to be

positive. Brutish her attacker may have been, but he was young, with a baby face and pampered appearance. She preferred to believe he was clean.

'Kate, I beg you, let me take you to a hospital.'

'In this state? If a doctor saw me, it would be as good as calling the police. We're quits, Michael.' After the intimacy, it was natural to be on first name terms. 'You've suffered, I've suffered. Let's not make any more trouble for each other.'

'What's happened is my fault. I deserve to pay for what I've done'

'Punishing you won't help me. For both our sakes, Michael, please promise to keep the outside world out of this.'

He looked into her eyes as if trying to understand. 'I won't argue with you now, you need to sleep. When you've rested you may feel differently. If you change your mind, I'll understand.'

She gave an involuntary shiver. He rearranged the bed covers, pulling them up to her chin.

Closing her eyes, she began to relax. 'No doctor, promise?'

'No doctor.'

'And certainly no police.'

He was silent.

'You must promise me.'

'I'll do nothing without your permission. Now get some sleep.' Still he lingered. 'Will you eat with me later, if I prepare us a meal?'

'If I feel like eating, I will,' she promised.

In the doorway, he paused. 'Kate, I don't deserve your forgiveness.'

Keeping a firm check on her emotions, she ordered him to go away.

Chapter 21

Kate was woken at dawn by a suffused light penetrating the thin curtains. She wondered at the transformation of the shutters but then became aware of the warmth and comfort of the bed. Something was missing – the hissing snake had vacated her head.

Tentatively her fingers explored the left-hand-side of her cranium. Her lip was still very swollen and an egg-like tumescence grew above her eye. Rising, she forced herself to confront her dramatic appearance in the mirror. The injuries to her jaw and brow were both plum coloured, as were her ribs. Purple fruits also adorned her neck, breasts, buttocks and thighs.

Not wishing to dwell on the evidence of her degradation, she dressed in the sweat shirt, jogging trousers and trainers that Michael had bought for her. It was the same outfit that she had worn last night, when they had shared a meal and bottle of wine in the cottage kitchen. Beyond a civilised politeness, they had spoken little. They might have been strangers forced to share a table in a public restaurant.

Their awkwardness was difficult for Kate to analyse. Only three hours earlier, his fingers had rubbed almost every part of her abused body. His gentleness had been completely asexual, yet, remembering, she became aroused. It was a reaction that shocked. Surely it was unnatural to be dwelling on sensual pleasure, when she was supposed to be traumatised from the sex attack?

After supper, Michael had insisted that he cleared away the debris of the meal and that she returned to the only bed in the cottage. He intended to sleep on the sofa. She was not about to argue.

The bed was comfortable and she had slept soundly, so much so that her usually fertile mind had been untroubled by dreams. Wondering how Michael's long limbs had fared on the two-seater sofa, she decided to exploit her freedom and make him a morning cup of tea. After her confinement, the prospect of being able to enter the kitchen and carry out a simple domestic task seemed like a very special privilege.

Not wanting to disturb him, she crept downstairs. Faint sound patterns coming from the room below, arrested her progress. There was a tinny familiarity about the sound. What she was listening to was chilling and unmistakable. It came from the headphones of the cassette player. Michael was playing the tape that had wound itself into her brain. She was afraid. Not for herself, but for him.

She burst into the room that had been her prison. Apart from the strips of light that gaped through the shutters, the room was in darkness. Fearful of what she would find, she snapped on the light.

He lay prone on the sofa with his long legs trailing on the floor. The cassette player was on the table, the sounds issued from beyond it. She recognised the solemn bars of the Death March. For a moment she thought he was dead. She ran to him.

'No, Michael, No!' At her touch, he raised his head. There was an emptiness in his expression.

'What's happened, Kate?'

She stared at him. The headphones were loose about his neck. The tinny music suddenly ceased. A short silence was followed by the well-remembered click, then it began again.

'Why are you doing this to yourself?' She shook him as she spoke.

'You said what I did was worse than being raped, and I had to find out how bad it was.' He gripped her hand. 'How did you survive it for all those hours? I couldn't keep the head-phones on. I should have been trussed-up like you were.' His fingers dug into her wrist. 'Tie me in the chair, *make* me listen,' he demanded.

She shook off his grip, and stopped the tape. 'I can't do that, Michael.'

'Why not? It's far less punishment than I deserve.'

She covered her ears with her fists. 'Stop it. I won't listen to you.'

'You're strong, Kate. You have to be, to have withstood this and come out sane. I didn't know. Forgive me.'

'You meant only to teach me a lesson, I know that.'

Her understanding encouraged him. 'That business with the pills. I wouldn't have let you take them. Christ, I must have been clean out of my mind.'

He broke down and, in a rush of tenderness, she cradled him in her arms, stroked his hair and offered an unspoken comfort. She could not bear to see him reduced to this.

But Michael had strength of character too. His arms went around her, returning the embrace, the pressure on her bruised ribs drawing an involuntary gasp from her.

He released her instantly. 'I'm sorry, that was so clumsy. How could I forget?'

They both stood up, feeling awkward and embarrassed.

'It's all right,' she smiled. 'It was just a twinge.'

They were back to the civilities of the night before.

'As soon as you're ready, I'll drive you back to London,' he offered. 'Or to your family if you prefer.'

There was a wicked satisfaction in imagining Robin and Ellen's horror at seeing her.

'I can't go anywhere looking like this.'

'You can't want to stay *here*?' he said in disbelief.

'Just for a few days. Until my face looks less of a mess.'

'If you're sure that's what you want.' His tone was a mixture of incredulity and hope.

'It would be best. For us both,' she added, before hurrying on to safer ground. 'I was on my way to make tea – would you like some?'

'Please.' He followed her into the kitchen. 'You owe me nothing, Kate. You don't have to protect me.'

'I think perhaps I do.'

Their eyes met. Hers were first to look away.

Kate insisted on preparing breakfast. They ate together at the small kitchen table. The meal, though lacking the wine of their shared supper, seemed far more intimate somehow. She poured tea from a china pot. He passed the toast. On a surprising number of occasions, their hands manage to brush.

He checked her damaged face and asked, 'How are the other injuries?'

'The ribs are still sore, but the wounds are clean and healing.'

'Would you like me to take another look?' He made the offer quite unselfconsciously.

Though not averse to another of his first-aid performances, she declined. 'I've already applied more of the antiseptic cream.'

'Pity.' He looked her full in the face as he spoke, but she didn't react.

When the meal was over, they stood side-by-side at the sink. She washed, he wiped. She threw crumbs from the window and they jointly identified the birds that flew down to gather them. With their ornithological knowledge exhausted, and their domestic duty done, she suggested a walk on the moor.

'It's rough walking,' he pointed out. 'Are you sure you feel up to it?'

'It's not my legs, only my skin that's broken,' she protested. 'I could do with some fresh air, it's been days . . .' Her voice tailed off. She had not intended to remind him of his culpability.

'I've been a brute, I know.'

He looked so pained she tried to reassure him. 'Let's think of this as a holiday. I needed one.'

'How can you make so light of it?'

'Would you rather I cried?'

He lay his hands on her shoulders and looked into her eyes. 'No, Kate, I'd much rather you smiled. In the future, I only want you to see you happy.'

The intensity of the moment, coupled with his mention of the future, made them both feel awkward.

Kate relieved the situation. 'Well, am I walking alone or are you coming?' The boldness of her invitation was at odds with the shyness she felt.

A sudden rain-squall beat a tattoo on the windowpane, pre-empting his response.

'What diabolical timing,' he complained.

'It's probably only a shower.' Kate peered through the window. 'It's quite bright in the west.'

Her optimism lifted his spirits as he joined her at the window. 'If it does clear-up, perhaps we could make for that high peak in the distance.'

'It's called High Willhays,' she told him, 'but I don't think we can walk there. It's part of the Ministry of Defence ranges. Public access is restricted.'

Her knowledge took him by surprise. 'How do you come to be so well-informed about Dartmoor?'

'I grew up in and around Plymouth and returned there to work after university. Dartmoor has been home territory for most of my life. It's quite a weird coincidence that you brought me here.'

'Any wilderness would have done, this was the least remote. The idea was to get away from the pressures of the city and restore my equilibrium.' He gave a wry smile. 'It had the opposite effect. When I rented this place, you were no part of my plan, yet from the time I came here I couldn't stop thinking about you. I had a crazy notion that I would never feel any better unless I made you . . .' He left the sentence uncompleted.

'Suffer?' she suggested.

'No, not that, not at first. All I intended in the beginning was to make you understand the damage that an ill-considered article could do, but once I got started, I couldn't stop. I don't expect you to believe this, or to understand, but your degradation gave me no pleasure. I didn't like what I was doing, so to continue was an effective way of punishing myself.'

It was a skewed kind of logic, but she didn't say so. Instead she discouraged him from talking about it. 'Please, Michael, there's no need. You don't have to offer an explanation.'

He would not accept this means of escape. 'Please, I need to explain. I'd made up my mind that as soon as you had some clothes I'd drive you back to London. Either that or give myself up to the police here. The choice was to be yours, but I didn't get the chance to offer it.' Sweat broke out on his brow. 'When I found you lying there, I thought I was looking at your corpse. It was the worst moment of my life.'

His voice dropped to a whisper. 'Even worse than finding Caroline. For a moment, I thought I was truly mad and must have murdered you myself.'

She recalled her own fear at finding him lying, unmoving on the sofa. 'Please, Michael, don't talk about it. I don't want to be reminded.'

He quietened her agitation by reaching out and taking both her hands in his. For a long while they remained like that, side by side, silent, watching the rain.

In the afternoon, the weather cleared. Their walk took them past small groups of grazing moorland ponies to a nearby stone circle. Under the mewing cries of a buzzard they pondered the prehistoric rituals that might have taken place there. They chose to ignore the darkening sky until large water-droplets sent them scurrying back, just ahead of the main rain-front.

She had walked away from what had been her prison without a backward glance. When the moor-stone cottage came into view, she saw it for the first time. It was built in the shelter of a granite outcrop. Its roof was thatched, and an unusual, two-storey porch graced its central door.

'It's delightful,' she exclaimed. 'I hadn't realised.'

'It dates from the 1780s, the time of the Enclosures. Externally, it's a perfect example of a small Devon farm house of that era. Of course, there have been structural alterations inside. Before the bathroom was installed, the first floor would have been divided into two rooms of equal size, similar to the ground floor.'

'I'd forgotten you were an architect.'

He grinned wryly and apologised for lecturing.

As they reached the porch of the cottage, the skies opened to turn the shower into a torrent.

'Home just in time,' she remarked.

'Home?' he said, with a surprised smile.

The colour that came to her cheeks had nothing to do with walking in the fresh air.

The walk had broken the ice and they were now perfectly relaxed. The rest of the day was spent in an amiable companionship. They read at the kitchen table, the material comfort of the sitting room being out-of-bounds by unspoken agreement in deference to Kate's feelings. In the evening, they shared in the preparation of the meal, polishing off a bottle of wine as they did so.

His manner was much altered: he smiled a lot and occasionally touched her hand or arm to emphasise a point. But it was the look in his eyes that was most changed. The glazed stare that had been so chilling was gone, to be replaced by one of adoration. Conscious of her temporary disfigurement, Kate valued the adoration all the more. She had observed a similar expression in Win Blakeney's eyes, when he looked at the lovely Lena.

Chapter 22

After they had eaten, tiredness overcame her. Though heady with wine, she grew quiet. He was sensitive to the change.

'What's wrong, Kate, are you feeling unwell?'

'Not unwell, just dead on my feet.'

'You're entitled, you must be shattered. It's selfish of me to keep you talking. Go on up to bed.'

She was considering whether she might kiss him goodnight, when he took the initiative.

'Perhaps I might come up to say goodnight?'

She readily gave her assent, but on entering the bedroom he found her buried to the chin in blankets. The layers of protection were a ridiculous modesty considering that only the previous day she had allowed him to massage her naked body.

'It's turned chilly,' she offered by way of explanation.

'Yes, the cottage does seem a bit damp. I must fix that broken window.' He made no move to approach the bed. 'Is there anything you need? A glass of water?'

'I'm fine, thanks. But what about you, where will you sleep?'

'Don't worry about me, just get some rest. Goodnight.'

'Thank you for today.'

He took this as his dismissal. As he reached the

door, she said in a subdued voice, 'I don't want you to spend another night in that room, Michael.'

He grinned sheepishly. 'It's OK, I've no intention of subjecting myself to the lullaby from hell tonight.'

'I'm glad of that.'

Her ploy had worked for now he lingered, as if loath to leave. She wondered how much encouragement she should give. 'You're far too long to use that sofa again. It's silly to be uncomfortable, you won't sleep.'

He hovered, half hopefully. 'What's the alternative?'

'This bed is enormous . . .' She hesitated, not wanting to appear brazen. 'It should be possible to share it.' And, to establish that she intended no euphemism, added, 'One side each.'

He needed no persuasion. Pretending to close her eyes, she watched every movement of his undressing. His body was well-toned, athletic. It was a physique with great pleasure potential. However, her expectations were quashed when, instead of joining her between the sheets, he carefully divided the blankets and lay beneath the top one. Constrained 'Goodnights' followed, and simultaneously they turned their backs on each other.

Her tiredness had lifted. She lay listening to his breathing and wondered if he were listening to hers. Though she lay still, she was restless within and could tell that he was not sleeping either.

'Michael?' she ventured.

His response was an immediate, 'What's the matter, can't you sleep?' But he remained turned away from her.

'No, and I'm sure you can't either. You must be cold under that single blanket. Get into the bed properly, it won't offend me.'

'If you're sure.'

She wished he weren't so delicate with her feelings. 'I'm quite sure.'

They lay between the same sheets, though the expanse of mattress kept them apart. Each willed the other to be the first to reach out, but the minutes lengthened and still they didn't touch. For each of them sleep was a long time in arriving.

Brymer and Diss arrived in Okehampton in the late evening. Before booking into the hotel, they called at the police station.

A Sergeant Bullimore greeted them. 'We've made a bit of progress in identifying likely cottages, sir,' he told Diss. 'In the area pinpointed, there's no more than three or four that are completely isolated. We've organised a couple of Land Rovers for the search in the morning.'

'Good. Can I see Inspector Pearce?' Diss asked.

'He's off duty at the moment, but suggests he meets you here at 0700 hours, tomorrow.'

'We'll need a WPC with us.' Diss reminded.

'The back-up team's been organised and it includes a woman constable,' Bullimore assured him.

Now that they were so close, Jack could not curb his impatience. 'If there are so few likely properties, why don't we take a look at them tonight?'

'All of them are out-of-the-way. As any local will tell you, sir, the moor is as full of hazards as any ocean. It's best to wait until daylight.'

Diss agreed, 'The sergeant's right, Jack. There's less likely to be a cock-up if we undertake the search at first light. A few hours more won't make a difference. Thanks to the homework the local lads have done, we'll nail him in the morning.'

Jack turned to the sergeant. 'What about an air search?'

'Waste of time, sir. Never fear, we'll have the kidnapper in the bag before most people have had their breakfasts.'

Jack hoped to God that he was right.

A stream of sunlight woke Kate. Unlike the previous day's dawn, there was no confusion, for she knew precisely where she was. Michael lay with his back to her, one knee bent. In her sleep, she had rolled against him, her left arm encircling his chest, her wounded breasts cushioning his bare back. Her leg was tucked about his, her right thigh making a lap for his buttock. Mortified, she set about disentangling herself, withdrawing inch by inch. But as her left arm came free, he clamped it with his own.

'Don't go, it feels too good.'

She should have known that he wasn't asleep, his breathing had been too light.

He claimed her hand, and held it pressed tight to his chest. The warmth of his body was comforting. Her anxiety faded, as had the desire of the previous night. She would have been content to drift back into sleep, but her confined right arm would not let her. Trapped awkwardly under her own body, it was too much a reminder of the discomfort of her bondage to be ignored.

'Michael, my arm's gone to sleep.'

He acknowledged her question with a drawn-out, "Uhmm" of satisfaction.

Turning to face her, he claimed the troublesome limb and began massaging it. The attention was so enjoyable that she didn't bother to tell him when the circulation was restored.

He pressed the palm of her hand to his lips. Now it was her turn to indicate satisfaction. His mouth found her swollen lip. Though the kiss was lop-sided on her part, their conjunction was the most natural thing in the world. After her mouth, he kissed her eyelids and the lump on her brow.

'It's called kissing you better,' he explained.

It made her feel like a child again, though she was very aware that these were nothing like a parent's kisses. They were far too disturbing.

Taking her hand again, he began licking the palm with a suggestive intent. When she offered her damaged mouth to be kissed again, he asked, 'What are we going to do, Kate?'

She captured his hand, taking the index finger into her mouth. It was the most eloquent answer she could have given him.

The ribbon tie at the neck of her night-gown was deftly released. He gave her breasts equal attention. His lips worshipped the places that the rapist had abused. Every action was tender, yet out of this gentleness came an arousal greater than any she had known.

'You've given me back my sanity, Kate. I wish I could do something to erase your hurt.'

She assured him that he could and, in confirmation, raised her arms to assist the removal of her night-gown.

To lie naked, under his gaze, seemed as natural as their first kiss. His lips brushed her bruised ribs, tracing them one by one. Then just as gently he kissed the fingerprint discoloration on her thighs, making her breath come fast and shallow. He eased apart her knees, breathing in the potent cocktail of desire and fertility she was exuding. When his tongue found the place immediately above the tampon's cotton tail she responded with a low moan.

'I want you, so much,' he declared, 'but I'll understand if it's too soon.'

His consideration was unnecessary, but though she might be careless of her own safety, she was suddenly frightened for his. 'It's what I want too, but we mustn't. I can't be certain that I . . . that he was clean.'

'Kate, my darling, don't ask me to behave like a rational man. I ceased to be that from the moment I met you. If there's a risk, then let me take it. I want you, and I want to make you happy. The rest is unimportant.'

Her hand found him, he was gloriously hard. It seemed a miracle that he could desire such a battered and misused body. Passion overrode caution. Inexpertly, she tried to pilot him home, forgetting the impediment of the tampon.

It was while they were occupied with this unromantic obstacle, that a fist hammered upon the cottage door.

'Police – open-up!'

They separated in some haste: the timing could not have been more perverse. Michael leapt out of bed, recovered his trousers and pulled them on.

'Don't answer it. Don't go,' she pleaded.

The hammering came again.

'I have to answer it, you know that.' His voice was flat, his expression defeated. Jaw set, he went to open the door. The honeymoon was over.

The party had set out from Okehampton Police Station in two cars for they were expecting to make an arrest. Pearce, the local inspector, drove the leading Land Rover with Nick Diss at his side. Jack sat in the back wondering if Kate would be sitting next to him on the return journey and, if so, what sort of state she would be in. Bullimore and the woman police constable followed in the other vehicle.

At their first port of call they found no trace of

occupation. The place was locked and shuttered, and there were no vehicle tracks in the soft ground. The next property on their list was approached by a five-barred gate and a winding track. The other Land Rover led the way now, and it was the woman constable who opened the gate. She gave a thumbs up, pointing to the fresh imprint of wide tyres.

They drove on and the cottage with its attendant Mitsubishi came into view. Jack registered the closed curtains and the solitary, shuttered window. His pulse quickened.

Over the radio link Pearce told Bullimore to pull over. 'Leave the Land Rover where it is to block the track. We'll go ahead on foot from here. Go quietly, we want this to come as a surprise.'

When they reached the cottage, it was Diss who took charge. 'Jack and I will check out the back. The rest of you guard the front door.'

Their reconnaissance discovered a broken side-window. The cottage lacked any rear access. It was built so close to the granite cliff that the rear wall was blank, without so much as a single window. They rejoined the others.

'There's no way out from the back, just a broken window at the right-hand side. Bullimore can keep an eye on that, just in case he makes a break for it. The rest of us are going in by the front door. OK, Sergeant, time to give him his early morning call.'

Bullimore's outsize fist thundered on the door. Half a minute passed in silence. Bullimore repeated his performance and sounds of movement were heard from inside.

Kershaw opened the door. He was pale faced, barefoot and bare-chested. The local inspector flashed his identification.

'Good morning, Mr Kershaw.' Pearce's West

Country accent made the greeting sound friendly. 'We're investigating the disappearance of Kate Rider, and have reason to believe that she is being forcibly held in this cottage.'

Michael's response was to open the door wide. Without speaking, he led them up the stairs.

From the bedroom Kate heard the voices, but not what was said. There was a tramp of heavy feet on the stairs. When Michael reappeared he was followed by a man in a raincoat, whose ginger hair looked familiar. From between two police uniforms, burst Jack Brymer.

'Kate!' he exclaimed, stopping in his tracks.

Kate had made use of the minute's breathing space to scramble back into her nightdress and fluff some order into her hair. Nonetheless, her battered appearance shocked Jack. Michael's attentions had made her feel so good about herself that she had forgotten her temporary disfigurements.

'What has the bastard done to you, Kate?'

Without waiting for an answer, he turned fist raised. 'I'll kill you for this, Kershaw,' he snarled.

'You've got the wrong idea,' Michael protested, standing his ground.

Jack lunged at him but was restrained by the ginger-haired man, whom Kate now recognised as Inspector Diss.

Pearce slapped a pair of handcuffs on Michael and began to lead him from the bedroom.

'He didn't do this to me!' Kate shouted. Her plea was ignored and Michael was escorted out.

A uniformed police woman appeared. She tutted and restrained Kate from leaving the bed.

'Don't fret, love. We've called for an ambulance.'

Kate was concerned only for Michael. 'What are they going to do to him?'

'They're taking him to the station. Don't worry,' the policewoman comforted. 'He can't hurt you now.'

Kate turned on her. 'Why don't you listen? He didn't cause my injuries.'

The woman patronised, by patting her hand. 'Don't fret about all that now. We'll get you to the hospital first.'

'I can't go to the hospital. I have to go with Michael.'

'There's no need for that. When you next face that sadist he should be standing in the dock of a criminal court.'

Kate had undergone all her recent ordeals dry-eyed. Now, finally, with the WPC's arm about her shoulder, she broke down and wept.

Chapter 23

Jack and WPC Cox rode with Kate in the ambulance. Though Kate had calmed somewhat, neither the policewoman nor Jack would listen to her protestations.

'Michael Kershaw didn't do this. He's a gentle man. An intruder broke into the cottage and raped me. Why won't you believe me?'

Such assertions did not suit their prejudices. Jack told her she was overwrought. The policewoman kept up a steady reassurance that she would be all right once she had seen a doctor.

A police surgeon was present during her hospital examination. Every bite, scratch and bruise on her body was located, and described into his hand-held dictation machine. It could not have been more impersonal had he been a pathologist and she a corpse on the mortuary slab.

An X-ray revealed that the damage to her ribs was restricted to a single crack. Despite her assurance that the injuries suffered were all external, the doctor insisted on an internal examination. Distressing as this invasive procedure was, far more sobering was the knowledge that an appointment was being made for her to be blood-tested for HIV and hepatitis.

The physical examination showed no reason for her to be detained and she was handed over to the police for a different kind of scrutiny. Cherishing the naive hope that she might see Michael, she went with them willingly. But disappointment awaited her at the police station. She was told that he had been charged and was being held in the police cells, pending a special magistrate's hearing.

Inspectors Diss and Pearce conducted her interview, with WPC Cox in attendance. They tried to take her through the abduction chronologically, but she kept returning to the assault, continuing to protest Michael's innocence.

'It was an intruder, not Michael who attacked me,' she insisted.

'Have I got this right?' Diss asked. 'You want us to believe that your attacker was an opportunist thief who turned into an opportunist rapist?'

'I didn't say that he was a thief. He was a backpacker, a foreigner who spoke limited English. From his accent I would say he must be German, or possibly Dutch. He broke in to find shelter, not to steal.'

'A bit early in the day to be looking for a bed, wasn't it?' Pearce scoffed.

'He wasn't looking for overnight accommodation, he was seeking shelter. There was a terrific thunderstorm going on outside.'

'A foreign tourist who goes in for breaking and entering. Interesting.' The Devon man's tone was disbelieving.

'Why do you find the truth so unlikely? He obviously thought the cottage was empty. Michael had taken the car, the lights were off, and there were no other signs of occupation. Getting in only involved smashing a small pane of glass and opening a window.'

'Wouldn't your intruder have seen the car tracks?'

Referring to the intruder as "your" made it sound as if she had invented him.

'He isn't *my* intruder,' she protested, 'and you seem to be forgetting the storm. It was raining hard, the tracks of the Shogun would have been obliterated.'

'So what did your visitor . . .' He corrected himself, 'sorry, *the* visitor look like?'

She was only too anxious to provide a physical description. If they found the real culprit they would have to believe in Michael's innocence.

'He's young, seventeen or eighteen, well over six-foot and tending to fat. He was clean-shaven with a smooth, baby face and grey eyes.'

They seemed to be listening, at last.

'Hair colour?'

'I'm not sure, he wore a woollen hat. His hair must have been cut short to have been hidden so completely.'

'And how was he dressed?'

'He was wearing what looked like army combat gear.'

Diss consulted the local man, but was told that, currently, there were no foreign troops using the moor for manoeuvres.

'I doubt he was a professional soldier.' Kate said. 'He looked no more than a teenager. Despite what he did to me, he had the air of an overgrown school boy playing at commandos.'

'He might well be a schoolboy,' the local man mused. 'I've personally booked a thirteen-year-old for committing rape. Some of these kids are lawless.'

Diss returned to the matter in hand. 'While he was assaulting you, did you try to protect yourself?'

She remembered the manacled wrists that had made her so vulnerable. To mention them would be to implicate Michael.

'I tried to resist, but that was when he hit me across

the mouth. It seemed safer to remain passive. I thought he wouldn't hurt me so much if I offered no opposition.' She wasn't lying, just being economical with the truth.

'When you tried to defend yourself, what did you do? Hit out at him, scratch?'

'I kicked out.'

'I see. You didn't use your hands?'

'No.' She didn't like the direction that his questioning was taking.

'And why was that?' Diss drawled.

'I can't remember.'

The two policemen exchanged looks and Pearce gave an exasperated sigh. He produced a sealed transparent bag from his desk. It contained a pair of handcuffs.

'Perhaps these will help you to remember.'

There was a long pause. Kate sat tight lipped, finally lost for words.

Diss took up the questioning again, he sounded weary. 'We're still waiting for a transcription of the medical report on your injuries, but I've spoken to the police surgeon. He says that the bruising on your wrists is consistent with the wearing of handcuffs.'

Still she remained silent.

'Kershaw left you in that cottage, handcuffed and unable to protect yourself. Isn't that what happened?'

Kate's chin went up. She was the victim and they were treating her like a criminal. 'He wouldn't have done, had he known he was putting me at risk.'

'Are you sure about that?'

'Of course I'm sure.'

Pearce took over from Diss. 'We found some interesting things at the cottage. Particularly in the shuttered room.' He picked-up a brown envelope from the desk, extracted some photographs, and handed them to her. They showed the wooden chair, still flying the cotton rags that had been her bonds. She averted her eyes.

Because of its associations, they had not gone back into that room. It was a sensitivity that had put Michael at risk, for they had left intact the very evidence that could convict him.

'Please, Miss Rider,' Pearce encouraged. I'd like you to take a good look.'

She obliged. 'What am I supposed to be looking at?'

Nick Diss exhaled, an expression of his exasperation.

'The medical examination found chafing on your arms and ankles. We know you were tied to that chair and abused by him. It's in your interest to assist us with our enquiry. Why, after such brutality, are you intent on protecting Kershaw?'

'I don't know what you mean,' she bluffed.

'There's no point in refuting the evidence. How long did he keep you tied up?'

'I lost track of time.'

'Was it minutes? Hours? Days?'

'A few hours, I think.'

'You're wasting police time as well as your own. I have to tell you that Michael Kershaw has made a full confession. We know that he abducted you from your London flat on Sunday night. We also know that you were brought to Dartmoor lying, gagged and handcuffed, in the back of his vehicle. When he got you to the cottage, he tied you to the chair shown in these photographs. You remained in bondage until Tuesday morning and, for the whole of that time, you were subjected to extreme physical and mental cruelty.'

There was little purpose in continuing with her lies. Michael was condemned out of his own mouth. All she could do was limit the damage he'd inflicted on himself.

'But he didn't beat, bite, kick or rape me. He had nothing to do with my physical injuries.'

Pearce, the other half of the double act, took over the questioning. 'How can you be so sure?'

'I'm the victim, how can I *not* be sure? You must have found evidence of the break-in at the cottage?'

'Certainly, we found evidence: the window broken from the outside, imprints of a pair of large walking boots, indoors as well as out.'

'What more do you want?' She decided she was dealing with idiots.

'We can't conclude that Kershaw wasn't involved. He blamed you for his wife's suicide. He was out to punish you. Perhaps he arranged for you to have a visitor while he was out.'

It was such an ugly suggestion, it hurt. 'That's not true,' she protested.

'The truth is precisely what we intend to uncover.'

Pearce tried another gambit. 'You do realise that your name will be withheld if Kershaw is charged with the sexual offence? We won't be able to give you that sort of protection if we nail him on just the other charges.'

She was scornful of this unsubtle attempt to win her co-operation. 'Was that intended as some kind of bribe? An inducement to lie?'

'Steady on, Miss Rider,' Diss soothed. 'Inspector Pearce was merely advising you of the considerable publicity that's bound to follow this case. Naturally we would prefer to spare you that.'

Kate was well aware of what press interest was likely to be: once more she would be powerless to protect either Michael or herself from another round of ugly and undeserved publicity.

Brymer was sipping a mug of tea in the police canteen when Diss joined him.

'She's not going to help us, Jack. The whole thing is crazy. He's made a full confession, even given us details we haven't even asked him for. There can be no doubt that he gave her a tough time, yet she's trying to gloss over everything. She's still pretending he didn't hurt her.'

'What exactly did he do to her?' Nothing Diss revealed could exceed the abuse Jack had imagined.

'Sorry, Jack, you're a newspaper man, and that information is strictly sub-judice.'

'Was he the rapist? At least tell me that.'

'It's unlikely. That's the only bit of the story they both agree on. The claim there was an intruder is borne out by what we found in the cottage: the broken window, the boot-prints.'

As a newspaperman, Jack was well aware that lightning *could* strike twice in the same place but he was still suspicious. 'Kershaw could have paid some-one to do his dirty work.'

'That he's an accessory is a possibility. But we've been there before, don't forget. We thought he was linked to the stalker business when he wasn't. Any-way it doesn't make sense. Why should he deny any knowledge of the rape and come clean on everything else? He's admitted to crimes against the person and is aware they carry custodial sentences. A charge of aiding and abetting rape is unlikely to lengthen the time he serves, so why deny it?'

The sleuth in Jack came to the fore. 'You won't get at the truth until you find that hiker.'

'We're looking for him. There's a helicopter out,

and the Devon boys are conducting door-to-door enquiries. They should turn-up something soon. Somebody must have seen him.'

'What if the bird has flown?'

'If he was on foot, he can't have gone far. Meanwhile, Kershaw has been charged with kidnap and grievous bodily harm.' The satisfaction in his tone did not match the expression on his face as he sipped at the mug of canteen brew.

'Grievous?' The charge surprised Jack. 'But Kate claims the mystery intruder was responsible for her injuries.'

'Mental torture can be GBH. He's admitted to that. Plus, we have some damning evidence.'

'Which I suppose you won't tell me about?'

'Sorry, Jack, I can't.'

'I gather from what you say that the rape was just part of her ordeal. He deserves to be put away.'

Jack ground out his cigarette in a way that suggested he would like to be extinguishing it on Kershaw's bare flesh.

'Don't fret – he will be. We have him on two counts.'

Thoughts of Kate's ordeal spurred Jack to her defence. 'Look . . . about Kate – she's probably confused. Any woman would be after the hell she's been through. Interview her again when she's recovered, she'll be more forthcoming then.'

Diss grimaced. 'Don't put your shirt on it, Jack.'

'What are you saying?'

'I'd say she is in love with the guy.'

Diss had voiced the suspicion that Jack had been trying to suppress. To hear it voiced so baldly gave it a legitimacy that disturbed him.

'Goddamnit, she hardly knows him,' he said gruffly.

'In my experience, knowing someone is more likely to impede than to aid infatuation.'

This was a cynicism that spurred Jack to an angry denial. 'Kate's showing a typical hostage response. She's identifying with her abductor, that's all.'

Diss knew when to back off. 'Maybe you're right. If so she'll come round, but at the moment I'd say that the chief prosecution witness is on the side of the defendant.'

'Witness? But if he pleads guilty there won't be a trial. She won't be called to give evidence.'

'That depends on what we turn-up in our rape investigation. There could be a further charge. But that's all you're getting, pal. I've said too much already.'

Diss drove them back to London. Jack sat with Kate in the back of the car. He hoped to be allowed to offer his support, but she ignored his every attempt to engage her in conversation. For the entire journey she sat with her head touching the side window, her damaged face averted.

It was a great surprise to him when, at journey's end, she invited him into her flat. But hospitality was not her purpose.

'Have you been in touch with *The Flag*?' she asked.

'Not yet. I wasn't following up a story. I came in search of you because I was bloody worried.'

'Please, Jack, don't tell them.' She made finger contact with his hand as she made the appeal.

'You're not thinking straight. Kershaw is under arrest. He's a man who's already made front page news, and he's admitted two serious offences against you. Every paper in the country will be covering this.'

'My God, haven't I done enough to him?'

He shook her by the shoulders. 'Are you crazy? You shouldn't be protecting him. Think what he's done to you.' He forced her to face a wall mirror. 'Take a look at yourself.'

What she saw was a grotesque of her usual regular features. The sight only made her more adamant. 'You're as bad as the police. What can I do to make you believe me? Michael didn't do this.'

Disliking her familiar use of his rival's forename, Jack accepted defeat. 'OK, I won't tell Colson any more than I have to. Not that I know much, Diss insisted that the details are sub-judice. But you'll have to accept that it will be open house when Kershaw is sentenced.'

She softened towards him. 'You won't use what you saw at the cottage?'

'No, it's your story. You're the one who should write it up. I'll bow out gracefully.'

She couldn't believe his lack of understanding. 'Don't you see? Because it *is* my story I *can't* write about it. It would make things worse.'

His sympathy evaporated. She had shown no gratitude for the rescue he'd mounted. Out of jealousy and anger came the desire to wound.

'Diss said that you were obstructing his enquiries. For God's sake, why do you want to protect that bastard?'

'He was ill. He's not a violent man.'

'Not violent! The man's a bloody sadist.' He gripped her arms and shook her. 'Is that what you like? Some women do, I know. Does degradation turn you on?'

She averted her face and his mouth found her ear. He nipped the lobe painfully and crushed her to him until she cried out from the pain of his bruised ribs. As suddenly as his anger flared, it was dissipated. He stood before her, hands hanging limply at his sides.

'Forgive me, Kate, I don't know what came over me.'

'I'd like you to leave, now, please.'

He tried to stay, to apologise again, to make it up with her but she was in no mood to listen. His goodbye went unanswered and he slouched out of the apartment into the wet street. Cursing Kershaw, he trudged miserably to Shepherd's Bush and the nearest Underground station.

Chapter 24

The story was every tabloid's dream. It had it all: sex, violence, revenge and deliverance. The victim was a vivacious young woman and the arrested kidnapper a successful member of the professional community. Both had already attracted considerable media attention. The other perpetrator, a mystery foreigner, was still at large and the subject of a police manhunt. What was more, the two villains' dastardly deeds were performed in a setting dramatically appropriate: Dartmoor, thanks to Her Majesty's Prison and Conan Doyle, was Britain's Transylvania when it came to reputation and atmosphere.

Kevin Colson was jubilant. It was the story of the year, and two of the protagonists, victim and rescuer, were already *Flag* property. However, his chief crime reporter was unusually respectful of the sub-judice aspects of the case. In this instance, Jack's loyalty had favoured Kate rather than his employer. The story he turned-in was undramatic and strictly factual, revealing no more about the events on Dartmoor than was public knowledge. Colson supposed that Brymer in his generosity was handing the main coverage over to Kate.

The day after Kate's rescue, *The Flag's* later editions carried the report of the kidnap exactly as Jack had written it, Colson not daring to tamper with his chief crime reporter's copy. The story gave Kate complete anonymity under the unsensational header: KIDNAP VICTIM RELEASED. The rape was not mentioned and the identities of victim and abductor were not disclosed.

Colson was less considerate. With an eye to his Saturday circulation figures, he splashed a promotional promise on the same page:

KIDNAP SENSATION – FLAG REPORTER KIDNAPPED
Kate Rider held in Dartmoor Hideaway.
Read tomorrow's exclusive. Only in The Flag.

Jack groaned when he saw it, but didn't have the guts to phone Kate and warn her of what Colson had done. She would see it soon enough.

Kate had absented herself from the office, pleading post-traumatic-stress. Besieged in her flat, she had not seen her paper's morning edition.

With a photographer in tow, Colson went in person to winkle Kate out. To reach the door of her flat *The Flag* delegation was obliged to beat a path through the ranks of their competition.

'You haven't given any statements to that bunch, have you?' Colson demanded aggressively, when she reluctantly granted him entry.

'Of course not, and I've no intention of doing so. Perhaps they'll end the siege when they realise they're not getting anything.'

'Good girl,' he approved. 'But I've a better idea. We'll move you away from here. Find you somewhere quiet. A country hotel, where you can write without distractions.'

'Write?'

'Wake-up, Kate. I'm referring to your story. It's

already promised to our readers, and they'll be getting impatient.'

The trap seemed to be closing but Kate concealed her distress. 'Sorry, Kevin, but I can't give you what you want. A trial by jury hasn't been ruled out, and the police have forbidden me to make any disclosures to the press.'

'I'm not asking for anything sub-judice. We can wait for the facts. What I want right now is the personal line. How you are, how you feel. The emotional angle is what our readers thirst for, and it's what you do best, Katie,' he coaxed.

She refused to be seduced. 'It's impossible. I can't do it.'

'What are you talking about? I'm not asking for anything that will affect the outcome of a trial. We won't mention Kershaw until the bastard is nailed.'

She didn't need this kind of pressure. 'Haven't you heard of post-traumatic-stress?' she demanded.

'Come on, Katie,' he soothed. 'You're a professional. Write this out of your system with an exclusive. It will be a whole lot healthier than accepting counselling from Victim Support. Be a good girl, I need you back at work. We have to steal a march on the competition.'

Unaware of Kate's protective attitude towards her abductor, Colson misread her reticence. 'OK, doll, I get the picture, there's no need to pretend a lack of enthusiasm. Just admit that you're looking for a fat fee and name your price.'

'As much as I enjoy haggling, Kevin, this isn't about money.'

'Have you been bribed by a competitor?' He was beginning to get angry, and so was she.

'No, I haven't, and I resent the accusation. My

story is not for sale. Not to *The Flag* or to any other publication.'

Colson simply couldn't understand her attitude. He cajoled, pleaded, bullied, and threatened, but she would not be shifted. Eventually, he admitted defeat.

'You win. You can give me the personal revelations when you've come to your senses. I'll settle for a pictorial exclusive at the moment.'

The photographer had taken no part in the failed negotiations. He interpreted Colson's words as the signal for action. Kate shied away from the invasive lens.

'Don't play camera-shy, darling,' he begged. 'We have to give the readers something to keep them happy. Your bruises, in glorious Technicolor, should help.'

Colson added to this insensitivity by pulling at the neckline of her shirt. 'At least give us a bit of dishabille. Just the top two buttons will do. If you won't describe the action then we'd better give *The Flag's* devotees a picture of your more intimate battle scars to help them imagine it.'

He uncovered the bite marks on the curvature of her breast.

'This is assault, Kevin,' she snapped, clutching defensively at her collar.

'So sue me,' he sneered.

To appeal to his better nature was useless; he did not have one. 'Get out of here, both of you,' she said wearily. When they showed no inclination to comply, she blustered, 'If you don't leave, I'll call the police.'

They went, but not before Colson issued a warning. 'Don't be tempted to do a deal with the opposition. You're still under contract to *The Flag,* and if you welsh on us, we'll take you to the cleaners.

I'll personally ensure that you're never employed as a journalist again.'

Kate found it hard to believe that she had once felt proud to be working for him.

Her father telephoned. 'What's all this about you having been kidnapped?' he demanded.

'You have the advantage over me, Dad. I haven't seen the morning papers.'

Her response seemed to rile him. 'Do you think it fair that we learn about this business from a public source?' he fumed. 'What's happened to you, Kate? You seem to be courting the worst kind of cheap publicity. It's all very embarrassing for us. Ellen is most upset.'

He seemed to think that the abduction was a publicity stunt. She restrained herself from saying, 'Sod Ellen,' but, smarting from the telling-off, could not temper the bitterness of her response.

'I'm not leading my life to suit your new wife, Dad.'

'That's very obvious. Though it certainly wouldn't hurt you to consider others a bit more. You used not to be so selfish.'

Her father droned on in similar, unsympathetic vein. Suffering the front-line fire of his disapproval, she could not bring herself to admit that she had been raped. In due course he ran out of commentary. Kate brought the conversation to a close and hung up. This kind of solace she didn't need.

Never had she felt more isolated and alone. Not on account of her father though. She was missing a lover.

It was only five days since Michael had appeared on her doorstep. In that brief period both their lives had been changed irrevocably. She found herself reliving everything: from his arrival at the flat on Sunday night to the Thursday morning police raid at the cottage, and all that had happened in between. The details ran through her mind in sequence, in much the same way as the nightmare cassette had replayed again and again.

It was the interruption to their lovemaking, rather than the rape, that became the most painful experience. She knew she had Jack to thank for that. Because Jack was well-intentioned, she felt pity rather than resentment. However, his chivalry could never be rewarded in the way he hoped.

The rape took on a different aspect. It had, after all, proved to be Michael's salvation. The shock that had restored him to sanity. But when the story broke in earnest, she and Michael would once again be subjected to the worst kind of publicity. This time, the coupling of their names would not merely be detrimental to his reputation, it might destroy him completely.

She spared a thought for her father. She could well imagine his reaction when the sordid details emerged. It was a bitter reflection that her unprincipled journalism had brought about the mess she found herself in. Imagining the sensationalist headlines to come, she felt sick to the pit of her stomach.

Tiring of their fruitless stake-out, the besieging reporters and photographers gradually drifted away, until by early evening they were all gone. The flat was out of provisions, but Kate could not summon up the courage to venture out. She was resigned to spending the evening in hungry isolation.

After a brief respite, the doorbell sounded again. Assuming her caller to be a persistent reporter, she ignored it. Eventually the irritation ceased. Just when she thought that the unwelcome caller had gone away, her name was shouted from the street.

'Kate, if you're in there, let me talk to you.'

The voice sounded familiar. Through a crack between the curtain, she looked into the street and was amazed to see Winston Blakeney standing there. Revealing herself, she indicated in sign language that she was coming down to let him in.

When the street door opened, he stared at the damage to her face, but made no comment on it.

'What on earth brought you here, Win?' she asked.

'There was a piece about you in the paper. Ma sent me to find out how you were.'

In the privacy of the flat, he gathered her into a compassionate embrace. The back of his fingers brushed the damaged side of her face from temple to mouth. His simple but earnest, 'I'm sorry,' sounded like an apology for all men brutish enough to do this to a woman.

Then she was clinging to him, blubbering. Her tears dampened the lapels of his well-cut suit. He said nothing, but stroked her hair until she was quiet.

'I used to think I was tough, in control of my emotions,' she sniffed.

'As Ma says, *it's better out than in*.'

She was touched by Irene Blakeney's concern in sending Winston. It contrasted sharply with her father's reaction. And her employer's.

Winston cast his eyes around the flat. 'You shouldn't be here on your own while you're in this state. Have you friends to go to?'

She shook her head despondently.

'Then you can't stay here. Pack a case, I'm taking you home to Ma.'

His kindness was soothing balm to her raw emotions.

'I couldn't impose.' The words contradicted what she felt. She was in desperate need of sympathy and understanding.

Win refused to take 'no' for an answer.

'Rubbish, it's no imposition. Get packed and we'll be off.' He raised an eyebrow. 'If you don't mind me fingering your undergarments, I'll give you a hand.'

She smiled at his suggestiveness.

'That's more like it,' he encouraged.

'I do need to get away,' she admitted. 'Reporters have been hanging around outside, and they're likely to go on hounding me. Perhaps I could just stay with you until I sort myself out?'

His handsome face lit with his devastating grin. 'No one will think of looking for you at Ma's. If you can find a better bolt-hole, we'll refund your money.'

She was not friendless after all. Her spirits lifted, and she returned his smile. 'Oh Win, you've made me feel better already. But I still don't understand, why your mother should concern herself about me.'

'You concerned yourself with us,' he reminded her. 'You unselfishly promoted my career.'

His reading of her motives was so generous that she instantly felt ashamed.

'More than that,' he continued, 'Ma has taken a shine to you. She says you remind her of herself at your age. Believe me, she wants to help.'

It was gratifying to find herself liked, particularly after her father's rejection.

Outside, they found no sign of lurking reporters. Even so, Kate feared they might be pursued. As an extra precaution Win drove a circuitous route to Wimbledon and was satisfied that no one had followed them.

Entering the road where the Blakeneys lived, Kate steeled herself. The painted board with gold lettering advertising Caroline Kershaw's little school had been removed. The comfortable private residence that had housed the nursery looked too respectable a setting to have been seminal to such violent events. Only a few short months had elapsed since little Toby's death. In that time both her career and Winston's had been transformed by the intervention of the tabloids, albeit in markedly different directions.

Irene Blakeney's greeting was affectionate. She showed not the least surprise that her visitor came bearing two suitcases. Still smarting from the memory of her father's disapproval, Kate felt envious of Winston. He was so fortunate to have been adopted by such a woman. For the first time in months she realised how much she missed her own mother.

The Blakeney's home was run by a married couple. Kate had not suspected the existence of live-in staff and her circumstances meant that she was more than a little shy about meeting strangers. Understanding her agitation, Irene gave an assurance that Alice and Thomas Avery had been with her for years and could be trusted absolutely.

Alice, the cook-cum-housekeeper, was a busy, bird-like woman of Scottish origin; Thomas, her husband, a jovial Londoner. Kate apologised to them for causing extra work, but Alice would hear none of it. She swiftly produced aired linen and Kate was ensconced in the main attic bedroom.

Like the other floors, the upper storey was tastefully furnished with antiques. From its Regency writing desk to its modern en-suite bathroom, the accommodation provided Kate with everything she could possibly need. Her room was perched at the top of the house and felt like an eyrie. From the tiny window in the gable, she could see the high-rise blocks of Croydon superimposed on the green of the Kent and Surrey countryside beyond.

Her unpacking completed, she rejoined Irene in the sitting room two floors below.

'I'm sorry to banish you to the top of the house,' her hostess apologised, 'but most of the second floor has been requisitioned by Win and Lena as their love-nest.'

The description *love-nest* conjured up the Devon thatch that had been both her heaven and her hell. Kate struggled to return Irene's civilities. 'It's a most comfortable room and the view from the third floor is spectacular. I can't imagine how I will be able to repay your kindness, Mrs Blakeney.'

'I'm so glad you like it. Call me Irene, please,' Irene said, intent on putting Kate at ease. 'There's no need for formality. Your company will be repayment enough. I get bored being on my own, and Winston's career takes him away from home more often these days. When he and Lena are in residence we always dine together and we'd like you to join us. We're a small family and it would give me great pleasure to include you in our little circle.'

It was a gracious invitation that Kate gladly accepted. It was so long since she had felt part of a family.

'We are going to be friends,' Irene declared. 'I am certain of it.'

Kate shared the sentiment. Though formed out of adversity, she sensed that this was to be an important and lasting friendship.

Chapter 25

Kate was apprehensive at the prospect of meeting Lena. She feared that the younger woman would regard her occupation of the Blakeney residence as gate-crashing. Had their roles been reversed, she might have resented the presence of her lover's female friend.

Certainly, Lena had once viewed Kate as competition, but secure in her consummated relationship she could afford to be above such pettiness. Kate's battered face aroused hitherto-unawakened feminist instincts, and the young singer was full of concern for her erstwhile rival. Dinner, therefore, was a companionable occasion. Irene and Kate sat opposite each other, Win and Lena sat side by side.

Kate could not help but notice how frequently the young couple's hands and bodies touched and was envious of the obvious magnetism between them. Irene, clearly delighted about the love-match, beamed her blessing upon them. Kate feigned a similar indulgence. It was a brave response considering her own deprivation. To be included in the warmth of what was essentially a family occasion triggered reminders of the austerity of Michael's present circumstances and the joys of those few harmonious hours they had spent together at the cottage.

Immediately after dinner, the young couple retired

to their quarters. Kate remained with her hostess. The kindness she had received heightened her already emotional state. Such turmoil of mind could not be concealed from Irene, who was a woman of considerable perception.

'Forgive me for saying so, my dear, but I see that you are not happy. From the damage to your face, it's obvious that you've been the victim of an assault. Beyond that, I can only guess what has happened to you. But if it would be of help to talk about it, I can be a very good listener.'

The offer was not made out of curiosity, Kate was sure of that, but from a real desire to help.

It was strange to be so at ease with a woman she barely knew. Perhaps Irene was the confidante she needed. At first hesitant, she began her story. She described her incarceration, and recounted, frankly, both her maltreatment by Michael and the violence of the rape. In talking, she found a relief she would not have believed possible.

At the conclusion of her story, rather than dwelling on her suffering, she embarked on a spirited defence of her captor. 'It's because of me that he's now facing a prison sentence. He was ill and not responsible for his actions; how can it be right to charge him?'

'I suppose that once the police are involved, things have to run their course,' Irene mused.

'That's the awful thing. Once he'd admitted everything to the police, I couldn't protect him. And, of course, the proof was there, in the shuttered room of the cottage: the chair with the harnesses, the handcuffs . . .'

Irene was more than a good listener, she was intelligent enough to recognise the implications of Kate's defence. The girl was hopelessly in love and desperate that her excuses for Michael Kershaw's behaviour should be validated.

'It's hardly to be wondered at that the poor man was driven to such extremes,' she remarked. 'Not after his wife's suicide and his outrageous treatment by the Press.'

Kate blessed her for her understanding. 'You're the first person to appreciate that. Can you believe that the police have even refused him bail?' This was a ruling that Kate found impossible to understand. 'It's not as if Michael is a danger to society. And he has too much at stake in terms of reputation and business interests to contemplate fleeing from justice.'

Irene produced the early edition of *The Flag*. Because the illustrious music critic, Larry Fines, regularly referred to Black Ivory in his columns, Win had set aside his former prejudice and the Blakeneys had become *Flag* readers. Irene read aloud from Jack Brymer's report. 'It says here, "an accomplice is being sought, and further charges are pending." If true, it explains why the police insist on holding him in custody.'

With a heavy heart, Kate realised that Diss and Pearce had chosen to ignore her evidence. 'They're intent on linking Michael with the rapist,' she told Irene, 'and it's all my fault.'

'You mustn't blame yourself. You couldn't prevent him from talking to the police.'

'What can have possessed him to confess so much?' It was the question Kate had been asking herself ever since the interrogation in Okehampton Police station.

'I don't know the man but it strikes me it was an act of deliberate self-destruction. He's guilt-ridden because of what he did to you.'

Kate grasped the significance of Irene's analysis.

'You think he's deliberately seeking punishment to atone for what he did?'

'I do. Most women would be flattered by such a show of devotion. It must mean that he cares for you very much.'

'That's assuming a lot,' Kate brooded. 'You're forgetting that he blames me for his wife's suicide.'

'Yet he made love to you.'

Kate had deliberately withheld the extent of their intimacy. 'What makes you think that he did?'

'Your whole attitude, my dear, you're obviously besotted with him. Was he such a wonderful lover?'

The directness of the personal question surprised her. Old ladies were not supposed to ask such things.

'We made love only once, on that final morning. Then the police came . . .' her voice trembled with emotion, 'before we actually . . .' She shrugged miserably.

'You poor dears, to be denied that solace when you had just discovered your love for each other. How cruel.'

The reference to their love came as a shock. Could something she had refused to admit to herself really be so obvious to an outsider? Kate wondered if Irene could be right about Michael's feelings, but she refused to indulge in what could prove a false hope and rejected the suggestion. 'You know what men are like. It could have been just lust on his part.'

'I would have thought his obvious remorse rules out your lust theory.'

'Perhaps that's what he was expressing – remorse, not love.'

'Time will tell which it is, my dear.'

Irene's platitude was a unwelcome reminder. Time was something Michael would soon be serving. 'He's to be incarcerated because of my investigative journalism. I can't bear to think of that.'

'You were only going about your job and acting professionally,' Irene protested.

'No, that's untrue. What I did was beyond the bounds of professional decency. It was quite despicable.'

'You shouldn't be so hard on yourself.'

'I have to be. Nothing can alter the fact that I had no right to pry into the life of a private individual. It was an invasion of privacy of the worst kind and it led directly to Michael's wife's death. I can never make amends for that.'

Irene brushed aside this negative attitude. 'You can make amends. You must find a way to help him.'

'How am I to do that? The police mounted an operation to find me in Devon, and they want their pound of flesh. You'd think they would be satisfied with Michael's confession, but they aren't. They're intent on connecting him with the rapist.'

'To allege that he masterminded the sexual assault is an heinous allegation,' Irene agreed. 'You've told the police that it's nonsense?'

'Of course I have. I'm the victim, you would think that my evidence would count for something, but it doesn't. Nothing I've said has persuaded them of his innocence. Until they find the real offender, Michael will remain their chief suspect.'

'They can hardly charge him with something as serious as rape without evidence. It would be thrown out of court.'

'What does the further charge matter anyway? Nothing can save him from prison. I'm responsible, yet I go free; he's the victim and is to be punished. Where's the justice in that?'

Irene commiserated. 'It seems to me you have both been punished enough already.'

'But it's worse for Michael. He has to survive a prison sentence.'

'From what you've told me about him, I imagine that strength of character will carry him through. That and the knowledge he has your support.'

Kate saw the empty years looming ahead. 'Even if he does care for me, what future can there be for us if he's sent to prison?'

'It might not come to that. After all, there are extenuating circumstances, and he has a previously unblemished record. What he needs is a good defence lawyer.'

Kate grasped the life-line Irene had thrown. 'Do you think there's a chance the sentence will be suspended?'

Immediately, Irene regretted her optimism. If it were to prove false then the outcome would be all the harder for Kate to bear. 'If he is sent to prison, we'll pray his sentence will be a light one.'

Kate had no faith in prayer. 'I'm not a religious person.'

'Then put your trust in the power of love.' Irene turned to practicalities. 'Now . . . you must visit him. Tell him what you told me. Tell him that you love him.'

'I couldn't do that, not without knowing my feelings are returned.'

The older woman's sound good sense would have no truck with negative attitudes. 'It's important you express your feelings.'

Kate said nothing.

Next morning, Irene and Kate breakfasted alone. Playing the night clubs meant that sleeping late had become a habit for Win and Lena.

'I have a suspicion that sleeping is rather

euphemistic for what they get up to in the mornings,' Irene chuckled.

Thinking of the antics that those beautiful black bodies were engaged in immediately above their heads proved not half so disturbing to Kate as what was emblazoned on the front page of the morning paper. Unfolding it, she was confronted with front-page twin portraits of herself.

The published photographs were those taken when Colson had gatecrashed her flat on the previous day. One showed her full face with swollen lip and downcast eyes. The other was in profile and emphasised the lump above her eye. Both looked as if they had been touched-up to exaggerate her injuries. But it was the nature of the headline that made her catch her breath: *Torture on Dartmoor, My Torment by* Flag *Reporter, Kate Rider*.

She read on in disbelief. The article, purporting to be written by her, alleged abduction and incarceration in a Dartmoor "prison". Rape and systematic torture were implied. A separate column, on the same page, reported less emotionally that Michael Christopher Kershaw, aged 35, partner in the well known city architects, Campbell, Kershaw and Mather, was charged with offences relating to the abduction of *Flag* journalist, Kate Rider. Bail had been refused as other charges were pending.

Kate, her face drained of blood, let the paper fall. Irene manoeuvred the wheelchair to be at her side.

'What is it, Kate. What has that scandal sheet of yours done now?'

'They've named Michael. And look—' She displayed the front-page photographs and headline. 'I didn't give them any of this. How dare they use my name!'

Irene read in silence, then suggested, 'You need legal advice. Shall I call my lawyer?'

'I can't take on *The Flag;* I couldn't afford the litigation. Which is precisely what they're counting on. Besides, if I did challenge them over this, it would mean even more publicity. Either way the paper wins.'

'So they know there's nothing to prevent them from getting away with it.' Irene's eyes flashed with indignation. 'The cheapskates!'

Kate was close to tears. 'Oh, Irene, what will he think of me?'

'Michael? You must try to see him, to explain.'

Kate made a helpless gesture. 'I drafted a letter for him last night, but this dreadful rubbish makes a mockery of everything I wrote.'

'You must convince him that this article has nothing to do with you.'

'Why should he believe me? Look at the evidence – apparently I've even provided photographs.'

'But this is evil.' Irene thumped the table with her fist. 'You're an employee, how can they treat you like this?'

'It's precisely because I'm employed by them that they're able to do it.'

'Then you should disassociate yourself from them as soon as possible.'

Where had it all gone so wrong? To be a journalist was all she had ever wanted. Friendship, marriage, a home, babies, none of those could compete with the excitement of her chosen career. She had courted fame, had dreamed of seeing her name prominent in print – a wish that had now been granted, though not in the way she hoped.

'My value as a journalist used to rest on my writing ability. *The Flag*'s reduced it to the selling power of my personal notoriety.'

Irene repeated her previous advice, 'Disassociate yourself from them, my dear. Do it today.'

Irene was right, never could she forgive the false attribution of these awful, first-person revelations. But tendering her resignation meant ending her career. Colson was vindictive. He would use his influence to ensure that she never worked as a journalist again.

Overtaken by events, her first letter to Michael was scrapped. The one she eventually sent was full of apologies and excuses. It lacked the spontaneity and affection of her earlier attempt. She might have been writing to a stranger.

The reply came, not from the recipient of her letter but from his solicitor. *The Flag* article had done for her. It had convinced Michael she was not to be trusted and her offer of help was spurned. Apparently it was not Mr Kershaw's intention to pervert the course of justice. There was no acknowledgement of her solemn assurance that she had neither written the latest article attributed to her, nor given permission for it to appear under her name. The solicitor's letter ended with a curt dismissal: *It is my client's wish that you desist from any further attempt to communicate with him.* To be so summarily rejected caused her the deepest trauma yet.

Up until now, for Michael's sake, she had found the inner strength to engineer an outer calm. To help his cause, she wanted to be the living proof that he had done her no lasting harm, so she had pretended that her mind was healing as fast as her physical injuries. But the solicitor's letter destroyed all that. Her confidence and the false facade of serenity were demolished.

Chapter 26

Colson was in a black humour. He stormed into Jack Brymer's office, brandishing Kate's letter of resignation.

'Did you know the little tart was going to do this?' he demanded.

Brymer was in no mood to be bullied. 'If you want to talk to me, you'd better go outside, knock on the door and start again.'

Colson literally snarled. 'Don't come all high-handed with me, Jack. If you'd handled this one properly, Rider would have been happy to pour her heart out to our readers. Instead she's bloody resigned.'

'She's *what*?'

'You didn't know? You really ought to keep a tighter rein on your woman.'

Jack had no intention of admitting to Colson that Kate wasn't and never had been his woman.

'If she's had enough then you're the fool whose driven her to it,' he accused. 'Did you really think you could get away with putting that dross out under her name?' He reached for the letter. 'What does she say?'

The letter of resignation was brief and to the point: Kate's contract expired in sixteen days and she was not prepared to renew it. Due to the trauma of recent events, she was unfit to undertake her normal duties and consequently would not be returning to work. It was the second paragraph that had made Colson wild: in it, she threatened the news-desk editor with legal action if he printed any more scurrilous material under her name.

Jack threw the letter back at him. 'What did you expect?'

Ignoring the question, Colson posed one of his own and then proceeded to answer it himself. 'You see what she intends to do? It's obvious, the cow's going to sell her story to the highest bidder and she knows that *The Flag* will have to join the auction. Christ, this is going to be expensive. We can't let one of our competitors buy her, we'd be a laughing stock.'

'You've got it wrong. Kate's not interested in money. She certainly wouldn't put herself up for sale as you suggest.'

Colson snorted his disbelief. 'You may be soft on the woman but you don't know what you're talking about. She'll be open to offers all right. It's vital we get to her before the opposition does. Competition will put up the price.'

'You're talking nonsense, that isn't Kate's style.'

'Style! Don't make me laugh. She was happy enough to perform on the casting couch for me. She can be bought, all right.'

Jack smarted at the casting couch reference. Though he doubted that Kate would have been so obliging to her insufferable editor, he entertained just enough doubt to feel insanely jealous. He clenched his fist and wished he had the nerve to plant it in Kevin's disagreeable face.

'She's pissed off with you, Kev, that's what her resignation is about.'

'Where the hell is she, that's what I'd like to know? She's not at her flat.'

'Why ask me, it's you she works for?' Even had he known Kate's whereabouts, Jack wouldn't have helped him.

'Come on, Jack, you chased across the country to rescue her. You're her Sir Galahad, she'll negotiate with you.'

'I don't know where she is.'

It was the truth, but he would be damned before betraying her to Colson.

'You could find her, you did before,' Colson wheedled.

'Sod off, Kevin. If the girl's disappeared, it's because she wants to be left alone. If you want to seduce her with your cheque book, you'll have to wait until she surfaces.'

'Haven't you been listening?' Colson yelped. 'Once she's out in the open every publication in the country will be on to her.'

'So, she's going to make herself rich. Good luck to her.'

'You're refusing to help?'

'I'm a crime reporter not your gofer. If you want her so badly, find her yourself.'

Despite his words, Jack had considerable interest in discovering Kate's whereabouts. But his search would be conducted as a piece of private enterprise, not under the banner of *The Flag*. Apart from anything else, she needed to be protected from Colson.

The Blakeney home was Kate's refuge from any further incursions by the media and particularly from her own ex-boss. But though she wanted to hide, she could not disappear altogether. The police still had a case to prepare for the judiciary and she had given her promise to inform Inspector Diss of her movements. The policeman understood her desire to escape media attention and gave his word that her whereabouts would remain confidential.

'Don't worry, the last thing I want to do is bring the press corps to Mrs Blakeney's door-step. But what about Jack? He'll be anxious about you. We don't want him instigating another nation-wide search.'

Nick Diss was not the man to ignore a debt and, over the years, Brymer had excelled as a useful informant. *The Flag's* chief crime reporter had proved himself a good friend to the girl too. He had looked out for her and tried to protect her. He deserved to be trusted with Kate's whereabouts.

'I'm sorry, Inspector, ' Kate said firmly, 'but I must insist you withhold my address from Jack too.' Kate regretted the disappointment this would cause and did not need to be reminded how much she owed Jack. She had forgiven both his interference and his recent rough treatment, understanding only too well, the cause of his violence towards her. But she could never be more to him than a friend to him and wanted to avoid further embarrassment.

Jack received the news of Kate's wish to remain incommunicado without emotion but Nick Diss was not fooled. Jack's pretended lack of interest could not conceal the hurt in his eyes. No one was more surprised than Diss that Jack Brymer, professed misogynist, had fallen so heavily for the girl. Usually, he avoided relationships; the only other woman to walk out on him had been his wife and then his reaction had been pure relief. This was different. Kate seemed to have become an obsession.

Her absence left Jack with a painful longing that manifested itself as indigestion and a lack of concentration. The sight of her partially naked and abused body had merely made things worse. Often in his fantasies he undressed her, but in contrast to the sadist who had inflicted those injuries, he loved her with a protective tenderness. If she would have him, he would be prepared to settle down with her.

His hunt for Kate started with her father but, on the telephone, Robin Rider was more concerned for his wife than for his abused daughter.

'You must appreciate all this has been a terrible blow for my wife. No one likes to be associated with scandal.'

Jack interrupted with some sympathetic noises. 'But have you heard from your daughter?' he asked.

'Kate telephoned from London and admitted that she was in some sort of trouble with that Kershaw chap. She warned me that the press had got hold of it, but was too inconsiderate to give any details of what had happened. Can you imagine what a shock it was for me and my family to find out about her abduction and rape from the newspapers?'

There was nothing to be gained from getting into an argument so Jack concurred. 'That was thoughtless of her.'

'Precisely. It was selfish too, she must have realised the worry it would cause.'

'Do you know where she might be staying at the moment?' This was the million dollar question. Even as he asked, Jack knew that he would not be lucky.

'We've no idea where she is. There's no answer when I call her number, so I assume she's gone away. If you do discover where she is, perhaps you could ask her to have the decency to get in touch.'

Hanging up, Jack could well understand why Kate had not looked to her parent for succour in her time of need.

His next approach was to Kate's landlord. He was willing enough to talk, but knew only that Miss

Rider's rent was paid up until the middle of the next month.

'In the terms of our agreement, there has to be a month's notice on both sides to end the tenancy. You don't think that she'd try to get out of that by doing a moonlight flit, do you?' He sounded worried.

Jack was just about to give an assurance of Kate's honesty when he thought the better of it.

'It might be wise to find out if her personal things are still at the flat,' he advised.

The suggestion that his tenant might indeed have done a flit, worried the landlord.

'Perhaps I should go around there to check?'

Jack had achieved the result he wanted. 'Good idea, better safe than sorry. Would you mind if I came with you? If her possessions are still there, they might throw light on where she's gone, and that's information that would be useful to us both.'

Unfortunately, the flat offered up no such clues. The landlord was relieved to find that its cupboards and drawers still contained items belonging to his tenant. Jack, trained in observation, noticed but did not mention the cleared dressing table-top, the absence of suitcases and the surprising amount of free hanging-space in the wardrobe. The radio that had been left playing at the time of her abduction was missing. All the evidence pointed to a planned lengthy absence.

Jack had to wait until Kevin was attending a meeting on another site before he extended his search to the workplace.

'What's happened to Kate's files and personal belongings? he asked Charlie.

'Still on her computer and in her filing cabinet, nothing's been touched.' Charlie hesitated. 'Well that's not quite true, Colson's been through everything with a fine tooth comb. Whatever he was looking for he didn't find, his temper made that obvious. What are you after?

'The same thing as he was, so I guess there's no point in looking again. I'd appreciate it if you didn't mention my interest to Colson.'

'Sure, and if you see Kate, tell her I miss her.'

Jack was missing her too, more than he could ever have imagined, but he was not into sharing confidences about it.

Nick Diss possessed the information on Kate's bolthole. Jack approached him as a last resort.

'I suppose you couldn't be persuaded to give me just a hint of where Kate might be?'

'Sorry, I'm not at liberty to say.'

'At least tell me if she's still in London.'

'Sorry, Jack, no can do.'

Jack was close to losing his temper. 'You pisser, Diss. At least deliver a message for me, you can do that. Tell her I'm here if she needs anything, she only has to call.'

The message he would have really liked to send was far too personal to be entrusted to a lousy copper.

Having distanced herself from Jack, Kate was developing a closer relationship with Irene Blakeney. Despite the difference in their ages they derived pleasure in each other's company and Irene urged her guest to stay for as long as it suited her. Kate accepted the extension of hospitality with gratitude. In her present frame of mind she needed a safe haven.

That Michael's rebuff had come, indirectly, via a formal letter from his solicitor, signified just how repulsive she had become to the man she loved. Her growing belief that all chance of happiness was destroyed induced a depression that descended like a dark cloud. She would have succumbed to it had not Irene taken her well-being in hand. The cheerful paraplegic was a natural psychologist, providing support without sympathy, denying Kate's right to feel sorry for herself.

Before Irene's accident, Alice had been the Blakeney's only full-time employee. After the smash, Irene's subsequent confinement to the wheelchair meant that she needed a man about the house. Alice's husband, Thomas, fitted the bill, for the couple were already resident in the basement flat. Thomas had been lured away from his regular employment, and upgraded from occasional handyman to permanent property manager-cum-chauffeur. At the time Kate came to stay, the housekeeper and her husband were in their late fifties. They had shared a home with their employer for so long that their relationship with her was an easy one. With Kate's consent, they had been entrusted with the truth of her identity. The couple at once became her allies, and were soon on first name terms.

Thomas' services enabled Irene to make regular sorties into the outside world.

Her most frequent excursions with him were into the West End. She encouraged Kate to join these outings.

Feeling too insecure to risk a public appearance, Kate declined. 'With my picture splashed all over the tabloids, I could so easily be recognised.'

Irene had an answer for every argument. 'Nonsense, my dear. You know what they say about losing oneself in a crowd? Well, the West End is the most crowded place I know.'

'I'd love to come, but what if I bump into someone

who knows me? I don't want my ex-editor tracking me down.'

Irene, however, was not to be thwarted. 'What would you say to a disguise.'

The suggestion was so delightfully cloak and dagger that it made Kate laugh.

'When I'm done, even your best friend won't know you.' Irene promised.

Such a whimsical scheme would have added spice to any adventure and, even in her less-than-frivolous state of mind, Kate could not resist the challenge. It was diverting to paint over the natural shade of her lips with Irene's brightly coloured lip-gloss, to don flat shoes, a garish head scarf and dark glasses. The outfit she wore had once been Irene's. It came from a wardrobe that she dubbed her "Active-legs Collection" and comprised the clothes she had worn before her accident.

The transformation was very effective. Kate declared that she had been 'radically reconstructed.'

Irene immediately borrowed these initials to dub Kate, 'Rhoda Radcliffe, my radically reconstructed companion.'

The change of appearance proved liberating in more than a physical sense. In the guise of Rhoda, Kate rediscovered the art of living. Delighted that the metamorphosis was proving so therapeutic, Irene insisted on developing it a stage further. At a very snooty Mayfair wigmakers, to an accompaniment of disrespectful giggles, Kate's sleek brunette bob was transformed into Rhoda's crowning, auburn glory. In this new persona, Kate went forth into the public world, of shops, theatres, concerts, restaurants and mingled with *Flag* readers, with complete anonymity. Irene devised a programme of amusements and diversions that left the younger woman little time to dwell on her wretchedness.

Kate felt undeserving of such attentiveness and more than a little ashamed. Measured against the permanent loss of independent mobility that was Irene's lot, her own lost love did not amount to much. At least, this was how she tried to reason. At an emotional level she felt very differently.

With some of her previous tenacity recovered, Kate turned her attention to looking for a job. Tactfully, she announced her intention over dinner.

'Do you have to, dear?' Irene protested. 'I so enjoy your company, and with my children soon off to Hollywood to become film stars . . .'

'Hardly stars, Ma,' Winston interrupted. 'We have singing, not speaking, parts. The movie is set around a night-club, and we're the background floor-show, that's all.'

'It will be madness for a Hollywood director to hide our lovely Lena away in the background. But I'll thank you not to interrupt me, when I'm propositioning Kate. I'm a selfish old woman and I don't want to be left on my own for six weeks.'

'And Kate is too unselfish to leave you, I'm sure.'

Winston's assertion was embarrassing. Although she was living with the Blakeneys, she still had her own flat to pay for and no income to meet that or her other bills.

'I won't desert you, Irene, but I do need to earn my living. I still have the rent to pay on my Holland Park flat.'

'Give it up, my dear, make your home with us. The attic floor will be unoccupied if you leave. Where's the sense in that?'

Lena, too, encouraged her to stay on. 'You're indispensable. We're getting more engagements all the time and we don't like to think of Ma being on her own.'

It was all nonsense, of course. Kate was not at all necessary to Irene's well-being. Alice and Thomas would make sure that their employer was never left alone. Kate suspected that the suggestion was intended more for her benefit than Irene's. After such a generous show of hospitality, it was embarrassing to explain her need to be financially viable.

'I'd love to stay on, but I can't live on your charity for ever. I have to find a job.'

Irene was thoughtful for a moment. 'You're a professional woman, Kate, one who values her independence. I won't insult by asking you to become a full-time Rhoda Radcliffe, but, there is a compromise you could make.'

Kate indicated that she was open to suggestions and Irene volunteered one.

'Why not operate freelance? You could write from here as well as anywhere.'

It was an idea Kate had been toying with. The consummate writer had been suffering withdrawal symptoms. 'You're right, of course. It would be best to stick to what I know.'

Irene had not finished. 'In return for your company, I could offer board and lodgings. Plus, of course, a dress allowance as befits the scintillating Rhoda. I don't expect an answer now, think it over and tell me later when you've had time to consider.'

Winston hugged his mother. 'Brilliant as usual, Ma. I think Kate has just been made an offer she can't refuse.'

It was not a difficult decision: the Blakeneys had adopted her and she them. Without a career to sustain her, a return to a solitary existence in the

Holland Park flat was unthinkable. And looming over everything was the prospect of the judgement on Michael; she did not want to face that ordeal alone.

Chapter 27

Win and Lena departed for Hollywood as planned. Irene saw them off without a qualm but Kate was apprehensive. The pair had undoubted talent, but essentially Black Ivory's success was down to Larry Fines. A tabloid newspaper had made them, and it or another could just as easily break them. Her own rise and fall proved that. When there was an opportunity for a sensational story guaranteed to sell more copy, no one was immune from press exploitation. If circumstances went against them, Win and Lena would be sold down the river too.

In London, Kate and Irene settled into a happy coexistence that was far from routine. Kate found the energy of the septuagenarian quite challenging, for almost every day Thomas took them on a fresh excursion. She appreciated that most of these ventures were undertaken for her own rehabilitation. Irene was far from the "selfish old woman" she pretended to be.

Even in this busy schedule, time was set aside so that Kate might pursue her writing. To begin with these sessions were sterile. She had little enthusiasm for the computer keyboard and missed the extensive resources available to a national daily. Previously, writing had been the reason for her existence; it was not an exaggeration to say that she had lived to write. In her changed circumstances, she needed to write to live and it altered her perception of her skills.

'I don't know what's happened to me,' she told Irene. 'I can't afford an attack of writer's block.'

'How do you normally begin?' Irene asked.

'I research a topic of current interest. But it's a different ball-game being free-lance. It's essential to know what the markets are, what style of material is likely to sell.'

'We'll send Thomas to buy a copy of every woman's magazine at the newsagents. Will that help you research your markets?'

Grateful for Irene's practical good sense, Kate accepted the offer.

Immersing herself in the world of the glossies and weeklies, she was relieved to find that her analytical skills had not deserted her. It was easy enough to identify what type of material would sell where. But a problem still remained, and she attempted to explain it to Irene.

'I've run out of fresh ideas. My creativity seems to have been suspended.'

Staring at the keys of her laptop, all she could think about was the imminent sentencing of the man she loved. Her favourite indulgence was to imagine that the police had never arrived at the cottage that morning. That there had been no interruption to prevent the consummation they had both desired.

If they had stayed together at the cottage, their days would have been spent exploring the moor, their nights reserved for exploring their love. Each union would have been sweeter than the last. Sometimes, she imagined their relationship as a marital one. But such fancies were of little comfort, serving only to intensify her frustration.

When, eventually, she did begin to write, it was not as a freelance journalist but as an autobiographer.

Obsessed with her feelings for Michael, she wrote about them, introspectively analysing her tangled emotions. His abuse had driven her to the point of suicide, but there was no self-deceit in the awakening she remembered.

That last morning at the cottage, cut, bruised and battered from another man's rape, she had desired him with an intensity that was unique in her experience. From out of her thoughts about Michael the words began to flow.

Living in such close proximity, it occurred to Kate that something of a mystery surrounded her elderly friend. Irene was an intelligent, witty, well-informed and generous woman; qualities that made her wonderful company. The strange thing was that, other than the people who served her in a professional capacity, she appeared to have few friends. Her doctor, bank manager, hairdresser, masseur and, of course, Alice and Thomas were her intimates. Apart from these people and an occasional visit from Lena's mother, no callers came to the house.

They were relaxing in Irene's sitting room when Kate tentatively broached the subject. 'Please don't let my presence in the house keep your friends at bay. If you'd like to entertain, I'll be quite happy to retreat upstairs to my room.'

'If I had guests, you would be one of them,' Irene assured her. 'You could don your wig and come to the feast as Rhoda.'

Irene's response was so natural and free of embarrassment, that Kate pursued the topic. 'Let's do it then. I enjoy playing Rhoda and it will be a chance for me to perfect the part.' She meant it, there was an escapism in dressing up. For a brief time she could shake off some of Kate Rider's pain.

'Are you finding it too lonely here?'

Kate protested at such a ridiculous suggestion. 'How could I be lonely in the company of someone as outgoing as you are. You've revitalised my life.'

'It's kind of you to flatter me, my dear, but mine is very limited company. I suppose you must wonder why I am a comparative recluse within these four walls.'

Kate had not expected such directness. 'I did wonder why you have so few visitors, but it's really none of my business.' Not so many weeks ago, as a journalist, she reflected ruefully, everything had been her business.

'You're living under my roof now; that gives you the right to know. Let me explain.' Irene manoeuvred her wheelchair. 'A large sherry is called for, it will help in the telling.'

The electric wheelchair was state of the art and it turned on a sixpence to propel her to the cocktail cabinet. She poured large doubles of the pale Fino, serving them in beautiful Jacobean wine glasses.

'You see, my dear, I did something a quarter of a century ago that ostracised me from decent society.'

Kate wondered if this was one of Irene's jokes. 'I find that hard to believe.'

'Who knows what we are capable of. Look at Michael Kershaw, successful architect and upright citizen, who turns abductor and ill-treats a young woman. Look at Kate Rider, beautiful, accomplished, self-sufficient yet falls hopelessly in love with the man responsible for her degradation.'

Kate looked down.

'I'm sorry,' Irene said, contrite. 'That was uncalled for, but it might help you understand.'

'I'd be flattered to be entrusted with your secret,' Kate said, intrigued. 'If you care to share it.'

* * *

Irene was born into the Anglo-Irish aristocracy, the only child of a youngest son. Declining fortunes meant that the family estate could support only his eldest brother, so her father became a career officer in the British Army. He married the daughter of the colonel of his regiment, but his young wife died in childbirth on the Indian sub-continent. Irene was brought up by a succession of Ayahs. Eventually her maternal grandparents intervened and insisted that she be subjected to the civilising influence of an English boarding-school education.

The children of her previous acquaintance had all been the offspring of native servants so that school in England had been a cultural shock. As a schoolgirl, she was both daring and attractive. Her keen sense of fun ensured that she swiftly achieved popularity with her peers. School days had been happy, and she was surprised to find that her teachers regarded her as clever. Her academic prowess meant she could get away with pranks that would have brought the wrath of authority on those less intellectually endowed.

An Oxford scholarship followed, but the war intervened. She donned a uniform, joined Intelligence and served in the bowels of the War Office. After the war, she returned to her studies and finally graduated in 1947. An academic career beckoned.

Despite her independence and the wartime opportunities, she had reached the age of twenty four, still sexually inexperienced. This swiftly altered when she met a devastatingly handsome father-figure, a visiting professor from Connecticut.

The existence of a wife in America and the considerable difference in their ages did not impede them. They threw themselves into a torrid affair.

Unwilling to trust to fate as her partner was prepared to do, Irene pinned her faith on Marie Stopes, but in her case that pioneer of birth control proved fallible. In the austere post-war period it was unacceptable for a single woman of her social station to have a baby. Before returning to America and his wife, her lover paid for an illegal abortion.

Presently she met Harry, a wealthy business man, quite different from the dons and academics of her acquaintance.

When she introduced her late husband into the story, Irene's eyes wandered to the large portrait in oils that hung above the fireplace. It was a board-room portrait, showing a man at his desk, stern and remote, but Kate knew, from the evidence of the silver-framed photographs on Irene's dressing table, that Harry-at-home was neither of these things. He was smiling and warm and looked adoringly upon his wife. It was this version of Harry that Irene's continuing narrative confirmed.

He was not as handsome as her American professor, but younger and far more romantic. He courted, wooed and won her. Yet not until their honeymoon was booked did they anticipate their legal union. Their marital home, a splendid period house in Regent's Park, was a happy one, for theirs was a love match.

There was no reason to postpone a family. Whenever they made love, which was frequently, she wondered if this was the beginning of their first child. When, after a year, she had failed to become pregnant, she began to worry. She consulted an eminent gynaecologist who ascertained that her abortion had been botched. She was no longer capable of producing a child.

Harry knew nothing about her abortion. She was

obliged to confess both her past shame and its present consequences in the same breath. She loved him too much to hold him to his marriage vows. When she offered him his freedom, he was hurt and angry. His hurt was not because she had deceived him, nor was his anger directed at her inability to provide an heir. He suffered because she believed his love to be so shallow that such circumstances could alter his devotion.

Their childless marriage was fulfilled in other ways. She repaid his generosity with an unstinting loyalty and companionship; gracing his formal occasions with wit and charm, and playing his whore in the privacy of their bedroom. They were faithful through twenty-one years of marriage. They never ceased to want each other, and the eroticism of their love-making did not diminish.

Harry's premature death from a sudden heart attack was a loss too great to endure. It seemed impossible that the widow, still youthful, some said beautiful, could live on without him. Friends came to rally her. Shockingly, several of her dead husband's friends offered solace of a very physical nature. She despised them.

On the first anniversary of her husband's death, a conversation with her daily-help changed her life. Winnie, an amusing West Indian, had been with her for years. She was a single parent, and, in the school holidays, brought her small daughter to work with her. Irene grew fond of Marsha, Winnie's little girl, and missed her when she grew to independence.

Eventually Winnie found a new man, who wanted to marry her. Clive was a fine fellow, not a no-good scoundrel like her previous men friends. He was a skilled workman, in a well-paid trade. His brother had set up his own building company in the USA and

Winnie's beau had obtained a work permit to join him there. All that was keeping him in England was Winnie's promise to go with him as his wife. This should have been good news, but Marsha got herself pregnant, and was determined to keep her baby. Unfortunately, American immigration were not keen to hand out visas to unmarried mothers and their offspring. It seemed that the daughter's misfortune would spoil the mother's opportunity.

Without pausing to consider, Irene offered to adopt Marsha, promising to look after both the young woman and her unborn baby. In considering this proposal, Winnie was torn between love for her daughter and her love for Clive. But aware that Mrs Blakeney's patronage would bring undoubted benefits to both daughter and grandchild, she agreed to the arrangement. Marsha was grateful to Irene for she did not want to be responsible for denying her mother a chance of happiness. So Winnie crossed the Atlantic to be with her man in Philadelphia, and Marsha moved into the Regent's Park house.

Five months later, Irene was present at Winston's birth. The surge of joy she felt when holding him expanded into an overwhelming love. In those first moments, she knew that she had to share this beautiful black baby on equal terms with his natural mother. She wanted him to be her son too.

It was to Irene that Win spoke his first "Mama". Blessed with two mothers, the little boy differentiated by calling the younger one "Mummy". Irene remained Mama, ultimately becoming "Ma". Both women delighted in the child, but their love nurtured rather than spoilt him.

Irene's friends were disapproving. They did not like being neglected, and could not understand her preoccupation with a black girl and her illegitimate baby.

Because a boy would need a large garden for his play, Irene sold the elegant period house with its views over Regent's Park and bought the more modern, spacious property in Wimbledon. The basement provided a staff flat for Alice and her husband Thomas.

Winston flourished, growing from cuddly baby into an affectionate child. It was around the time of his third birthday that Marsha acquired a new suitor. Irene realised with dread that the stability of her little family was threatened. Terrified of losing both Marsha and her son, she was obliged to act. She considered bribery, for she possessed wealth enough to buy off any number of Marsha's would-be lovers, but it seemed a dishonourable course.

'Instead, I wooed Marsha myself.'

Her listener's reaction to this statement did not go unnoticed.

'You think it unlikely that a woman in her fifties could win a sweet girl of twenty-one from a virile young man? It was not so very difficult. Marsha already loved me and we'd always been physically demonstrative. It was easy to push these demonstrations of love into something more intimate.'

Kate was startled by the revelation. 'You became *lovers*?'

'In every sense of that word.' Irene was proud of her conquest. 'I had one tremendous advantage over her boyfriend. I was a woman, familiar with what gives women most pleasure. I became so expert that I could make Marsha's body sing. Marsha was a mother, but no man had succeeded in awakening her sexuality. I did that. After all,' she added wickedly, 'a prosthesis has one big advantage over the real thing –

it doesn't wither and can perform all night if necessary.'

'Did Marsha realise that you became her lover in order to secure Winston for yourself?' It was not the lesbian relationship, but its motive that disturbed Kate.

'Did I give the impression that it was only Winston I wanted? My possessiveness extended to his mother. I loved Marsha, too. I admit that ulterior motive drove me to become her lover, but I soon rejoiced in that role. She was a lovely girl, and I did not have to pretend the pleasure her body gave me. I looked a lot younger than my age, and Marsha returned my attentions. In every sense she became my partner, as dear to me as Harry. I was victorious, the suitor was sent packing. But there was a price to pay.'

Irene paused to top-up their glasses.

'I think I can guess what that was. Your affair must have been difficult to keep secret.'

'Not difficult, my dear, impossible. And it was no ordinary lesbian relationship. My lover was my own adopted daughter. I was ostracised. A series of ugly letters arrived by post. With a rather flawed logic, they accused me of practising incest with my *black whore of an unnatural daughter*. A few friends stood by me, but their support did not include Marsha, and so, in the end, I alienated them too. Husbands were the worst: they felt threatened and ordered their wives to have nothing to do with me. I became persona non grata. But I was proud, I turned my back on them all. No, not quite all, there was one, Imogen Peters, a friend from those far-off schooldays, who stuck by me. She suffered as a consequence.'

'Where is Imogen now?' Kate asked, 'I'd like to meet her.'

'She died last year. I miss her dreadfully. After the

accident she was an absolute brick. Do you know, I was so busy mourning Marsha's death that the loss of my legs seemed insignificant. It was the other way round for Winston. He was so preoccupied with my spinal injuries that he was spared the worse grief of bereavement. He was only a boy, barely seventeen, when we lost his mother yet, at that dark time, he repaid all the love I'd cherished on him, and with interest.'

'Did Win know the extent of your relationship with Marsha?' Kate wondered aloud.

'How could he not – we shared the same bed for fourteen years. To him, our fond behaviour was entirely natural, we were a family. When he was old enough to understand, we told him that what we shared was a physical love. Our explanations caused him no concern, we had raised him to believe that all love is beautiful.'

Kate declared her approval. 'I think that's wonderful.'

'So, you see, Kate, it's no exaggeration to say I was cast-out from decent society. My so-called friends deserted me a long time ago. It's a state I became accustomed to. I have since become very selective in my companions, which is why we see so few visitors.'

Kate felt honoured that Irene had shared such confidences. It meant that she was numbered among the select few whom Irene considered friends.

'It's a privilege to be told your story. I'm sorry that people were so bigoted and didn't understand, but it was their loss,' she told Irene.

'Thank you for saying so, my dear, but I didn't tell you my history to make you miserable.'

Kate's eyes had filled with tears. She was not in the least embarrassed to accept the comfort of Irene's embrace.

It was not the tragedy of Irene's life that made Kate weep, but the abundance of its fulfilment. She had enjoyed three great passions: love for her husband, so intense that she could allow no other man to step into his shoes, love for Marsha, so complete that she had willingly sacrificed her place in society to preserve it, and love for Winston that was ongoing and unselfish.

The affection for Win, Kate had witnessed at first hand. She saw how the elderly woman's eyes lit up when he entered the room; she heard the pleasure, unmistakable in her voice, whenever he telephoned, and her obvious pride whenever she spoke of him.

It seemed to Kate that Irene was capable of commitment and had a capacity for loving that was lacking in herself. As a child she had loved her parents as much as any child might. She still could not think about her mother without missing her. Yet her love for her father had not stood the test of his second marriage because she was jealous of his involvement with his new wife's family.

Irene spoke freely of passion and erotic love. There had been little of either in her own life. Sex had never driven her in the way that it drove others of her acquaintance. Not that she was frigid, she found love-making pleasurable enough, but her response had always lacked sincerity. The sexual act provided her with little more satisfaction than could be obtained from the enjoyment of delicious food and a fine wine. No sex ever matched that pumping of adrenalin when chasing a good story. No post-coital relief ever so sweet as seeing her own articles in print. She used to wonder if there was something wrong with her.

Michael, had been the first man to make her want

to give everything of herself. That was what made his rejection so painful.

She wept at Irene's story because it made her feel so much less of a woman than the elderly cripple who had told it. She had never given of herself completely to another person as Irene Blakeney had done, nor did she possess Irene's capacity for other kinds of love. Her affection for Winston did not preclude his mother from caring for others. Already she was devoted to Lena, while Alice and Thomas were treated with an affection that elevated them far above the status of mere employees. And to herself, a relative stranger, Irene had responded to her needs and extended the sort of unselfish friendship she had never before experienced.

Kate regretted her own inadequacies, the selfishness that for all her adult life had made her put career before people. Even her two long-term lovers had not remained her friends. Now her career was in ruins and she was left with nothing. She mourned what she had never had. Her sadness went much deeper, for it was accompanied by the gnawing belief that with Michael she could have found a love as intense and as all-encompassing as Irene's for Harry and Marsha. The loss of his love would impoverish her life forever.

Chapter 28

The call came through to Jack's office just before mid-day on Monday.

'Mr Brymer? This is Anthony Parsons. You asked me to phone if there was any news.'

It had been several weeks, and the name meant nothing to Jack. 'Sorry, did you say Parsons?'

'Yes, I'm Kate Rider's landlord.'

Jack felt a tingling at the base of his skull. 'You've seen her? Is she back?'

'No, that's why I'm calling. She was in touch by telephone to say that she would be moving out. There was no problem, she's paid the rent in full, in lieu of notice.'

'When does she plan to collect her possessions from the flat?'

'Oh, they've gone, everything was taken away last week.'

Jack cursed under his breath. 'Last week? And you've only just found out?'

'Not exactly. I met with Miss Rider's representative when the flat was being cleared.'

Jack struggled to control his temper. 'But if that happened a week ago, why have you left it so late to phone me?'

'I'm sorry. I misplaced the business card you gave me, and it's only just turned-up.'

The bloody fool knew he worked for *The Flag*, he

was hardly ex-directory. Despite the frustration, he made an effort to remain polite. 'You mentioned her representative – do you remember his name?'

'It was a woman, and I made a special note of it – a Mrs Radcliffe.'

That it was a woman came as a relief. If Kate was shacked-up with a girlfriend, there was hope for him yet.

'Do you have a telephone number, or a forwarding address?'

'No, I did ask for one, so that mail could be sent on, you understand. But Mrs Radcliffe was unable to provide one. Apparently, Miss Rider expects to be moving around.'

'What about the Radcliffe woman, do you have her number?'

Of course the idiot didn't, all he could provide was a description.

'Mrs Radcliffe was a very attractive woman – young, elegantly dressed and with a striking head of auburn hair.'

'What transport did she use?'

'She came in a new Mercedes. The man drove.'

'Man? You didn't mention a man. Was he the husband?'

'He wasn't introduced, but I doubt it. He was much older, with more than a trace of cockney accent. At first I thought he must be a chauffeur, but they seemed very chummy, as if he had come along to help her as a favour. I distinctly remember her calling him Thomas.'

It wasn't much, but it gave him something to go on.

Jack spent the rest of the day ringing every Radcliffe in the London telephone directory. He began with the entries that carried the initial T, and then continued with the rest. At every number that answered, he drew a blank. Only at a single house, did a Mrs Radcliffe admit to having striking auburn hair, but that was in her youth, before the ageing process had turned it grey. After this disappointing lack of success, he started working his way through the directories for the home counties.

Jack wasn't the type of man to make a fool of himself over a woman, not even one as attractive as Kate. After the divorce he had made a decision not to get involved again; he didn't need the hassle. As for the physical side, he didn't crave it. He got his kicks from the job, and sex could always be bought when deprivation reached frustration level. But that was a level soon arrived at when he thought about the missing Kate. Part of him wished he could forget her, as it was obvious she did not reciprocate his feelings. She hadn't even appreciated the efforts he had made to find her when she was abducted. Probably all it would take to get her out of his system was one good fuck. But, after a few drinks and in more sentimental mood, he admitted to himself that he wanted much, much more than that from Kate Rider.

In her Wimbledon retreat Kate was now immersed in a rehabilitation process. In part this consisted of a personal fitness programme of morning exercises, but more significantly it involved the recording of events at the cottage and of everything that had occurred between herself and Michael. Striving for truth, she revised the episodes until they appeared on her computer screen with such blinding clarity that everything else in her life dimmed in comparison.

Kate's apparent burst of apparent creativity did not go unnoticed.

'It's good to know you're able to write again, Kate,'

Irene remarked. 'Am I allowed to see what you're working on?'

'I'm afraid I'm a fraud. It's not work, it's something purely personal.'

'Tell me about it, dear.'

Irene had every right to know – the freelance articles had been her idea. Kate was supposed to be supplementing the Blakeney benevolence with an income from part-time journalism, but weeks had passed and she had not written a single word for the commercial market.

'It's an account of my abduction. I began because I wanted to be absolutely clear in my mind about what happened. As it's progressed it's become an obsession. I'm trying to reconstruct my feelings, to analyse them.'

'It sounds absorbing.'

'That's the trouble,' Kate admitted somewhat shamefacedly. 'I find it impossible to turn my mind to anything else. I'm afraid I've written nothing that could be offered for publication.'

'The therapeutic exercise sounds more valuable. Does it help – to bring such things out into the open?'

'It's not exactly cathartic. Sometimes, when I read over what I've written, it makes me feel wretched. But it helps me to remember that on the last morning at the cottage I felt more alive than at any time in my life before. It's hard to imagine ever feeling like that again.'

'You're a winner, Kate,' Irene encouraged. 'You proved that at the cottage. Michael may be lost to you for the moment, but he isn't dead.'

'He's shut me out of his life, which amounts to the same thing.'

'When he knows you've waited for him, he'll learn

to trust you again. I was a middle-aged woman when I won Marsha, you are young and desirable with your prime still to come. If you really want Michael, then fight for him.'

They were stirring words, that made Kate admire the older woman's spirit. 'I wish I were more like you, Irene.'

'That's a pretty compliment, but it's nonsense. You're too spunky a young woman to be so defeatist.'

This conversation was like a raking over of ashes, exposing a small ember to the air. Irene made sure that this glow was fed fresh oxygen whenever they talked of Kate's future.

Early in his enquiries, Nick Diss realised that Kate Rider, who could have been his star witness, was not prepared to contribute to his case against Kershaw. Far from bearing her abductor malice, she was intent on protecting him. She had even gone on record as denying that she had suffered any lasting damage, mental or physical, as a result of her treatment in captivity. This, of course, was nonsense, for her ordeal had cost her a promising career. Prior to the kidnap, she had been launched as a tabloid journalist. Currently she appeared to be employed as a paid-companion to an elderly cripple. From what he knew of Kate Rider, that transformation would have been impossible unless she had undergone a personality change.

Diss and his fellow officers from the Devon force had listened to the tape they had found at the cottage. Broadcast through a speaker to a room full of people, it had sounded disjointed and amateurish, but the listeners had recognised its potential for causing mental torture. If the victim were tied to a chair with those same repetitious sounds blasting her brain cells, the effect would be mind-blowing.

During an interview with Rider, Nick Diss had exploited the tape by playing it to her. He'd been bastard enough to make her listen to it through the headphones, in the hope that it would shock her out of her complacency over Kershaw. As he had said to Inspector Pearce, 'When you want results, most means can be justified'

Kate proved to be one feisty lady. She had gone along with the experiment, even making light of it. However, her involuntary reactions had told a different story. Both policemen had noticed her hesitation before putting on the earphones, and the way she flinched after only a few seconds of the tape confirmed what it was doing to her. It made no difference to her stance though; she still insisted that Kershaw had done her no harm.

As far as the rape was concerned, the Devon police favoured the conspiracy theory. Nick wasn't so sure. The accused still strenuously denied being an accessory, and they had been unable to convince the victim that the appearance of the intruder had been anything other than an unlucky coincidence.

Diss hated loose ends and the failure of his team to turn up the rapist was a source of professional embarrassment. Despite extensive enquiries on the moor, not a single witness to his existence had been found. The local police thought it impossible that a distinctive-looking, lone foreigner could have roamed their patch, apparently engaged in out-of-season hiking, yet unseen by anyone.

Reviewing the case, Diss had to concede that the hiker's trail was cold and the evidence connecting Kershaw to the rape was entirely circumstantial. Diss was as keen as his West of England colleagues to add a charge of accessory to Kershaw's indictment but they had insufficient evidence to satisfy the Crown Prosecution Services. Their only chance was if the victim had a change of heart.

Aware that Kershaw had refused to see her, the Inspector travelled to Wimbledon to interview Kate again. They sat opposite each other in the comfort of Irene's sitting room.

'Doesn't it strike you as odd that we were unable to come up with a single sighting of a stranger on the moor, that day?' was his opening question.

'Not particularly. The weather was foul, there would have been no one out there to see him.'

'But he would have needed to eat,' Diss pointed out, 'and to find a bed for the night.'

'I told you, he had a large rucksack. It would have been possible to carry everything he needed, even a tent.'

'Ah, yes, the rucksack – I wanted to ask you about that.' Diss tried a more subtle way of testing her original statement. 'You said the man had entered the cottage by the broken window.'

Kate did not see where this questioning was leading. 'It was the only way, the front door was locked. You saw the broken pane by the window catch, and the footprints he left.'

'You described him as a big fellow, it would have been a bit of a squeeze, getting through that small window with a large rucksack on his back.'

Kate bridled. She understood that he was trying to discredit her evidence.

'All I know is that when he entered the room he was carrying a rucksack. Why would I tell you that if it wasn't true?'

'Have you considered that the rucksack might already have been in the cottage? Perhaps your assailant wanted you to think he was a hiker who had chanced upon the place.'

The imagined reconstruction angered her. 'Why do you insist on trying to implicate Michael? Don't you think I would have known if he had planned my attack? He was in shock when he found me, no amateur could have acted so convincingly.'

Her interrogator noted the tender use of Kershaw's Christian name.

'But you were in shock too. Were you really in a fit state to assess Kershaw's reactions?'

'You disgust me. You've failed utterly to find the real villain, so you take the easy option and accuse an innocent man.'

Diss raised his eyebrows at her use of "innocent" but, choosing to ignore the insult, he tried to reason. 'Look, no one saw this man, either before or after the attack. Doesn't that strike you as suspicious? To disappear so effectively suggests planning, and the help of an accomplice. Consider the facts: prior to the day of the rape, the accused kept you tied in such a way as to restrict all movement, yet, illogically, when he left you alone in the cottage, you were restrained with no more than a pair of handcuffs. Shackled to that chair, rape would have been impossible unless your attacker freed you first. The handcuffs made you more accessible.'

'If my attacker had been in league with Michael, as you seem to believe, why did he run off when he heard the vehicle return?'

'To make you believe precisely what you *do* believe: that Kershaw had no involvement in the attack.'

'You're wrong, I know you are. There's no connection between them.'

'Kershaw denies seeing the intruder, yet you claim

it was his vehicle that frightened the rapist away. How can that be?' His questioning was relentless. It was as if his enquiry had become a personal vendetta.

'The cottage door was locked, my attacker left the way he entered, through the side window. Michael approached from the front. Visibility was poor and the light was fading. It would be surprising if he *had* seen him.' Kate glowered at the policeman. 'Why do you keep on about this? Michael's pleaded guilty to the rest, isn't that enough for you?'

Diss decided it was time to back off. 'It will have to be, and perhaps it's for the best. Had Kershaw been charged with the rape and then contested it, you would be facing a cross-examination in the witness box.'

'If that happens then I'll protest his innocence and do everything I can to win him sympathy with the jury,' Kate warned.

Diss was uncomfortable. It was as if Kershaw had succeeded in brain washing the woman. Her belief in his innocence of any complicity came over as genuine. She was sincere enough to convince any jury. He would have to settle for the other charges.

Diss prepared to leave, but Kate was eager to quiz him on procedural matters.

'What happens next?'

'Kershaw has pleaded guilty to two offences that carry custodial sentences. Without a contested charge, the case will go to a hearing.'

'What does that mean?'

'The facts will be presented and a judge will dispose of the case.' Having played the interrogator, he was glad enough to be able to provide the information she sought.

'How long will it take?'

'Not long, though as the criminal charges he faces are serious, all the circumstances will have to be considered before the sentences are passed.'

'Sentences in the plural?'

Diss had no wish to cause her unnecessary grief. 'Don't worry. Whatever he gets, the sentences will run concurrently.'

It was the probable length of the incarceration Kate agonised over. 'Can you tell me how long his sentence is likely to be?'

'Hard to tell. It depends on whether his barrister can convince the judge that this was an aberration. In view of the particular events surrounding his wife's demise, they'll go for extenuating circumstances, state of mind and all that.'

'Could that absolve him from responsibility?'

'It's unlikely,' Diss said, dashing Kate's brief flutter of hope. 'In all the police interviews he's been perfectly lucid. No psychiatrist would be prepared to testify that he's suffering from a severe mental disorder.'

Kate did not need to be told that Michael was sane. He had suffered a temporary breakdown, he was not mentally ill.

'So there's no way he could walk away from the court a free man?' She knew before asking that this was wishful thinking.

'Not a chance, though given the unusual background to the kidnapping and as he has no previous record, he's likely to get off lightly. He shouldn't get more than two years.'

He believed he was offering comfort, but her face paled.

'Two years? But he's not a *criminal*.'

Converted into days, hours and minutes, this length of incarceration seemed an eternity to Kate.

Diss did not bother to argue the issue of Kershaw's criminality. 'If he behaves himself, there'll be remission. That can be up to fifty percent on a sentence of that length. With the time he'll already have served in custody, he could be out in under a year.'

In her most optimistic moments she hoped his punishment – their punishment – would be measured in months, and with remission be reduced to a matter of weeks. Courtesy obliged her to thank the inspector for his information, but at heart she hated him for dashing the optimism engendered by Irene.

Kate had a dream that night. It was she who stood in the dock but the proceedings were confused and only after the verdict, when the judge donned the black cap, did she realise that she was on trial for the murder of Caroline Kershaw.

The following night she dreamed again, only this time the details were different. Now Michael, not she, stood in the dock charged with murder of a person unknown. He was strangely at ease, speaking in a strong and measured voice. He looked as she remembered him. This dream became repetitive. Always, the accused pleaded not guilty. Always, the prosecution would describe, in lurid detail, the offences perpetrated against an unnamed victim. Then the judge donned a black cap and pronounced the death sentence. Michael went white and collapsed, a broken man, aged so much as to be unrecognisable.

A few nights later came a variation–– the victim was identified. The murdered woman was herself. She begged to be allowed to enter the witness box, to prove that she was alive, but her plea was ignored. The truth dawned: she could never testify on

Michael's behalf because she had become an invisible presence in the courtroom. She was dead. Waking from these nightmares was a resurrection of sorts, but one at which she did not rejoice.

Chapter 29

Nick Diss had agreed to ring her when sentence was passed and he kept his word.

'Kershaw's been lucky, it's just eighteen months. With full remission he'll serve no more than nine.'

Kate did the arithmetic: with the six weeks already spent in custody, it meant that by mid-August he would be a free man.

'Where have they taken him?'

Diss named a prison in Kent.

As soon as the call ended, Kate wrote to the prison governor, requesting permission to visit.

When the reply came, two weeks later, it was as she feared: Michael was again refusing to see her. It was a bitter disappointment and undeserved, for she had done nothing to betray his trust; the treachery had been all *The Flag's*. She wondered about the numerous other lives the unscrupulous newspaper had ruined with its lies. She knew she would never be able to forget her own destructive contribution.

Once the sentence was known, her nightmares ceased, though her days continued to be plagued with the pain of Michael's continuing rejection. He obviously believed her to be insincere and unprincipled, and was not about to let her prove otherwise. Despite the rupture in their relationship, his sentence was also hers. Like him, she needed to be strong if she were to survive it.

Day merged into weeks, weeks into months. The expectation that the time would drag proved unfounded. First the Blakeney household was enlivened by the return of Win and Lena from California and then, in the late spring, Kate accompanied Irene on a holiday to the South of France.

When Irene's husband had been alive, it had been customary for the couple to spend several weeks each summer at his company's villa, situated in the unspoilt Provençal hills not far from Bormes. As a major shareholder, Irene continued to enjoy this privilege and after Harry's death she holidayed there with Marsha and Winston as her new companions. For a while, the accident put paid to these French idylls but more recently, with Thomas and Alice to assist her, Irene returned to Provence regularly. The Villa Ferigoulet held many special memories and the annual visits had become something of a pilgrimage.

At the beginning of May, the Wimbledon house was shuttered and locked and the household, Kate included, departed by motor-rail for the south of France. Owing to Black Ivory's busy schedule, Win and Leda were unable to join them.

The luxury of the Villa Ferigoulet surpassed anything in Kate's previous experience. Irene's Wimbledon home was gracious and expensively furnished but it did not flaunt her wealth. In contrast the villa was opulent to the point of decadence. Each of its six bedrooms had an en-suite bathroom, garish with gold fittings. The main *salle* was some fifteen metres long with a series of French windows leading to a vine shaded terrace of similar dimensions, beyond which was a heated swimming pool of Olympic proportions. The hill on which the villa was perched was shared by only one other property and enjoyed breathtaking views to the distant Mediterranean.

On their first morning, Irene appeared on the terrace in a towelling robe and swimming costume. In London, she habitually wore long skirts and previously Kate had never seen her legs. Though they were thin because of muscle-wastage, there was no mutilation.

Thomas carried his employer into the pool and despite her useless legs, Irene proved herself to be a strong swimmer. Kate watched in admiration until Irene demanded that she join her.

Changed into a black one-piece costume cut high at the thighs, Kate felt embarrassed. It did not seem right to be emphasising the perfection of her legs when her friend's were so withered.

As she stood at the pool's deep-end preparing to dive, Irene called up to her. 'You have a lovely figure, my dear, and that swimsuit sets it off to perfection.'

Kate acknowledged the compliment with a smile and wave and plunged in. Favoured with hot sunny weather, this was to be the first of many sessions spent together in and around the pool.

The days passed, each one more relaxing than the one preceding it. Kate's skin turned a golden tan giving her the appearance of bursting good health that was at odds with her mental state. Though she had left her laptop in London, she had come on holiday with a supply of exercise books in which to scribble. The account she was writing had developed beyond the introspective to become a damning attack on invasive press practices. The bitterness she felt towards *The Flag* was given full vent.

They were in the third week of their holiday when a surprise telephone call made Irene very animated.

'We have an invitation,' she explained. 'That was

Pierre Bellac, the owner of the neighbouring villa and son of an old friend. I didn't expect to see him as he usually comes down in high summer. The dear boy saw Thomas in the Mercedes and realised we were in residence. He's invited us to dinner tomorrow night.'

The "dear boy" turned out to be a suave Frenchman of about fifty. His black hair was flecked with steel and he cut a distinguished figure in his well-tailored suit. Welcoming Irene with kisses, he spoke in rapid French before turning his attention to Kate.

'Irene,' he said, in perfect English, 'what a treasure you are to bring such a youthful delight into our midst.'

Taking Kate's hand, he looked approvingly into her eyes before bestowing a light touch of lips to her finger tips.

'I shall not call you Kate,' he pronounced when Irene introduced them. 'You are far too lovely for such a plain name. I shall call you Katerina.'

Pierre proved a fascinating host and conversationalist. He owned art galleries in Paris and Nice, was the author of books and articles on the twentieth century art of the so-called School of Paris and was regarded as an expert on the work of Maurice Utrillo.

Discussion drifted from English to French and back again. Kate had been unaware of the extent of Irene's linguistic skill and was impressed. Too self-conscious to trust her little-used A-level French, her own contributions were made in her native tongue. It was a struggle to follow her companions' Gallic chatter and she mostly caught only the gist of what was being said. Irene was the first to appreciate her difficulty.

'We're being thoughtless, Pierre. In future we must use only the Queen's English in Kate's presence.'

The following evening, they returned Pierre's hospitality and he dined with them at the Villa

Ferigoulet. Having apparently exhausted his reminiscences with Irene, he was particularly attentive to Kate. Irene had volunteered very little about the man beyond his wealth, occupation and divorced status. Her journalist's curiosity made Kate dig for more.

'Have you owned your villa long?' she asked.

'It belonged to my mother. Her family originated in Provence.'

'You must love returning. It's so beautiful here. Do you speak the Provençal patois?'

'Regrettably, very little. It is rarely used these days. If you want to hear it spoken you must let me take you to Arles where a few ancients keep it alive. It still survives in place-names, of course, such as your own Villa Ferigoulet.'

'And what does Ferigoulet mean?'

'The place where thyme grows. So, Katerina, it is appropriately named.'

Kate agreed, for the whole hillside abounded with the pungent herb.

Before Pierre departed he begged a favour of Irene. 'Tomorrow, if you can spare her, I would like to borrow your guest and show her the old monastery at Cartreuse de la Verne.'

Irene replied in a rapid French that Kate did not follow.

Pierre laughed and gave Kate a bow. 'I have your guardian's permission, so will you do me the honour of accompanying me?' he requested.

She had no objection to spending the day with the personable Frenchman.

They drove to the Carthusian monastery through hills covered in vines, olive trees and cork oaks. As Pierre commented, there was little else in that part of Provence. The ruin's medieval origins could still be discerned despite the eighteenth-century classical detail. Though Pierre made an informative guide, Kate could not help wondering what Michael, the architect, would have made of the site.

Their stop at Cartreuse was brief. Pierre's chief object in driving her in that direction was to lunch at a favourite restaurant nearby. Steps from the dusty road led to a stone terrace dotted with metal tables sprouting mushroom sunshades. Inside, the simplicity of the check tablecloths belied the sophistication of the menu and excellence of the cuisine. The meal extended throughout the afternoon. Her companion was witty and charming, and, plied with champagne, Kate found herself flirting with him quite spontaneously.

On the way home, Pierre stopped the car at a viewing point on the *corniche* and pointed out several landmarks. Before driving away he embraced her, kissing her full on the lips. His masculine arms were so comforting that she was almost reluctant to be released.

It was no surprise when he ignored the gates to the Villa Ferigoulet and drove on to his own door. She was not only prepared for his amorous advances but welcomed them. For months she had been hungry for love. Pierre was not Michael, but he was intelligent and distinguished and an admirable substitute.

With a Frenchman's gift for playing the lover, he was generous with his compliments and appreciative of each new inch of flesh surrendered to him. It was as his tongue found her nipple that it all went wrong. What she had been enjoying suddenly became distasteful. She knew she could not go through with the liaison.

Pierre interpreted the sudden resistance as a game

and began to impose himself more determinedly. With the German youth she had been unable to defend herself – this time she could. She fought him off with fists, feet and fingernails.

The injury to his pride was worse than his disappointment. 'What's the matter with you?' he demanded, dabbing at a scratch on his cheek. 'You signal that you want to make love and when I oblige you attack me. Are you what the English call a cock-teaser?'

She had no answer. It was a justifiable anger, she had indeed led him on. When he went to his bathroom to find antiseptic for his wound, she adjusted her clothing, found her shoes and fled. Although there was no likelihood of pursuit, she ran the several hundred yards to the Villa Ferigoulet.

Her hope of reaching her room without being seen was dashed for Irene was sipping a Pernod on the terrace. She immediately noticed Kate's *déshabillé* state.

'Where's Pierre? What's happened?'

Kate had become accustomed to confiding in Irene, and blurted out, 'I made a terrible mistake! I thought I wanted Pierre to make love to me, but I couldn't go through with it.'

Irene made murmurings of commiseration, but secretly was rather amused.

Next day, two floral tributes were delivered to the villa. One was addressed to Katerina; the card said simply, *The misunderstanding was regrettable, my apologies*. The note in Irene's bouquet read, *I have to return to Paris urgently. Your young friend needs to grow up, she doesn't know what she wants*.

'After the disappointment you dealt him, Pierre's leaving. I imagine he's too embarrassed to show his face. The French dislike being denied their conquests.'

Kate felt guilty. 'I'm sorry, it's all my fault. I've deprived you of your friend.'

Irene gave her a hug. 'Nonsense, if anyone is to blame it's me. It was a misjudgement on my part. I guessed he would try to seduce you but he's an attractive man and I thought you might find the diversion pleasurable.'

'Any normal person would have done. What's wrong with me, Irene?'

Irene knew but didn't express the thought. There was nothing wrong with Kate that Michael Kershaw couldn't put right.

Chapter 30

The Blakeney party returned to London at the end of May and with them arrived a draining heatwave. Sensibly, Irene abstained from her usual gadding about town. Instead they spent companionable afternoons beneath a shady apple tree in the garden. Irene read while Kate wrote. They both missed the pool at the Villa Ferigoulet.

Kate continued writing throughout the summer months. Though her main creative effort still went into writing her account of the recent events, she managed to sell articles about Provence and Provençal customs to a travel magazine.

Her personal record had expanded to include the jottings of press criticism written at the Villa Ferigoulet. The Dartmoor sequence became the sequel to what had gone before and fifty-thousand words grew into over a hundred and fifty thousand. She redrafted and pared, until her fragment of biography was contained in a manageable, hundred thousand words. Satisfied at last that it was finished, she submitted it to her most constructive critic.

A drawn-looking Irene returned the manuscript at the breakfast table next morning.

'How was it?' Kate asked, trying not to sound over-eager. 'A load of morbid rubbish, I suppose.'

'My dear Kate, you suppose wrong. Your *magnum*

opus may have taken many months to write, but I read it at a single extended sitting.'

'But you must have sat up all night to do that,' Kate stammered aghast.

'I did, but believe me, it was no sacrifice. To borrow the reviewer's cliché, it was *unputdownable*. You were right about it being a harrowing read. I've been reliving your experiences, and there are places where it made me cry.'

'So you found it depressing?' It was a verdict that should have caused Kate no surprise.

'On the contrary, I found it uplifting. It contains as much honesty and kindness as trickery and cruelty. Above all, it's an inspirational love story, though I have to confess, that aspect made me weep too.'

Irene's opinion was terribly important to Kate. 'You're telling me you liked it?'

'Of course. You write well, I feel as if I know Michael personally. My only criticism is that you've been too severe with yourself.'

'I tried to be honest. I couldn't dodge responsibility for my part in Caroline Kershaw's death.'

'You've told a cruel but beautiful story. It deserves a wider audience than an old woman in her dotage. It should be published, Kate.'

The suggestion caused the author a mental shudder. 'I could never do that. Part of it is as private and personal as a diary. Besides, what I discuss belongs to Michael too and nothing would induce me to invade his privacy again.'

'And what if Michael Kershaw gave his permission?'

'That's as likely as him walking through that door. He's made it quite clear that he wants to disassociate himself from anything concerning me.'

'If you truly believe that, then why have you spent

all these months writing your shared story? I'm no literary critic, but it's obvious that he's your intended audience. You wrote it for him.'

'The manuscript is about more than just me and Michael,' Kate protested.

'Certainly it is. You expose the devious workings of the tabloid press, but you do that to exonerate him and to some extent yourself. He *should* be given the opportunity to read it.'

Irene said no more, leaving Kate to ponder her words. Later, resuming her attack, she was aware that Kate was wavering.

'Even if I sent it to him, he wouldn't look at it.'

Kate's objection was made without conviction, and Irene seized the opportunity.

'Send it? Nonsense, when he comes out of prison, you must take it to him.'

'Irene, he doesn't want to see me. I have to respect his wishes.' Even as she spoke Kate hoped to be contradicted by the older woman.

Irene did not let her down. 'Would you really give him up so easily?'

'It's not my choice, you know that. But he's rejected me and I have to come to terms with that.'

'How can you talk like that when you know you can't live without him?' Irene scolded. 'If I'd taken such a defeatist attitude, I would have forfeited those happy years with Marsha and lost Winston into the bargain.'

'I don't want to lose him. Tell me what I should do.'

'That's the spirit,' Irene encouraged. 'Convince him of your loyalty – show him your manuscript.'

'If only it were as simple as that,' Kate sighed. 'Is my writing really so convincing?'

'Don't pretend modesty, my dear. You're a professional, you must know how good it is. Only a fool would miss the sincerity, and I can't believe that a woman of your intelligence would fall in love with a fool.'

Irene had a knack of telling her precisely what she wanted to hear.

Although these were to be her last words to Kate on the subject, Irene could not put the manuscript out of her mind. The more she thought about it, the more she was convinced that it was an important work. There was another factor to consider: writing was as important to Kate's well-being as the air she breathed. Such a commitment deserved success. Irene determined to become active on the author's behalf, to become, in effect, her agent.

She took her problem to Robin, the son of her old friend, Imogen Peters. Years earlier, Robin had been the junior partner in a once-illustrious publishing house. Though its name still survived, like most of the independents it had been bought up and absorbed into a publishing conglomerate. Robin, as the youngest and most dynamic member of the old management team, had been retained. She had not been in touch with him since his mother's funeral, and was gratified at the warmth of his telephone response.

'Irene, what a pleasant surprise. What can I do for you?'

'There was a time when you used to call me Aunt Irene, do you remember?'

'Of course I do, but you're far too youthful to have a man in his fifties claiming you as an aunt.'

'Are you really that age, Robin? Where do our lives go?'

Robin was aware of Winston's success in *show business* as he called it. He expressed an admiration for Lena. 'What a stunning girl. Tell him from me, he's a lucky young tyke.'

Irene reciprocated by enquiring after Robin's own family. It was agreed that they would meet for lunch to discuss her business proposition.

It was the end of July, and Michael's release was imminent. A plan formed in Kate's mind that she had not even shared with Irene. She rang Paddington Green Police Station, only to be told that Inspector Diss was on summer leave and not expected back for two weeks. She railed at herself for not getting in touch with him earlier.

She toyed with the idea of contacting the prison authority, but rejected it as she did not want Michael forewarned. Surprise was the only weapon in her armoury.

After dithering for a day, she finally rang Jack Brymer.

'Jack, I need your help.' She knew it was the sort of appeal he could not resist.

'Kate, where in the hell have you been? I chased up every Radcliffe in the phone book looking for you.'

Though she could not imagine how he knew about Rhoda Radcliffe, she let his reference to her pseudonym go unremarked and his question unanswered.

'Can we meet?' she asked.

'Just name the time and place.'

The enthusiasm of his response reminded her of the way Jack felt about her, but there was no one else to turn to.

The rendezvous, a cafeteria at the Royal Festival Hall, had been Kate's choice; the stark, impersonal ugliness of the South Bank buildings being preferable to the cosy intimacy of a private restaurant. Arriving early, she found Jack already seated at a table. He looked up as she approached, then looked away for she had come disguised as Rhoda and he did not recognise her.

The classy dresser with the auburn hair stopped at his table. Remembering the description given by Kate's ex-landlord, Jack sprang to his feet.

'Mrs Radcliffe?' He blurted, then penetrated the disguise. 'Kate, is it really you?'

She sat down opposite him, and he reached out to take her hand.

'I've missed you,' he said gruffly. 'Couldn't you have let me know where you were?'

'I'm sorry, but life had become too difficult and I needed to make a complete break. I've been staying with a friend and her family, she's been very good to me.'

'I tried to be a good friend and would be still, if you'd let me.' Such sentimental declarations did not come easily to Jack.

'I know you're a friend, Jack, and you must think me ungrateful.'

He did, but lied by denying it. The pressure on her hand became a caress.

'It's so good to see you, you can have no idea how good it is.'

His sentimentality embarrassed her. She regretted that he still appeared to harbour the same expectations as before. To avoid misunderstanding, she came straight to the point.

'Michael Kershaw is due out of prison soon. I'd hoped that Nick Diss, your detective friend, could tell me when, but he's away on holiday. Could you get the information, Jack? I know you have contacts everywhere.'

His face was an open book, and she read the obvious disappointment there.

He released her hand. 'I thought you said you needed to break with the old life.'

'I can't help it, I can't forget him.' She hung her head, not because she was ashamed of her feelings for Michael, but to avoid the hurt in Jack's eyes.

'If they'd found your rapist, Kershaw would have been charged with aiding and abetting, did you know that?'

She bore his cruelty because she was responsible for his disappointment.

'If my rapist had been found, Michael would have been cleared.'

A waiter came to take their order. Neither of them were hungry and they opted for salads.

'Are you saying you won't help me?' Kate said as the waiter withdrew.

'I'd do almost anything for you, Kate, but I wish you'd not asked this of me.'

They sat in silence until the food came, then only picked at it.

'When I have the information, how do I pass it to you?' he asked suddenly.

He was rewarded with a smile that churned him up inside.

After lunch, he saw her to the station and, when they parted, the brushing of her lips on his cheek was bitter-sweet.

Jack had intended returning to work but instead he walked purposefully to the nearest telephone kiosk. There he extracted a printed card from his wallet – a card he had removed from another kiosk in another part of town. *Kate The Kitten offers professional masseur service to discerning men, satisfaction guaranteed,* it read. Very deliberately he dialled the sequence of numbers printed on the card. Never had he felt in greater need of satisfaction.

The satisfaction provided by the aptly-named substitute proved temporary; Jack's chagrin was more permanent. Far too self-centred to settle for Kate's happiness at the expense of his own, he was tempted to obstruct her reunion with Kershaw. However, Kate had been right in her assumption – the desire to re-establish his links with her proved too strong. Against his better judgement, he decided to do as she had asked.

He took some consolation from the thought that prison experience might have sharpened Kershaw's resentment. If Kate were cold-shouldered, then he might still be in with a chance. Encouraged by this selfish hope, and having obtained the information Kate needed, he telephoned her.

'I suppose I ought to wish you luck,' he said, sounding subdued, 'but Kershaw doesn't deserve you. I want you to know that if it doesn't work out, I'll still be here for you.' It cost him a lot to say that. His pride was of the past.

She didn't know what to say. To tell him the truth, that even without the existence of Michael he would never be in the running, would have been too hurtful.

'Thank you, Jack.'

She was going to add that he was a good friend, but knowing that in the circumstances this would not please him, she amended it. 'You're a good person.'

He gave a bitter laugh that rattled around in her head, long after the call was over.

Chapter 31

Michael's release was only days away, and the immediacy of the event crystallised Kate's intention. She would wait for him at the prison gate, giving him no chance of avoiding her. Whether he would listen to what she had to say would remain to be seen.

Irene applauded the enterprise. 'He is bound to be moved by seeing you standing there. Figuratively speaking, you've been waiting for him all the time he's been incarcerated.'

'Standing by my man,' Kate paraphrased, with an ironic laugh.

That he would be softened by her demonstration of loyalty was precisely what she was counting on.

Irene was keen on giving all the assistance she could. 'Borrow the car. If you drive him home, he'll be a captive audience, so to speak.'

'D'you really think he would let me?' Kate had not dared to think beyond the exchanging of words with him in the shadow of the prison wall.

'He might, if you make the offer.'

'Then I will take the car. Thank you.' She was conscious that this might be her last opportunity to offer Michael anything.

'That's the spirit. You must remember to take your book with you.'

Irene persisted in elevating the manuscript to the

status of a book; her reason for so doing was something that Kate was in ignorance of.

'I can't foist my manuscript on him. He won't be ready for that.'

Her literary outpourings represented a final chance to make her case. She had to keep something in reserve.

Though reluctant to admit her intrusion into Kate's affairs, Irene had been waiting for an opportunity to re-open the subject of the manuscript.

'I have a confession to make. You may not thank me for the interference, but I've been making some enquiries on your behalf.'

'Enquiries?' Kate couldn't imagine what her friend was talking about.

'Your book made such an impact on me. The images are still so strong, I can't shake them off.'

'Go on,' Kate prompted, frowning.

'Please don't be cross. I know I shouldn't have done so without your permission, but I've approached an old friend, a publisher . . .'

'A publisher? Irene, how *could* you. It's not intended for publication, you know that.'

'I know how you feel, certainly, but I believe you to be wrong. It's such a poignant story, you will never write anything finer.'

Irene could see from Kate's expression that she would need to call on all her powers of persuasion. 'It deserves to be read, other people will find it fascinating too. It would be a sin for it to be abandoned and forgotten. Robin, the publisher I have in mind, is the son of my old friend Imogen. I've talked to him about it and he's very interested. He mentioned an advance of £25,000 . . .' Her voice tailed off.

'Without reading a word of it? He was pulling your leg.'

'Oh no, my dear, he respects my judgement, and was in earnest. I took the liberty of giving him a brief verbal synopsis, he was very excited by it. Robin believes that public interest has only to be rekindled to make it a best-seller.'

Kate was aghast. 'Public interest is precisely what I must avoid. I'll definitely lose Michael forever if I go down that route.'

'Give Michael the opportunity to read it. Then you can decide together on whether it should be published. It's not for you to make all the sacrifices. Michael owes you something, Kate. You gave up your career because of that man. Surely he wouldn't begrudge you the restoration of your professional pride?'

Although Kate had her doubts, put like that, it sounded almost a reasonable proposition.

Irene had offered the Mercedes, but Kate preferred to borrow the compact Ford that Alice and Tom used as a runabout. Leaving London in the coolness of dawn, she took the most direct route to the M25 and headed into Kent. Jack had said that prisoners were released in the early morning, between the hours of eight and ten, and she would not risk being late.

She arrived in the town with time to spare. After locating the prison, she drove to the river and parked. To kill time, she walked along the towpath beneath the Archbishop's palace. It was turning into a perfect mid-August morning with only the gentlest breeze to stir the leaves and ripple the water. She found a bench and sat, contemplating the moving river and being serenaded by the chirrup of sparrows in the nearby trees.

Not daring to consider the future, it was as if she existed in a time warp, suspended between the stones of history and the flow of nature. Not until the pulse of morning traffic built to a loud rumble did she think about Michael. The moment had come to take up her vigil at the prison wall.

There was a small gate, set into the larger one, and she had been waiting only ten minutes when it opened. Every nerve in her body was on alert. She was conscious of a drumming inside that pounded too fast to be a heartbeat. A figure emerged, carrying a suitcase. She did not want it to be him. Despite the months of waiting, it was too soon, she was not ready for him yet.

He was smartly dressed, his suit well-cut. His face was pale, but otherwise he looked fit, and actually younger than she remembered. He paused only a moment, as if breathing in his freedom, and strode in her direction. Her mouth was dry, she shrunk back into the car-seat.

He looked towards her, shading his eyes against the sun. Then, incredibly, he raised a hand in greeting, he was actually smiling. But the hope was dashed even as it surfaced: the greeting was not for her. She had not even been noticed; Michael was walking past her towards another car parked further along the road. He was walking out of her life.

Her body moved into action: her lips and tongue shaped his name and her voice projected it through the open window. He stopped, turned and frowned. A moment's hesitation, then he came back at more of a saunter than a stride. The smile was gone. When he bent down to the window, their faces were almost on a level. She could not read his expression, but could see the involuntary movement of muscles about his jaw. She felt her own face crumple and fought back an emotion that threatened to overwhelm her.

'Good of *The Flag* to organise a reception.'

His sarcasm was cutting.

'I don't work for them anymore.'

'What, moved upmarket? Which tabloid do you grace with your columns now?'

The irony was wounding, she wanted his good opinion. 'I'm no longer a journalist.'

The expression changed, his voice softened. 'So what are you doing here, Kate?'

'I came to take you home.'

It was an arrogant assumption. He stared at her analytically.

'Will you wait for a moment?' he asked.

Without understanding, she nodded her agreement.

He turned away, to walk to the other car. Its driver, a plump balding man, got out. She watched in her wing mirror and witnessed their brief embrace. They were talking, looking towards her car. Then they were shaking hands, and Michael was sauntering back to her. He came to the passenger's side, gave a wave towards the other vehicle, stowed his case on the back seat, and got in.

Too nervous to speak, she started the engine. Her foot slipped on the clutch, and the car stalled.

'Would you like me to drive?' Michael offered.

Kate gratefully relinquished the driver's seat.

'You said you were taking me home – which home might that be?'

Not dwelling on the ambiguity of his interpretation, she hastened to explain. 'I was offering to drive you to your home. Or do you want to go to your friend's?'

'My friend?'

'The man who came to collect you.'

'No, he was taking me to Putney, too.'

'Did he mind you coming with me?'

'No, though he was curious about you.'

'What did you tell him?'

'That you were a friend. He's my brother-in-law, and it might worry my sister if she thought I'd fallen into Kate Rider's clutches.'

She supposed that his acknowledgement of her as his friend was facetious too.

They both fell quiet as he negotiated the rush-hour traffic of the unfamiliar town. It was a silence that continued all the way to the motorway.

The words that she had been practising for days would not come. Instead she asked.

'Why didn't your sister come to meet you?'

'She's at home with the children. They have a young family, and they don't want their kids to know their uncle is a gaol-bird.'

'Please, don't call yourself that.'

He took his eyes from the road to glance at her. 'It's what I am.'

To conceal her awkwardness she asked about his nephews and nieces, their names, ages and where they lived. It was something safe to talk about.

'For someone who's no longer a journalist, you certainly ask a lot of questions,' he observed.

Their conversation stayed strictly impersonal all the way to Putney. While stationary at some traffic lights, he looked at her and asked, 'Is it true that you're not with a newspaper?'

'Perfectly true.'

'What happened?'

'I couldn't go on, I was no better than a marionette with my editor pulling the strings. It became important to repair my life.'

The car swung onto the drive of a town-house. A FOR SALE sign leaned at a drunken angle from a border. Michael applied the hand brake and switched off the ignition. A gentle summer shower spotted the windscreen and he made no move to get out.

For want of something to say, she stated the obvious, 'You're selling the house.'

'I won't be needing it. I'm going abroad.'

The news stunned her and she could make no response.

The rain eased, she expected him to go. Instead he asked, 'Will you come in?'

The invitation was so unexpected. All she could think of was that this house had been his marital home, and the place where his wife had committed suicide.

'I don't think so. You'll want to be with your family.'

'There's no one here. I particularly asked to be left alone for a day or so.'

He had provided her with an excuse to disguise her cowardice. 'I understand. I'll go, and leave you to your privacy.'

'No, you must come in, there's something I have to say.'

It was she who had the things to say, but had been unable to. Obediently, she followed him.

There was no mustiness; the house smelt fresh and well-aired. It was obvious that someone had been caring for the property in his absence. A vase of vivid bronze chrysanthemums adorned a table. He read the card that lay beside them.

'Well there's a surprise. They're from Faith, Sandy Mather's wife. He was one of my business partners.'

Kate remembered Irene's account of being newly widowed, how some of her late husband's friends had been eager to offer physical solace. She wondered if, in contradiction to the fidelity of her

Christian name, Faith Mather had flaunted her services in similar fashion. The suspicious mind of the journalist still rules, she thought ruefully.

Michael perused a second card. 'Apparently, my sister's stocked the fridge with essentials, so I imagine that I can offer you refreshment. Coffee, tea?'

'Shall I make it?' It was an offer she immediately regretted, recalling that the kitchen was where Caroline had ended her life.

'You can help if you like. A home-made cuppa will be quite a treat after prison brew.'

His lightness of tone suggested that he was prepared to talk about his experiences in prison.

'Was it very bad?' she asked.

'It was bearable. It wasn't the loss of freedom so much as the lack of privacy that made it grim. I suppose I was lucky. For most of the time, my cell-mate was an inoffensive, small time embezzler who was quite civilised in his habits.'

'I didn't want you to go to prison.' It was such a bald statement, not at all the script she had intended.

'The sentence was poor restitution for the crime. I deserved far worse for what I did to you.'

Kate cherished his words as proof that he had been thinking about her.

'Don't say that. I'm more to blame for what happened than you are.'

He didn't disagree, but made his way to the kitchen where he busied himself with making tea.

Kate followed as far as the doorway. Her eyes were drawn to the cooker – a brand new electrical stove.

He followed her glance. 'You didn't expect me to hang on to the instrument of my wife's death, did you?'

She flinched at the directness of the reference. 'No, of course not.'

She sought the comparative neutrality of the adjoining room.

The tea was strong and they drank it without speaking. She was aware of his eyes on her.

Nervously, she broke the silence. 'You said that you had something to say to me.'

'Yes, it's time you heard my confession.'

For one moment of doubt, she thought he was about to admit involvement in her rape. But his revelations proved to be of a quite different nature.

'When you investigated my wife, you missed something very significant.'

He paused, but she gave no encouragement. Her exposé of Caroline Kershaw was the thing above all else that she did not want remembered.

'What you failed to uncover was that Caroline had been diagnosed manic depressive. She had made four earlier suicide attempts and spent several spells in mental hospitals.'

This disclosure did nothing to ease Kate's conscience. The opposite, in fact; it meant she had exploited a sick woman.

'Oh, my God, Michael. I never knew that.'

'You see, dicing with her life was Caroline's way of responding to pressure. You weren't responsible for her death, believe me. My accusations were an attempt to exorcise my own guilt. I needed a scapegoat – you were high-profile and conveniently available.'

He turned to stare out of a window and she was reminded of the recurring nightmares, when he stood in the dock but did not look at her. He might, indeed, have been addressing a jury in the street outside.

'Her first attempt on her life occurred when she was just a school girl. She panicked over her approaching A-levels and took an overdose of

Paracetamol. After being stomach-pumped, she was moved to a mental hospital as a voluntary patient.'

If Caroline had been unable to cope with school exams, Kate wondered how she had managed to graduate.

Michael seemed to read her mind. 'She learned to cope with academic pressure, and became an undergraduate. One of her lecturers became her lover. He was unmarried, and she viewed the relationship as serious. Lover-boy had other ideas. When she discovered that he was sleeping with a fellow student, she slashed her wrists.'

Still facing the street, he continued Caroline's painful history.

'She was sectioned after that, and spent months in a mental hospital. When she came out, she completed her degree at a different university. Several seemingly-stable years followed. She was distrustful of men and avoided further sexual relationships. When an aunt died, she inherited some money, almost enough to make her independent of employment. She had no need to pursue a high-powered career, so took on the management of an up-market charity shop.'

'Was that when you met?'

'Yes, it was. She was twenty-nine, beautiful and elegant; I was three years younger and flattered by her interest. The architectural practice was taking off, we had secured our first big contract and I had just been made a full partner. It was an asset to be seen at social functions with an intelligent and decorative woman on my arm. She wore wrist jewellery and long sleeves, I didn't discover those razor scars until I got her into bed. They scared me, but it was too late, I'd already proposed marriage. In any case, she seemed fully recovered from her past traumas and perfectly at ease with herself.'

He paused, to drink some coffee. 'Our first year was idyllic. I congratulated myself: I had an intelligent wife with an amiable nature; bed was enjoyable, the union was a success. She was thirty, and wanted children. We were already financially secure so there was no reason to postpone a family.'

Kate's cup clattered in its saucer. She did not want to be reminded that she had destroyed his happiness.

'She didn't become pregnant, so we both took fertility tests. I was fine, but she was found to have been born with a deformed womb. She would never carry a baby.'

Kate tried to make the sympathetic noises that might be expected, but they stuck in her throat.

'The news destroyed her. She sank into a state of depression. Out-patient treatment was no help. She took another overdose, followed by ten months of misery before she got any better.'

Kate could see from his grim expression how he was reliving that misery in the telling.

'When at long last she accepted that there could be no babies, she decided to do something useful with her life. She trained as a social worker. It was a crazy choice for someone unable to cope with stress, but she wouldn't be told. I didn't expect her to survive the training, but she proved me wrong. She qualified, found a job and two years later was promoted to a position of considerable responsibility. The work was demanding though, and the physical side of our marriage suffered.'

Kate had travelled a similar route: as an ex-career woman, she knew how it was possible to be fulfilled by work to the exclusion of all else. She remained silent, not wishing to interrupt his narrative.

'Then the little girl was murdered. The press held Caroline responsible and the cycle of breakdown and attempted suicide started all over again. But eventually, she pulled through.'

This time he fell silent for so long she felt obliged to fill the gap. 'That must have been when she started the nursery school.'

'The nursery was my suggestion. I thought it would be a safe option and for a while it was. Caroline was happy. After two years of celibacy, we resumed normal marital relations.'

Kate was glad he did not refer to it as making love.

'Then,' he continued, 'little Toby was killed in the road accident.'

He turned from the window to look directly at her.

'Don't you see, Kate? She blamed herself. It didn't take your articles to push her over the top. She was barely aware of the things you wrote. I knew she would try to take her life, her past record warned of that, yet I did nothing. You know the rest. Believe me, Kate, her death wasn't your fault. If it was anybody's it was mine.'

There would be no joy for Kate in relinquishing the burden of her guilt only to have it fall on Michael.

'You couldn't be expected to watch over her all the time,' Kate protested. 'You weren't your wife's keeper.'

'There were friends and family who could have shared that responsibility with me. She should have been protected from herself. By doing nothing, I provided the opportunity for suicide.' He gave her a harrowing look. 'Prison gave me time to think, I began to understand my actions towards you. That first time we met, my wife wasn't even buried and I found myself wondering what it would be like to make love to you.'

Kate felt the blood suffuse her cheeks.

'When your scurrilous newspaper carried those photographs, it was all too close to the truth. I was angry and felt betrayed. I didn't want to admit that I was culpable and it was all too easy to transfer the blame for Caroline's death to you.'

'Is that when you decided to abduct me?' she asked.

'No. What I told you at the cottage was true. I went there to escape, but the solitude drove me crazy.'

'I understand, Michael, I really do,' she said softly, wanting to reach out and comfort him.

'Don't you see, Kate, I wanted you with me, but I was too crazy to understand why. If instead of abducting you, I'd turned up at your flat with a bouquet of roses, what would have happened?'

He was waiting for an answer, and she found the courage to reply honestly.

'I think we might have gone to bed together, though in rather different circumstances from those at the cottage.'

He let out a low groan. 'What a fool I've been. I wanted you from the moment we first met, but refused to admit it, even to myself. I should have made love to you, instead I set about torturing you.' His eyes burned into her. 'What are you doing here, Kate? You don't owe me anything.'

She longed to go to him, to put her arms around him, but sensed this was not the moment.

'Michael, this isn't necessary. Please don't dredge it all up again.'

'This is my confession, you have to hear it all.'

'I don't need to, you have my absolution. You were ill. Not responsible for your actions.'

'I wasn't ill before Caroline died, I have to take responsibility for her death.'

'Please, don't think like that,' she begged.

'Do you remember your second morning at the cottage?'

She remembered her degradation only too well: he had found her sitting in a pool of menstrual blood.

'I saw what I was doing to you. I should have stopped it all then, but was too cowardly. I knew that I'd committed a criminal offence against you and was scared of the inevitable repercussions. Instead of releasing you, I played for time. By leaving you handcuffed, I made you easy prey for that maniac who broke in. The rape was my fault.'

Her protest was ignored. He bowed his head. 'I can't shut my eyes without picturing your injuries.'

'Look at me, Michael, I'm healed. The bumps and bruises have vanished and I didn't contract anything nasty. More than that, I've come to terms with what happened, and you must too.'

He laughed bitterly. 'How am I ever to do that? Prison helped me to know myself: I'm not the self-controlled, well-balanced and fair-minded bloke I imagined. In reality, I'm a self-deluding coward, an abuser of a vulnerable woman.'

She shook her head vigorously, 'You're not, you're a human being with human weaknesses. You were ill. When you recovered, you made amends: you wanted me to go to the hospital and you were prepared to face the police. Have you forgotten that?'

'And how easy it was for you to persuade me to do neither of those things.'

Irene had said she must be bold, she would be. 'Michael, listen to me. I'm glad you took me to the cottage.'

He refuted her claim with a shake of the head. 'You can't mean that.'

'I do mean it. And my greatest regret is that we were prevented from making love.'

'Was that real? There have been times when I thought I imagined it. Were you really going to give yourself to me, after everything that happened?'

'Yes, it was what I wanted,' she continued in a whisper, 'and still do.' How far she had come from her intended script.

He looked incredulous. 'Kate, I'm bad news, all I've done is hurt you. I've even cost you your career. For your own good you have to stay away from me.'

In contradiction to his words, he closed the distance between them.

'What if I don't want to stay away?' Her breath was coming shallow and fast.

'I don't deserve you.'

She recognised the echo of Jack's sentiments, "Kershaw doesn't deserve you".

'Is that why you wouldn't allow me to visit you in prison?'

He nodded his head. He was very close to her now – close enough for her to feel his breath on her face.

'It was cruel to reject me,' she admonished.

Their bodies were almost touching, but still his hands remained by his side.

'I thought I was being kind. You'd been hurt too much.'

His eyes roamed over her breasts. 'Where that scum bit you, were you permanently marked?'

'No.' She shook her head. 'Not a single scar.'

At last he touched her. It was a gentle brush of fingers across her cheek, but when he pressed his lips to hers it was with a hungry ferocity.

'Tell me again, Kate, he said, as the kiss ended. 'Is this what you really want?'

'Yes,' she said, her voice hoarse. 'Oh, yes.' She

reinforced the assurance with a desire equal to his own. When their lips separated, he spoke of things that she was happier to hear.

'In prison, I scarcely remembered that I'd lost a wife. All I could think about was that I'd lost you.'

It was a declaration so momentous that she wanted to match it with one of her own. But all she could think of to say was, 'You hadn't lost me, I wanted to come to you.'

'And I punished us both by refusing your visits.' He held her away from him, to look into her face. 'Let me love you, Kate. Let me try to make amends.'

The love word had been spoken. She was smiling now.

'If you'll let me love you too.'

They kissed again and his desire became urgent.

'Come to bed, Kate, and I'll do my best not to disappoint you.'

She experienced the stairs as an ascent in slow motion. It was a solemn pilgrimage. She was aware of each riser, each muscle movement that propelled her upward. But, reaching the bedroom, the sight of the double bed sobered her.

'Is this the room you shared with Caroline?'

The question sounded like an accusation, and it arrested his progress.

'This is *my* room,' he insisted. 'Everything of Caroline's has gone. My sister has cleared the house of all her belongings.'

To prove his statement he opened doors and drawers. The voids she saw made her feel no better.

'Can't we go somewhere else?'

She knew she was playing for time. As with the Frenchman, Pierre Bellac, her mind was refusing what the flesh was so willing to give. She wondered if the rape followed by the untimely arrival of the police posse had traumatised her so deeply that she would be unable to perform the sexual act.

He held both his hands in his. 'Don't spoil things for us, Kate. Caroline is the past. *You* are the present. *We* are the future.'

He stood looking down at her, his desire obvious.

'My wife was beautiful and born to tragedy. You, Kate, are gutsy, adorable, generous and born to be loved.'

His words made it all right. Wanting to be the generous and loving woman he described, she took him in her arms.

Chapter 32

It was evening before other appetites drove them from the bedroom. They prepared a Parma ham salad from the food stock found in the refrigerator. Michael insisted they sat side by side while they ate. They went on touching because looking was not enough.

Despite the richness of their physical and emotional bonding she knew so little about him. 'Tell me about your work as an architect,' she encouraged.

'It's mostly bread and butter stuff,' he said modestly. 'Commercial buildings: the usual high-rise, concrete and steel monstrosities. I don't regret that I won't be adding any more carbuncles to the world.'

His remark puzzled her. 'I'm sure your designs aren't carbuncles, but what do you mean about not adding any more?'

'Didn't I say? Like you, my career is finished. An award-winning firm of architects is too high-profile to have a director with a prison record. Campbell and Mather have offered to buy me out and I've accepted.'

He spoke calmly and without bitterness but the revelation crushed her.

'My God, Michael. Are you really telling me your career is over? How can I live with that on my conscience?'

'I thought I'd convinced you,' he said, with some exasperation. 'You're not to blame.'

'*The Flag* is, and I was their agent.'

'You were manipulated by that toe-rag of a newspaper just as I was.'

She would not be comforted. It seemed as if *The Flag* had become a shroud, enveloping them both and stifling their prospects of happiness.

'Kate, don't cry. We have to think positively, that's what I've been trying to do. Ever since my student days it's been my ambition to produce the definitive book on world domestic architecture. The research would mean extensive travel and as a practising architect there's been no time to do that. Now, with no professional commitments, there's nothing to stop me undertaking the project.'

'Is that what you meant when you said you were going abroad?'

'Yes, I planned my itinerary in prison.' He looked straight into her eyes. 'Come with me, Kate. I'll handle the technical material and the drawings. You can collaborate by turning the book into something more literary.'

She hardly dared believe he was serious. 'You really want me with you?'

'I've no intention of going without you.'

An awful practicality struck her. 'Michael, I've been out of work for months. I've no money to go gallivanting around the world.'

'But I have. With the compensation from the company and the sale of the house I'll be awash with liquid assets. If you agree to be partner in my project, I'd naturally expect to cover all expenses.'

It felt as if she were bathed in glorious sunshine. It made her wanton in her desire for him. 'Can I entice you back to bed?'

'I was about to make the same suggestion. I'm expecting you to stay the night.'

His possessiveness was unnecessary, for she had no intention of leaving.

It was late when she called Irene with an apology. 'I hope you haven't been worrying. It was remiss of me not to phone earlier.'

'I take it you're still with Michael.'

'Will it be all right if I stay? It means that I won't be returning the car until tomorrow.'

'How can you think of such mundane matters at a time like this?' Irene teased.

With Michael's tongue exploring the interior of her ear, Kate was finding it difficult to think of anything.

She wanted to share her happiness. 'Everything has been resolved, Irene. I can't believe it.'

'You sound elated,' Irene observed. 'I'm so glad it's turned out all right.'

Irene's penetrating tones escaped from the cordless phone. Overhearing her remark, Michael raised himself on an elbow to listen.

'Not just *all right*, Irene,' Kate said. 'That would be a complete understatement. In fact everything is better than wonderful.'

'Still understated,' Michael called out. 'It's beyond ecstasy.'

There was a chuckle from the phone. 'What are you trying to do, make an old lady jealous? Enjoy, my dears.' There was the click of disconnection.

'Who's Irene?' he asked.

'My dearest friend, my confidante and adviser.'

'Now you're making me jealous? From now on I want to be your dearest everything.'

And he proceeded to prove it.

In the morning, Kate woke happy and relaxed. She snuggled closer to Michael. 'It feels as though we've been together for twenty-four months rather than twenty-four hours.'

'I won't be a contented man until we've shared twenty-four years,' he whispered in her ear, his hands rediscovering her body.

'By then your book will be acknowledged as the definitive tome on domestic architecture,' she asserted confidently. 'Your name will be up there alongside Lutyens and Wren.'

'That's the sort of reputation I'd like. But it's a bit premature to think like that when it's still to be written. Tell me. have *you* ever tackled a book before?'

Secure in her love, it did not occur to her to lie. It seemed the opportunity to tell him about her manuscript. 'As a matter of fact, I have written something of book length and a publisher's showing an interest.'

'You must tell me what it's about.'

She felt suddenly shy. 'Can't you guess?'

'Is has to be a handbook on how to make a man happy. You're well qualified to write it.'

He made other frivolous suggestions before demanding a clue.

'It's autobiographical,' she admitted.

He guessed immediately. She felt his previously relaxed body go rigid. 'You wrote about us?'

Wide-eyed, heart sinking her, she could only nod.

'Christ! How could I get you so wrong? Are you just a cheap little publicity seeker intending to make money out of a miserable *kiss and tell*?'

Before she could respond, he sprang from the bed, gathered up her clothes and threw them at her. 'Get your things on. Get out of my sight.'

She tried to reason but he would not listen.

'If you're not gone in five minutes,' he snarled, 'I'll throw you out.'

* * *

After the euphoria of Kate's call, Irene was totally unprepared for the anguished young woman who returned to her bosom next morning.

'Kate, what has he done to you?'

Kate broke down into sobs. 'Oh, Irene! It was so perfect, so incredible, and I've thrown it all away.'

'I don't understand, you sounded so happy on the telephone.'

'I was a fool not to realise how fragile his trust was.'

Irene was completely nonplussed. 'What on earth happened between you?'

'What happened? Everything that is glorious . . . and the one thing that is unendurable.'

'I'm sorry, Kate, it's all too cryptic for my fading brain. You'll have to explain.'

'I couldn't believe it, he wanted me as much as I wanted him. We made love for most of yesterday and were so good together. Everything was so natural.'

She was not exaggerating. It had been a total consummation – an uninhibited expression of love. To Kate, whose previous orgasms had been nothing more wonderful than climactic flushes, such fulfilment was a revelation.

'Goodness, after the deprivation of prison, all that strenuous love-making must have been an exceptionally rich diet for him.' Irene was never less than blunt. 'If there was no disappointment in the physical aspect, what on earth went wrong?'

'I can hardly bear to tell you,' Kate said with a snuffle. 'We knew so little about each other, we began to talk. I was so hungry to know all about him.'

'And you discovered something detrimental?'

'No, it wasn't like that at all. I told him about my manuscript.'

'It upset him?'

'He was furious. The idea of making our story public property disgusted him.'

Irene was beginning to regret her exploration into publishing. 'But surely you explained the purpose of your manuscript?'

'I tried, but he wouldn't listen.'

The recollection increased Kate's misery and she gave way to tears. Irene sat patiently, much troubled by her young friend's distress and her own innocent culpability.

Eventually, she was calm enough to continue. 'He was so angry, it was pointless trying to reason. If I hadn't dressed hurriedly, I believe he would have thrown me into the street naked.'

Irene ventured a criticism. 'It sounds to me as if he behaved like a brute.'

Kate did not comment. 'I was too emotional to drive away. I just sat in the car, half hoping that he would come out of the house and apologise, but he didn't. It seems I've managed to ruin everything.'

Irene felt frightened for Kate. Michael Kershaw's violent mood swings suggested something deeply unbalanced in his personality. She regretted the months spent nurturing her friend's hopes. For her to try and wean Kate from her dependency now would be an about-turn hard to justify.

'Have you considered that he might still be mentally ill? He received no treatment after his breakdown, and then had to cope with prison. Perhaps he's never fully recovered.'

Kate shook her head. 'He was never mentally ill. He had a slight breakdown, that's all.'

'Hardly *slight*, my dear, we mustn't forget what he did to you.'

'He's not ill, Irene, I would have known. He was

utterly calm and composed when I collected him from the prison. He showed emotion when talking about his wife, but that's hardly surprising as he feels responsible for her death.'

'He said that?'

'Yes, but it's nonsense. If he's responsible, it's only by default. He blames himself for not preventing her suicide. Believe me, Irene, if you were to meet him, you would find him entirely rational.'

Irene was not easily convinced. 'Throwing you out of his house was hardly a rational act.'

Kate had to concede that nothing in his behaviour had prepared her for that.

'Telling him about the manuscript was what did it. I think he suspected me of bedding him as some kind of cheap publicity stunt.'

'Publicity stunt? To what purpose?'

'To promote the sales of my book. It's the only plausible explanation.'

Irene spread her hands helplessly. 'I'm sorry my dear. It looks as though my well-intentioned interference had gone badly astray.'

Kate was generous. 'It's not your fault, or his. How was Michael to know that I wrote to establish his innocence, not to damage him.'

'He should have given you the opportunity to explain.'

'Why should he? With first-hand experience of how disreputable *The Flag* can be, he probably imagines that anything I wrote about him would be similar inaccurate garbage.'

Like a pair of analysts reviewing a case, they discussed Michael and attempted to understand his motives. They were in agreement that the tragedy of his wife's past helped explain his unwillingness to trust a woman. Caroline had not been entirely honest; she had concealed her history of mental illness until after he had asked her to marry him, which was hardly surprising, though unfair to him.

Kate continued to find excuses for his behaviour. 'The article that *The Flag* falsely attributed to me must have compounded his view that all women are untrustworthy.'

'But you disassociated yourself from that scurrilous piece,' Irene reminded her.

'I tried to. I wrote when he was in prison, but he never acknowledged my letter. With my past record so suspect, it was an appalling insensitivity to mention my manuscript and the prospect of publication. It must have sounded as if I were writing purely for commercial gain – the ultimate betrayal as far as Michael is concerned.'

In a sudden burst of clarity, Kate saw that Michael's reaction, rather than being extreme, was entirely justified. The cause of their rift was a deep mistrust, based on past experience.

She resolved not to be defeatist. 'I love him too much to let our relationship founder due to a misunderstanding.'

Irene was coming round to feel somewhat less hostile towards Michael. 'Then you must see what you can salvage.'

'How am I to do that?'

Irene said promptly, 'Parcel up your book, and send it to him. If that doesn't renew his trust in you, then nothing can.'

'In his present frame of mind he wouldn't read it.'

Kate had a vision of Michael unwrapping her words, only to consign them to the consuming flames of a bonfire.

'He'll calm down. What if I undertake to deliver the manuscript personally? If he hasn't the goodness of heart to indulge a frail old lady in her wheel-chair, then he really is a heathen brute and not worthy of you.'

Irene, in her wisdom, believed that the manuscript was the key to repairing the troubled relationship. So be it. Kate parcelled and posted her work. There was no need for a covering letter, the account was complete, there was nothing she could add. It was upon the honesty and articulation of those typed pages that she must pin her hopes.

Michael was her one-man jury, judge and executioner. The manuscript had been her downfall; now let it be her salvation.

After a telephone call some four days later, Irene found Kate in a state of some distress.

That was Inspector Diss,' Kate explained, grim faced. 'The Devon police have discovered a corpse. They think it's the body of the rapist. He wants me to travel down to Okehampton with him tomorrow to identify some clothing.'

'Did he say how the man had died?' Irene could read the fear in Kate's eyes.

'It's starting all over again, isn't it? If he was murdered, they'll suspect Michael, I know they will.'

'Did the inspector say there was foul play?'

'No, but my attacker was a healthy young man. What else could it have been?'

'An accident perhaps? Call Diss back, you'll be fretting about this all night if you don't.'

She rang, but Nick Diss had left the station. As Irene predicted, Kate got little sleep that night.

An unmarked car, driven by a WPC, collected her at eight a.m. Diss sat with Kate in the back. He was apologetic.

'I'm sorry to rake-up this business, but we have to

tie up the loose ends. We'll try to make it as painless as possible.'

She sought reassurance. 'You won't need me to identify the body?'

'The body is beyond identification. It's been out on the moor all these months, at the mercy of buzzards and the elements.'

She shuddered but had to force the question, 'Does that mean they can't tell how he was killed?'

'Killed? It was an accident. The pathologist's examination confirmed that. He must have fled the cottage that evening, and walked straight into a bog. He'd only gone a quarter of a mile. He was unlucky, I'm told that the particular spot is only treacherous after heavy rain. With the bulky rucksack on his back he wouldn't have been able to struggle out.'

Despite the relief, she shivered. 'He must have called for help. I didn't hear anything.'

Diss understood the significance of her words. 'A quarter of a mile is a long way for a shout to carry on a stormy night, and you were inside the cottage.'

'Do you know who he was?'

'A positive identification was made from papers found with the body. You were right about the nationality: the passport confirmed he was German, and the sole pattern of his boots matches the casts of prints taken outside the cottage.

'If you know all this, why am I needed?' Kate said, frowning.

'You're the only person who can positively link the possessions with the rapist.

We prefer things to be neat and tidy when we close the file on a case.'

At Okehampton police station, the dead man's belongings were displayed on a trestle table: the rucksack and boots, the jacket and trousers in combat camouflage, and woollen hat.

'They look the same, they must be his. There can't have been two men out there dressed so similarly.'

A local officer invited her to take a closer look. Her stomach lurched as she recognised the enamelled badge that was pinned to the turn-up of the hat. When the rape was taking place, that badge, with its emblem of a soccer ball and set of initials, was what she had focused on. It was an image she was not likely to forget.

Diss congratulated her. 'You did a good job, victims of violence are rarely so observant.' He seemed to be forgetting her journalistic training.

It was lunchtime. Though she did not feel like eating she could not deny Diss and the WPC sandwiches in the police canteen before the drive back to London. While they were engaged in eating, Inspector Pearce relayed the news from the German police in Düsseldorf that the young hiker had been a wanted man in his own country.

'He was a factory worker and member of a Neo-Nazi organisation,' Pearce reported. 'He disappeared shortly after the rape of a university student in his home city. The man-hunt extended to the countries bordering Germany, but not to England.'

'So I wasn't his first victim?'

'No. The German student's description of the attacker tallies with yours. Apparently you suffered practically identical injuries. From the dates the Germans have given us, it's probable he'd been in England no more than twenty-four hours before committing the offence against you, so he didn't waste any time.'

The WPC expressed the woman's view. 'Good

riddance, I say. Once he started down that route he wouldn't have stopped until he'd killed somebody.'

Kate was triumphant, though her satisfaction was for different reasons than the policewoman's.

'Now do you believe that Michael wasn't implicated?' she demanded of Diss.

He was immediately defensive. 'We got it right, didn't we? We didn't charge him with complicity. That's all that matters.'

It wasn't all that mattered to Kate.

Chapter 33

A week elapsed. Tension grew with each dragging hour. Kate was convinced that Michael had destroyed the manuscript without reading it.

Irene urged patience. 'Give him a few days more. If he hasn't contacted you by next week, I'll see he gets a replacement copy.'

Next day, a telephone call made this contingency unnecessary. Kate was sunning herself in the garden when Irene came trundling out in the chair to announce that a certain Michael Kershaw had phoned and left a message.

'You spoke to Michael, and he didn't ask for me?' It didn't sound like good news to Kate.

'I offered to fetch you, but he said he preferred to wait until he can talk to you face-to-face. I'd say that was a good omen, wouldn't you? He's coming to the house this evening, at eight o'clock.'

Kate demanded that Michael's words were repeated verbatim, hoping to read something of significance into them. But he had given no clue as to the purpose of his visit. She was too apprehensive about the meeting to harbour any hope that might prove false.

Shortly before the appointed hour, Kate presented herself in the sitting room, casually dressed in a deep-blue silk shirt, teamed with cream trousers.

Irene appraised her. 'You look charming, my dear,

but don't you think one of your shorter skirts would be more feminine?'

'It's my integrity I want to convince him of; I'm not trying to sell my body.' Kate regretted her tart response even as the words left her mouth. 'Forgive me, that was unpardonable. I know you're only trying to help.'

'You know best, my dear, but I can't help being an interfering old woman. If I promise to behave myself, will you introduce us?'

'Of course. But I don't expect you to disappear. It's your sitting room.'

'You can't conduct your meeting in my presence,' Irene protested. 'You need privacy.'

'Then we'll use the garden room.'

'That's hardly appropriate; Alice will be rattling around in the kitchen next door. You must take him upstairs to your room.'

Kate felt suddenly shy. 'How can I take him to my bedroom after what happened?'

'You're being childish. It's your living room too.'

'Anyway, I doubt if privacy is necessary, he's probably coming to return the manuscript. That's all.'

'And what if he's coming to make love to you?'

The most Kate could hope for was that he was coming to talk. 'After he threw me out? That's hardly likely.'

'Are you quite sure about that, my dear?'

There was no opportunity for further discussion. Though it was still a few minutes short of eight o'clock, the doorbell sounded.

He stood on the doorstep, composed, dark suited and handsome, carrying a document case that was too slim to contain her manuscript. By way of greeting they exchanged no more than names, and she invited him up to the sitting room. Her choice of outfit had not been so bad. The well-cut trousers afforded him a provocative view as she went ahead of him up the stairs, and she sensed his gaze.

Irene was her usual welcoming self, though her remarks were deliberately loaded.

'You're such a frequent topic of conversation in this house, Mr Kershaw, it's hard to believe this is your first visit.'

'I'm glad to be here, though I'm sure you flatter me.'

Irene approved the modulation and pitch of his voice, the firmness of handshake and the unwavering eye contact.

'You young people have a lot to discuss,' she said. 'Why don't you take Michael up to your room, Kate. You can be as private as you want up there.'

The unsubtle suggestion raised the colour in Kate's cheek. Irene observed how their visitor monitored this reaction. Kate was too nervous to look at him, but Michael Kershaw was devouring her with his eyes.

In the intimacy of her room, Kate closed the door timidly, suddenly affected by a shortness of breath that had nothing whatsoever to do with the climb.

Such was his own agitation, he failed to notice hers. He strode to the window,. appearing to give his attention to the view. However it was the view inside that he had come for. He turned, his eyes travelling brazenly over her.

'A lovely sight,' he commented, aware of the ambiguity of his remark.

In no mood for word games, she had to know. 'Did you read it?'

'It wasn't what I expected.'

'No?' There was a lump in her throat which prevented her speaking more than a single syllable.

'You were wasted on the gutter-press, you have talent. It was right to look for a publisher.'

It was such a reversal of attitude that she was stunned into silence.

He raised his eyebrows, demanding a response. She knew he was testing her.

'I didn't go to the publisher, Irene did that, and without my prior knowledge. I never intended it to be published. What I wrote is far too personal.'

He ignored her defence. 'Did Irene talk terms?'

She would not be trapped. 'An advance was mentioned, but it's immaterial, it's not for sale.'

'How much was offered?'

She told him, wishing that he would not persist with these questions.

'If we made it a collaborative effort and organised the right kind of publicity it could be much more.'

Kate was uncertain of his meaning.

He opened the document case and passed her a colour-printed A4 sheet. It was obviously the artwork for a book jacket. Central, occupying two thirds of the frame, was a carefully-detailed, miniature cottage with thatched roof, stone walls and a two-storey porch; one of the windows on the ground floor was shuttered. The drawing was overlaid with the frame of a giant chair, ribboned with rag ligatures and fettered with handcuffs. On both sides of the main design were the silhouettes of a man and a woman. They were too large in scale to enter the house, too small to fit the chair. To the left of the house, they stood side by side but separate. To the right, the silhouettes merged into a single outline. It was impossible to decide whether they were looking into the picture or out of it. Above was a night sky, filled with stars.

'The title, when you've found one, mingles with the stars.'

Though she gripped the illustration firmly, her hand trembled.

'You produced this?'

'Yes, that's why I didn't come before, it's taken days to get right.'

'But why?'

'I studied graphic design for a year, before I switched to architecture.' It was not the explanation that she was seeking and he knew it. 'Your book with my cover! Think of the free publicity. There would be an auction to buy the rights.'

She stared at his illustration, wondering when she would wake up.

'Aren't you going to tell me whether you like it?' He moved closer as if wishing to study the design too.

'It's clever. Striking. You're a talented artist.'

'But you don't want to use it?'

More than ever, she was convinced that he was playing with her. 'Use it? I can't believe you're sincere about wanting the manuscript published.'

'After my recent behaviour, you have every right to doubt me. But I'm completely serious. After all, you agreed to collaborate on my book. It seems only equitable that I contribute something to yours.'

Utterly confused, all judgement gone, she blurted out, 'But it would make us public property, you would hate that.'

'This isn't a rushed decision, I've given it careful consideration. We're both casualties of the tabloid circulation wars. What you've written sets the record straight. The publicity won't be welcome, but I'm prepared to put up with it if we can bring *The Flag* to half-mast. This time it will be us manipulating the media, not the other way around – think of the satisfaction of that. Then there's the little matter of our reputations: your manuscript restores our good names. Though, on that point, I'd like to suggest some revisions. You deserve to come out of it better.'

She wanted to be convinced, but still could not be sure that he was in earnest.

He continued his sales-pitch. 'It's a brilliant exposé of the disreputable practices of a tabloid newspaper. Presumably everything concerning *The Flag* is accurate? There's nothing that could be construed as libellous?'

She flushed at the suggestion. 'Of course not, it happened exactly as I describe it.'

'Good, then publication will be a sweet revenge for both of us, not to mention the added incentive that as a collaborative effort it should amass us a small fortune.'

Her emotions were raw. She could understand his desire for revenge but not his preoccupation with money. 'A fortune out of misfortune, wouldn't that be ironic!'

'Don't we deserve some recompense for the damage done to our lives?' he demanded, observing her closely.

She felt hurt for he had made no mention of the manuscript's more personal aspects.

'I'm waiting for your answer, Kate, what do you say, are we to be partners in this publishing venture?' His eyes searched hers as if probing for a hint of hostility. 'Think of the opportunity, it could be the beginning of a whole new career for you. Don't you want to be a best-selling author? You're quite adept at handling the emotional bits, you have a talent for fiction. Your next work will probably be a commissioned novel.'

His words crushed as effectively as any blow. 'Fiction? Are you accusing me of being disingenuous?' The words came out strangled with emotion. Her fingers crumpled his design until it became a tight paper ball. Silent tears welled, and ran in salty pendants down her cheeks. Dark spots appeared on her silk shirt where they dropped.

Then he was holding her, his body hard against hers. Her vision was too tear-laden to discover the extent of his emotion.

'I wanted to believe in your sincerity, Kate. You can't imagine how much I wanted that.' He raised her chin, gently, as he had done on the first day they met. 'Forgive me, my darling, I had to push you. I had to have proof that you meant everything you wrote.'

'I wrote from my heart. I wrote for you – for us. Not for publication,' she sobbed.

'I know that now. But I was too insecure to believe that such an unconditional declaration of love was intended for me.'

'Every word is true, Michael.' She offered her lips by way of confirmation.

'I believe you,' he whispered throatily. 'Bless you for writing it.'

He used the side of his forefinger to wipe her tears, then applied his lips to stem them. When she threw her arms about him, he whispered that he loved her, that he wanted her. She returned his avowals and, still embracing, they found the bed.

In removing her clothes, he saw the fading bruises on her upper arm.

'What are these?'

She heard the suspicion in his voice, and the fragility of his trust pained her. Taking his hand, she fitted his fingers onto the blemishes, it was a perfect match.

'You shook me and threw me out of your house. Remember?'

'Christ, did I really do that to you?'

He attended to the recent bruises with lips and tongue. When he turned his attention to her breasts, he traced the invisible, older injuries. He nuzzled with great accuracy, for the other man's abuse was mapped onto his brain. He moved to the ribs, long healed and, in a repetition of the journey he had made that last morning at the cottage, parted her thighs.

He made no preparation before entering her and she did not attempt to caution him.

'Trust me, I won't come inside you,' he promised.

A powerful force was born in them both and their copulation was bruising in its ferocity, destructive in its intensity. But it was doubt, not love, that was destroyed.

Her action, as he signalled his withdrawal, was not involuntary, only unpremeditated. Thrusting her pelvis towards him, she clasped his buttocks, her nails indenting the smoothness of his flesh.

Both knew that however exciting, poignant and fulfilling their future love-making might be it would never again reach that peak of intensity – and neither would they wish it to.

Michael groaned, first with pleasure, then with dismay. Raising himself on an elbow, he looked into her eyes.

'Why? I intended to be careful.'

'You said you wanted proof. I wanted my proof to be convincing.'

His laugh was triumphant. 'Oh, Kate, how could you go on loving such a miserable unbeliever?'

'I live in the hope of converting him.' She was smiling now.

'Thank God you persevered. And thank you for organising such a glorious road to Damascus for me.'

Later he stroked her abdomen with the back of his hand, upward strokes that began at her dark triangle and finished at the indentation of her navel. The gesture was consciously symbolic, a directional encouragement to the multitudes of microscopic voyagers.

'Will you still come away with me, Kate? I can't go abroad without you. I need your sweetness for sustenance, your body to love and your brain to help me with my project.'

'You chauvinist!' she protested.

'Not at all, I'm a feminist through and through, and I adore you. We'll work by day and make love all night,' he promised, 'and after Europe we'll move on to Asia, America and Africa. I want to love you all over the globe. What do you say?'

'I want to be with you. You must know that.'

The commitment was made. It was sealed in the time-honoured fashion of lovers.

It had grown dark. Through the uncurtained window they could see stars and the sliver of a new moon.

'Before we go abroad, we must sort out a publisher for your manuscript. I'm serious about this, Kate, that damned paper has blackened too many reputations with its lies. Surely you feel the same?'

Kate visualised Kevin Colson's smug face and the various indignities he had subjected her to. 'Yes, it would be good to give a tabloid a taste of its own medicine.'

'Would Irene object if I stayed the night?'

'No, she'd be most understanding.' She didn't add that it was Irene who insisted they conducted their meeting in the privacy of the bedroom.

They lay on their backs, with Michael's arm about her. His splayed fingers resting lightly on her left breast felt like a territorial claim.

'I still can't fathom how you succeeded in transforming my brutality into something beautiful,' he mused.

'You were never brutal.'

He stilled further protest with a kiss. 'I want you to be published, Kate. You've worked our story into a small masterpiece. You're a writer, a fine one, and your talent deserves to be recognised.'

He was thanked for his generosity with all the means at her disposal.

Irene prepared for bed, she had been clock-watching for hours, and it was almost midnight. She could sleep now, secure in the knowledge that only physical intimacy could have kept Kate and her visitor so long in the attic suite. Though his sandy colouring was wrong and there was no facial resemblance, Kate's lover reminded her of Harry. He exuded the same strength, moved with the same certainty. Like Harry, he would know how to satisfy a woman.

It was pleasurable to think of them making love. She felt the same about Win and Lena. It gave purpose to the house to think of those young and beautiful bodies enjoying each other under her roof. Giving and receiving love, as she had with Harry, in the Regent's Park house, as she had with Marsha, in the very room that Win and Lena shared.

Kate's happiness would be Irene's sacrifice. She would lose her companion to Michael. There were no impediments, they would naturally want to be together, and Kate had said that Michael had talked of going abroad. With Win and Lena away on their extended Australian tour, she would be lonely. She consoled herself with the certainty that Win would be home next month, and that Kate's commitment to Michael did not rule out their continuing friendship.

After the accident, there were those who had written her off, but now, ten years on, life still offered riches, and she intended to stick around to enjoy them.

At the top of the house, Kate and Michael planned their campaign of revenge.

'We could call a press conference to discredit *The Flag* for flagrant breaches of the voluntary press code,' Kate suggested tentatively, uncertain how Michael would react.

He hugged her. 'At the same time, we could exploit the press conference to restore our credibility and promote your book.'

The surging adrenalin was something familiar to Kate, the journalist. Newspapers had been her life but now she was ready to crusade against them. 'If just a sector of the media-circus give us sympathetic coverage, it might be enough to persuade the government to launch an inquiry into press practices. Wouldn't that be something?'

Michael kissed her. 'It's a campaign well worth fighting – let's go for it, Kate.'

Their lives had purpose again. Together they would turn that purpose into a cause.

It was obviously a celebration. The usual pints were supplemented with doubles of single malt.

'So, how does it feel, *Chief* Inspector?' Jack Brymer asked.

Nick Diss grinned. 'Bloody good. But I have you to thank for the promotion. If we hadn't shared information on that extortion racket, I couldn't have cracked it.'

'You know my motto – You scratch my back and I'll . . .'

'That's partly why I asked you here, Jack. I'm assigned to something big, a scam involving illegal immigrants. It's being organised, right here, in West London. Are you interested?'

Jack lubricated his throat with the bitter, and allowed the malt to do the chasing, before he responded. 'Sounds right up my street, tell me more.'

Several chasers later, their crime-talk concluded, Nick asked, 'Have you seen anything of Kate Rider recently?'

Jack was not about to disclose meeting her at the Festival Hall. It hadn't been flattering to learn that Kate had only come on to him to get information about Kershaw. He resented being cast in the role of Cupid.

'I've decided she's a lost cause.'

'Pity. Feisty lady, fabulous body,' Nick declared, caressing his pint.

Jack communed with his glass. 'That's the problem, too bloody gorgeous. It would have ended in disappointment; a woman with a beautiful body rarely makes a good lay. The plain ones try much harder – they have to.'

'Wouldn't know about that, old son. I'm a married man, remember.'

The recollection of his marital status reminded Nick that he had a home to go to.

'Time I was off. We'll keep in touch on the illegals, yes?'

'Sure. Always good to do business with you, pal. We make a good team.'

Jack lit another cigarette and contemplated a last

drink. His brain was already working on ways of following up the immigration racket. It would be a tricky investigation, and, as Diss had warned, it could be dangerous. The surge of adrenalin made further alcohol unnecessary. Maybe it was for the best that Kate had spurned him. An emotional entanglement would have been too much of a distraction.

If the fruit he fancied grew on inaccessible branches, then it made sense to move on to another tree. Jack was in a mellow mood as he meandered his way home.

THE END

OTHER RECENT PUBLICATIONS FROM ASPIRE

BRIDGE OVER THE PAST by Jane de Launay
ISBN 1 902035 10 0 Paperback £5.99

THREEPLAY by Hamish Macfarlane
ISBN 1 902035 13 5 Paperback £5.99

FORTHCOMING PUBLICATIONS FROM ASPIRE

TRIAL BY CONSPIRACY by Jonathan Boyd Hunt
ISBN 0 473 05123 0 Hardback £15.99

IN THE SHADOW OF SADDAM
by Mikhael Ramadan
ISBN 0 473 05305 5 Hardback £15.99

TITANIC II by Andrew Crofts
ISBN 1 902035 11 9 Paperback £5.99

Apire Books are available from bookshops, supermarkets, department and multiple stores throughout the UK, or can be ordered from the following address:

Aspire Publishing
Mail Order Department
8 Betony Rise
EXETER EX 2 5RR

The price includes postage and packing.